"This sensitive portrayal of a young girl's loss of innocence has much to tell us about American culture as well. The writing is poetic and precise; the novel is mesmerizing."

—Lee Smith

"A bittersweet story . . . disturbing . . . memorable."

—*Detroit Free Press*

"Benz so deftly puts us into the mind of a fifteen-year-old that we are fifteen again . . . not to be missed."

—*Greensboro News & Record* (NC)

"Maudy Benz fully explores the fears and desires of a young woman trapped in a seemingly helpless situation. But North is a survivor, her strength and wisdom growing out of her adoration for First Lady Jackie Kennedy. In this moving first novel the acute observations of a young woman coming of age and the historical facts and references to the Kennedy years are riveting and memorable."

—Jill McCorkle

". . . [A]n enormously talented writer."

—Bob Shacochis

"For anyone who has forgotten, Maudy Benz's *Oh, Jackie* is a powerful reminder of just how thoroughly fantasies of romance and sexuality fill teenage hearts and minds—and continue to fill adult hearts and minds, despite increasing conflicts with reality and an ever larger toll on actual lives."

—Gwenda Blair, author of *Almost Golden*

"Benz's images are fresh, honest, sometimes raw descriptions that nourish belief in North and her voice."

—*The Independent* (Durham, NC)

Oh, Jackie

MAUDY BENZ

BERKLEY BOOKS, NEW YORK

OH, JACKIE

A Berkley Book / published by arrangement with
Story Line Press

PRINTING HISTORY
Story Line Press edition published 1998
Berkley trade paperback edition / September 1999

The Penguin Putnam Inc. World Wide Web site address is
http://www.penguinputnam.com

ISBN: 0-425-17044-6

BERKLEY®
Berkley Books are published by The Berkley Publishing Group, a division of
Penguin Putnam Inc., 375 Hudson Street, New York, New York 10014.
BERKLEY and the "B" design are trademarks belonging to Penguin Putnam Inc.

PRINTED IN THE UNITED STATES OF AMERICA

10 9 8 7 6 5 4 3 2 1

Acknowledgments

Thanks to Lee Smith, Jill McCorkle, Robert Sam Anson, and Jan Alexander for reading the manuscript as it developed. To Todd Lewis for computer heroics. Thanks to Doug Marlette for helping me find my wonderful agent, Deborah Schneider. Thanks to Dana Gioia who always gave me hope. And to Michael Mezzatesta who believed in me. To all my friends at Bennington who saw me through. To my mother and my father who talked books to me when I was a child. To my cousin Katy for her love. To Moreton and Anna for reading the novel as friends.

Much thanks to Robert, Joseph, and Jenny at Story Line who listened and soothed. My deepest gratitude to Judith Palais at Berkley for her insightful editing and her attention to detail in this Signature edition. And to Daphne and Conrad for living with me through the writing and editing of this book.

For my father, Carl Alfred Benz,
who loved the English language and me

Between the hammer strokes
　　　　our hearts survive
like the tongue
　　　　that between the teeth
　　　　　　　and in spite of everything
goes on praising.

> Rainer Maria Rilke,
> from the Ninth *Duino Elegy*
> translated by David Young

I went through some pretty difficult times, and I kept
my sanity.

> Jacqueline Bouvier Kennedy Onassis

Contents

Oh, Jackie

Prologue

Once upon a time, there was Camelot. A queen and a king in the home of the free. There were babies in the White House, and a pony grazed the lawn. The sun shone down. Radiant. She was dazzling, too. Jacqueline. Mother to her children. Like a child I needed her. During the summer of my fifteenth year.

The day Oswald shot her king she wore a pink suit. His blood marked the place where his head lay. That night she would not take the suit off. Friends begged her, *Please, for appearances*. She stayed dressed in the suit, as if to say: it happened. It happened. She wore the suit into the night. Friends and family gathered around. She told the whole story. Again and again. She took the suit off.

She knelt beside the coffin and kissed it with Caroline by her side. She gave her hands to her children, steady hands. She gave her face to the nation and she did not yield to her full grief in public. She became my mother then, in my fifteenth year. When my world broke.

The camera traced her every gesture. The angle of her chin and her heels clicking on the avenues as she walked in big strides. She never faltered, held her head high. He would have smiled proudly down. At this funeral for a king. He would have called out: O beautiful wife.

She fashioned a new life, accused of avarice, vanity. Another assassin fired killing Bobby. She sought safety and found it, saving her children and herself. Flash bulbs, cameras, paparazzi. She lived through it and rose above.

I knew where she was from moment to moment. Her sunglasses

on, in Crete and in Malta. Her long mane of thick black hair tied back, dressed in a halter dress with a necklace like bells. She wore Greek sandals wound like silvery ropes around her ankles. I traveled with her around the world always knowing where she was with the broken pieces sounding inside like chips of bone rattling inside a glass bell. I listened for her. I watched the newspaper for a glimpse of her face. The one face that said yes to the new life. Even if it could only be a half life.

When she found a new life I believed in one. I married and had my babies. When they grew older I opened my dress shop. You look like Jackie Kennedy, a customer said every few weeks. I smiled my pleasure. Made dresses she could have worn.

I feel like Jackie O in this, a mother giggled from my tiny dressing room. Ivy paper on the walls. Pictures of my husband and children alongside my fashions on my desk. And pictures of Jackie.

I collected pictures of her beginning in 1963, the year I feel pulling me back in time. A photo of her in a short skirt exiting a sports car, revealed her athletic legs, her sensual beauty caught by film. As my body had been caught by film back then. Long legs shown to the world, said to me: To have a beautiful body is no shame. Jackie's life said to me: Live, North. Live. She had been my courage once and now, as I tell the story of my fifteenth year.

Queen Mom

I packed for the summer and my transistor radio played Little Richard's "Jenny Jenny Come Along With Me," a song the disc jockeys didn't play often, I guessed, because Little Richard wore lipstick and mascara and dressed like a woman in sequined outfits. But I loved the way he sang *Ooo* in a falsetto at the end of each line of the song. The quick beat moved me and the idea of going with a boy, especially going in a car, made me feel warm. Oh, I loved to ride fast, so I started to dance across my room. "Ooo Jenny Jenny."

Quick piano chords moving my feet, I turned a circle with an arm above my head, then out in front of me, pretending my fingers were touching the feather-soft fingertips of a boy and his touch came and went with the beat of the music. I grew so excited the skin on my arms beaded with goose bumps. But I wasn't cold. No, I was not cold and my phantom boy was turning too in a circle. "Ooo Jenny Ooo."

For a minute I felt lost in my phantom boy's arms, and I imagined him pulling me down on my bed, onto the blue flannel bedspread that looked shiny like lake water. I sank onto my bed as if he had pulled me down where our hearts could beat side by side in syncopated rhythms. Lying still, I waited for him to touch me but he was only a boy in my mind; so I closed my eyes and wished for him to be real while Little Richard sang: "Come with me."

Then I slipped my hand inside my pink short-shorts, inside my white cotton underpants, to touch myself the way I had touched myself last night when I imagined my phantom boy so clearly, when I had moved my fingers in fast circles. *Ooo.* And my heart was a motor accelerating, my arms and legs rising into air and space to spin around thoughts of him. Tall and handsome. Until suddenly my arms and legs beat automatically like wings.

The whole time I imagined him deep inside me, the way Deena Williams—who had gone steady with Bryce Sherman for three years—had described their lovemaking. This was a secret Deena told after drinking two glasses of champagne at a wedding reception, a secret all the girls in my school had committed to memory along with the Gettysburg Address. Deena said she felt her body had no ending; there was no stop sign and no caution light, just the ever increasing speed of love. I moved my hand faster, trying to bring back last night's ecstasy until my mother's voice broke through the walls of fantasy.

"North, are you packed up?" she called. I jerked my hand from inside my underpants and sat up quickly, letting go of my dream boy's image. I heard the professorial tone in my mother's voice giving a crisp edge to the words she spoke. "North, answer me!" she called. Standing up fast, I felt dizzy so I steadied myself on the bed post and breathed deep. Then I walked over to open my bedroom door.

"Almost ready," I shouted into the hall. I wanted to call my mother *Queen Mom*, a nickname I'd given her, but never used to her face. She would have impaled me with her eyes, and upbraided me with her tongue, too. So I assured myself, *North, at least you won't have to listen to her directions all summer long*. She and Dad were leaving for Europe on a jet that evening. I would be spending the summer with my cousin Dee Diehl at Glass Lake. I envisioned the boys who would be living at the lake for the summer. I saw myself dancing in the loop of a boy's arms, with his hand wrapped around my fingers as tight as a glove.

"North, turn down the radio!" Queen Mom called from Hades, her name for the kitchen in July. She claimed it grew so hot there you could bake chicken without turning the oven on. But she had a dramatic name for everything that irritated her. I was "Princess" sometimes. "Princess doesn't want to go to school? . . . Get in the car," she'd order. She could have been a prison wardeness without any training. She called the Huron River the River Styx, and she closed her eyes and folded her arms across her chest every time my dad drove us across the Huron River Drive bridge.

"Chuck, stop here and let the boatman take me," she would say, "so I'll never have to teach another blank-faced, dizzy-headed kid." Her thick lips with the tangerine lipstick smudged on the curled out-lines parted slightly so I could almost picture the coin of death on her tongue. She said the tedium of teaching English at Washtenaw Community College had grown unbearable. "Dumb jocks," she said. "I teach testosterone-poisoned hulks." She believed she might be hired away any minute by the University of Michigan. But I knew her lack of a Ph.D. in English prevented this. She'd quit her graduate program to marry Dad back in the days of their true love, which I never had witnessed.

"North, turn down that racket. How can you think with that racket going on?" She called now from the vicinity of the bottom of the stairs.

"It's not racket," I shouted. "It's rock and roll." But as she stomped up the stairs I stopped twirling, and turned the radio down on the chorus of "Surfin' USA."

"You've got fifteen minutes." Her words shot in from the hallway and I heard the swishing of her legs against her skirt as she walked by my room, moving those hips that had pushed me from the womb fifteen years before on a blistering July first. Could my mother's hips heave me forward into the future? The clothes seemed to flutter in the closet as she passed by my room. Her power, her intelligence, hung in the silent hallway behind her, thick like air before a storm. I told myself, *North, in a few hours you will be far away from here. You will be at Dee's, without Queen Mom to rule you.*

At Glass Lake giant oak trees and cotton woods towered on the grounds surrounding my Uncle Judd and Aunt Joan's summer home. Their family seemed almost as rich as the Kennedys, with their ser-vants and speedboats and fast cars.

I had fallen in love with Uncle Judd's Thunderbird the first time I laid eyes on it on Christmas day in 1961. It looked like the car President Kennedy rode in for his inauguration, with cream-colored seats and a white steering wheel, as round and shiny as a halo. Uncle

Judd's other car, a Stingray, was one of the fastest cars on earth. Since Uncle Judd bought it in 1962 and the first time I saw it I knew I wouldn't be happy until I rode inside. I squeezed my eyes closed and imagined its sleek body, as flat as a shark. The Corvette emblem, a shiny metal decal of two crossed racing flags, shone on the swelled back of the car's body beneath the twin rear windows.

From downstairs the mantel clock chimed a warning. Before Queen Mom issued another decree, I checked to make sure I had packed the clothes we had listed together. Striped shift, white shift with pink swirl design, white terry cloth bathrobe, green brocade sheath. Sleeveless tops, all colors. Underwear. I packed my double A cup bras I wore because my breasts had been so slow developing. My left breast was a small white cone with the right one next door, as flat as any man's breast with a nipple at its tip, small and peaked like a pink Hershey's kiss.

My cheeks flushed when I read the next words: *sanitary belt and napkins*. Little nervous waves capsized in my stomach. I thought I would never start my period. Yet I went to the closet and pulled out the lilac colored box with *Kotex* written in white scripted letters across the side. I'd dented the box at the top perforated corner trying to claw it open during false alarms.

If and when I started, it wouldn't be like the movie they showed us every year at school. A gorgeous blond floated across the screen, waltzing through fields of pink and white lilies. The day she started she happened to have pads in her purse so that despite her heavy flow she smiled throughout Math class and scored a hundred on her pop quiz. Never did a single drop of blood stain her panties or the back of her skirt. Not once did one red dot fall onto the bathroom floor as she changed pads, the way it did when my mother had *the curse*. All our mothers used the word "curse" to describe their periods. But if you believed it, you might also believe that the day you started your good luck would fly right out the window to the moon.

Sometimes I asked questions of my friends who had started. Madeline Spears said her period felt like giant hands wringing the muscles in her stomach. Sally Teague told me in a whisper that her legs ached for three days before she started each month, and when she touched her breasts they felt like bruises. Periods sounded like something to be avoided. Like a Christian Scientist I'd will myself not to have them. Was there some sex to be, in between a woman and a man? An Amazon warrior, maybe? With breasts beating on my naked chest like tom-toms. Madeline Spears said Amazons were a myth. And that you had to start sooner or later. Sometimes I secretly and strangely wanted mine. Boys would want me more then because of "animal instincts for procreation." That's what our science teacher had said. When my period arrived one day I'd become a woman. In Africa girls my age were already having babies, or so some boys at school had said. But I just wanted a boy like the boy in my fantasy to drive me in a car. Fast.

"North, five minutes," my mother shouted from her bedroom down the hall.

"Coming," I called, glancing around the room for things I might be forgetting. Smokey Robinson was singing "A Hold on Me" on the radio. He sounded love-cursed, singing of bad love, mad love.

The news commentator announced the best news then. He said Jackie Kennedy would have a baby right while she lived in the White House. Her doctors had said her schedule would be lighter during the summer so that she might rest before the baby's birth in October. I imagined her trim body changing shape beneath a zillion stylish shifts, each one with a larger bulge beneath, rising up like a beach ball. Then a Zeppelin. And then the baby's birth for all of us to admire. Until that day she would spend more time at the family home in Virginia. She would not be allowed to horseback ride or play her usual athletics. Who would exercise her horses? Maybe they'd gallop wildly in the paddock, excited about the baby, too. Or get jealous. Horses could be jealous for attention like people.

I pictured her reading in the quiet of her New England retreat. I thought of her face hidden behind a book cover and peeking up above the page, her eyes so dramatically etched with such dark thick lashes she didn't need to wear eye make-up. The green of her eyes shone like emeralds beneath her lush brows. She looked like a fashion model in every picture I'd seen, and I believed her to be the most beautiful woman in the world. And young enough to have babies in the White

House! JohnJohn was born a month before the President's inauguration, and she had appeared, miraculously sleek and lovely, at the inaugural ball. Slow dancing with the President lovey dovey like a teenager, she dazzled the eyes of all the guests with a sophistication equal to her French name Bouvier.

When she graduated from college she could speak several foreign languages fluently. During the T.V. tour of the White House, she spoke intelligently about each room she passed through in a voice that sounded bubbly, like champagne. Wearing a claret-colored woolen dress with a three-stranded pearl necklace, she had described her attempts to restore the White House to its authentic design. Now and then she told stories about the previous presidents as she stood before their portraits. I believed that each one would have been very honored to have her speaking so highly of him. I knew, too, that if she had been asked, she could have given the tour in Spanish or French or Italian without rehearsing the changes.

When the President came on the show at the end of the program he called her *Jackie* for the first time publicly and I saw how much he loved her, how deeply he admired her accomplishment. Jackie had more than two syllables, the way he said it in this long ascending wave.

I read later in a magazine that she never asked for a "better camera angle" or a retake of a segment. She simply was not conceited at all about her beauty, or what she had done. The same article said that the President had his appearance retaped once so as to smooth it out. She let him stand in the light, and only when the light spilled over onto her did she let herself shine right there beside him, brilliantly. He smiled from ear to ear as he listened to the crowds across Europe and America chanting: *Jackie, Jackie*.

All this attention did not keep her from her children. She spent hours with them, playing in their nursery, riding with Caroline who had her own pony, Macaroni, grazing on the White House lawn. A fairy tale unfolded in America. But she was there behind the scenes making it happen. Everything and everyone she touched emitted a grace I'd never known to be possible. When I realized I wouldn't see her face on T.V. or in the newspaper this summer, already I missed the bursting smile that would mark her next intelligent, stylish decision.

I remembered a picture I had seen in a *Life* magazine, showing her dressed for a ball in Paris, France. Rummaging through the magazines on my bedside stand, I found the right issue and opened it. There she was, standing tall beside the President before the dinner party she and the President had attended in the Hall of Mirrors at Versailles. The lined-up mirrors reflected images of her shoulders that grew smaller and smaller, moving off to infinity, a concept from Math class that made sense for a moment then.

Her sleeveless white silk gown showed her athletic arms sheathed in above-the-elbow gloves with accordion pleats. Her dress had little mirrors in the shapes of moons and stars appliquéed onto the fabric, and I thought it was like wearing a night sky filled with glittering stars and beaming planets. I couldn't stop staring at her. A tiara crown with a center moon and two wave-shaped side pieces glimmered through her dark hair. From her ears giant sparkling teardrop earrings fell. My mother called again and I opened my desk drawer, removed my scissors, and cut the picture out.

Jackie Kennedy reigned in America as a real queen and she was more regal than any queen in Europe. Looking at her made me feel that becoming a woman might be exciting. Especially if you met a man like the President with whom you had beautiful babies. Especially if you could speak different languages and receive high marks at a very challenging college. And still look so attractive. I told myself, *North, maybe anything is possible. Anything and everything.*

"North," my mother's voice rose an octave. I wrapped Jackie Kennedy's picture in white tissue paper, placing it into the gathered side pocket of my suitcase.

"I'm coming. One second," I shouted.

As I closed my suitcase I glanced at my desk, at the tower of books my mother had instructed me to read this summer. Most were selections from her Introduction to English Literature class: *Silas Marner, The Waste Land, Sons and Lovers*. I considered taking *The Waste Land* because it appeared thin; I felt I could read one page a night and finish by August. But then I told myself, *North, just this once let yourself be a normal teenager. Jackie Kennedy needs to read because she needs to rest. But you need to shed your studious habits, just for one summer.*

I walked over to the bedside stand and held *The Waste Land* in my hand. It was light despite the depressing sounding title. I didn't want to think about barren things, deserts and planets that whirled out in the uninhabitable universe. I snapped *The Waste Land* closed on top of the tower of books and quickly scooped them all into my arms. At my dresser I stuffed them in the bottom drawer under some t-shirts I had outgrown.

Bumping my red American Tourister suitcase down the stairs on its side, I hit it against the wall several times, leaving scrapes in the finish. I found my dad leaning against the archway of the dining room. He was standing loose-limbed like Humphrey Bogart, smoking a Pall Mall and acting like he didn't hear me struggle on the stairs. He puffed on his cigarette and the red cinder at its tip glowed. For a moment he seemed stopped in time like a picture in his tan chinos and blue oxford cloth shirt, his body slumped against the wall. He possessed a faraway look in his eyes, as if he could see beyond mountains, and suddenly I understood how my mother had fallen in love with him.

"Honey, your mom's in the car. You ready?" he asked, looking toward the window.

"Yeah, but first take some pictures," I said.

"I'll take a few." He grinned at me.

"Let me take one of you and Mom so I don't forget what you look like." I elbowed him in the arm. He smiled at me. I thought he and Queen Mom might return from Europe completely changed. She might visit Buckingham Palace and become convinced she belonged there. All the times I had shouted *Go away* at her haunted me; I remembered my face twisting, how deeply I meant it. But to leave me forever! The thought made my throat ache and my stomach turn thunderously.

Dad snapped a Polaroid of my mother and me in front of our Mercury station wagon. When he handed it to me it developed in my palm. Presto. Queen Mom and I appeared on the glossy gray square.

The shadow from Queen Mom's straw hat covered everything except her mouth which, turned my way, looked ready to command. My knees knocked together in the middle of my long stork legs, white as ice. My legs were so white I thought I would look like vampire dinner in my bathing suits.

From the back seat of the Mercury I watched the sun sweep over the fields in waves like in "America The Beautiful." The grain turned gold as if spun by Rumplestiltskin himself, and thin strands of wheat bent in the wind like tiny wires. The sky filled with white clumps of clouds that resembled cotton balls. Everything flew by in shapes like geometry, fields of corn in black earth squares, a blue circle of a farm pond and the black asphalt triangle formed by another road coming into ours at an acute angle.

At the intersection of I-35 Dad hesitated, as if he didn't know which way to turn. I wished he would flash a hard feverish stare at the road and crush the gas pedal in one foot stomp.

"Gun it," I challenged suddenly, my voice shrill.

"O.K., Parnelli. That's Parnelli Jones, Mary, right there in our back seat. She wants me to lay a patch." He laughed his laugh, all throat, an almost singing.

"Yeah, Dad. Burn some rubber. It's hot enough." I leaned forward in my seat. Parnelli Jones had won the Indianapolis 500 the week before in a record time. Still, I would rather my dad had called me Stirling, after Stirling Moss who was a driver who pushed himself to extreme limits. He was forever ending up in accidents that sent him to the hospital. Once he was in a coma for a week and then recovered miraculously. When I snatched secret chances I sat behind the steering wheel of the Mercury, pretending to be Stirling driving a fast car down a long straightaway.

"Stop wisecracking, North," my mother scowled, proving to me that I was neither Parnelli Jones nor Stirling Moss. I was merely a fourteen-year-old passenger in our wreck of a Mercury. "Save the tires, Chuck," she added drearily.

The Mercury lurched as Dad pushed on the accelerator. He didn't burn rubber, but the car gained speed and my stomach lifted as the speedometer touched sixty. When I squinted, the fields, roads and cars flew by in splashes like the colors in the abstract paintings they showed in big color pictures in my dad's art magazines. The forward speed of the Mercury threw me somewhere outside myself, somewhere up the road ahead when I could drive a car, pressing my foot to the floor.

Time whirled by faster with each mile per hour we gained; I sensed the ninth grade trailing off behind me. And I wanted my first real kiss to happen, wanted my lips to press against a boy's lips—not just for an instant, but for minutes at a time. And the place between my legs seemed to open where I felt a wetness inside my underpants; then my left breast pointed through my A-cup bra. When I saw the drawn-up nipple, I slumped forward to hide it beneath the white puff of my cotton blouse. Still, I felt so excited I could almost sense a boy's arms tightening around me. I imagined looking into his eyes, closer and closer, until his skin was a beige blur. I could feel his phantom breath as he asked me, *would you take a ride in my Chevy.*

"Fast enough to please you, Parnelli?" my dad spoke from the front seat. But he could have been talking to me from Mars I felt so far away in the fantasy, the boy's arms curled around me.

"Yes." Like a hiss my answer seemed to speak to the phantom boy. But I told myself, *straighten up.* Because my mother's warnings about becoming *boy crazy* played in my mind. "Girls who chase boys end up in trouble," she said. What if boys pursued me? Was I supposed to hide in a closet all my life and end up with soft bones?

Beside us the Irish Hills rolled by, smudged green hills with soft slopes that seemed to belong to a foreign country. Herds of sheep grazed on the hills looking like giant rocks until they started moving around, bleating. The scenery couldn't hold me and the car seemed as quiet as the center of a mountain. I studied my parents, and they, too, resembled stone. I stared into the basket weave of my mother's straw hat until I couldn't bear the little weaving pattern—like the one in potholders we made at Y Day Camp—any longer. I leaned forward and asked if I could listen to the radio.

"Then we all have to listen," my mother barked.

"Please," I begged.

"Boredom is a side effect of affluence, North." Queen Mom glared over the seat back at me, moon-faced. She complained almost non-stop about needing money, and entertained liberal ideals utterly out of sync with her *nouveau riche* upbringing. My Grandparents North, her parents, were almost millionaires and their money was made from cars, the machines my mother called *strictly utilitarian objects*. My Grandfather North devoted his life to climbing the corporate ladder at the Ford Motor Company. My mother's inheritance financed this trip to Europe.

"Oh, c'mon, Mary," my dad said. "You won't have to listen to rock and roll music all summer. You'll probably miss it by August." His words were magical; so rarely did he take my side.

"All right. If it's played softly. We're almost to Judd's, anyway," she said in a Jane Mansfield voice, the voice she used whenever she spoke of Uncle Judd. She admired him for his income as a successful plastic surgeon. Money was the North family god, even if *in absentia*. Sometimes when I saw her staring his way at a family party I saw love in her eyes, and believed that one turn of his head, one flicker of his finger, would have called her across the plain of relatives to his side.

"I wonder if Judd still has the 'Jess picture'?" my dad said. Dad shot the picture when I was ten, running naked and wild in a meadow with the neighbor's pony, Jess. At his art opening in the Hearst Gallery in 1961 when he first showed it, Uncle Judd lifted his chin and slacked his jaw to study my pose. The crowd filtered out of the gallery, but Uncle Judd stayed. He whispered in the corner with the gallery director and a society lady who wore spike heels. I hovered beside the refreshment table not far from them, staring at the empty plates, the used wine glasses, rims smudged with all colors of lipstick. It looked like the aftermath of a party for Caligula or one of the other Roman emperors who threw up after huge meals.

"Buying innocence, Judson?" the society lady asked.

"Have to support Chuck." Uncle Judd chuckled like Ward Cleaver, as the gallery director set a red dot beside the photograph, making it his.

"Another Humbert," the lady hissed, walking away, her heels

hitting the floor like nails. I gulped down an entire cup of lemonade punch, and eyed my mother with a let's-leave-now-glance. She shot me an icy stare, then walked across the floor like a model on a show ramp, arms swinging. Uncle Judd smiled her toward him. Her skirt rose above her knees. She walked with her neck first, like a giraffe. He lifted her hand in his, wrapping a big arm around her waist. She looked at the photograph. "Jess and North in their birthday suits," she said with a laugh of abandon.

That night I vowed I'd never again pose for my father. Yet when he asked me to model in a bikini the very next week I agreed because it was a bathing suit. And the sessions freed me, let me be another girl, more glamorous than studious North Wagoner. I said: *Look, art's where you do things you wouldn't ordinarily do*. Yet I wondered what Uncle Judd did with the picture. I suspected I was an exhibitionist for stripping with Jess. *Old Jess*. He always wore *his* birthday suit and no one blamed him.

"What's an exhibitionist?" I asked my father.

"Someone who does things in public for attention," he answered, finally finding a rock and roll station on the radio. Johnny Mathis sang "It's Not For Me to Say."

"That's Jess and me. In the picture," I said.

"That's an art photo, North. You were supposed to be the universal sexually free child." My father talked this way about photography. He talked like Montaigne or Rousseau reincarnate and I wanted to cover my ears.

"Turn the radio up," I said loudly. Dad obeyed. "It's Not For Me to Say" played louder, Johnny Mathis sounding gay.

"He told me he hung it in the living room. At Glass Lake." My mother pulled a finger along the edge of the dashboard. She sighed like Hamlet's mother. Too big. I wondered why she hadn't tried harder to please Uncle Judd years ago; everyone in the family knew she had dated Uncle Judd before he dated my Aunt Joan. How many times had he kissed her? How far had they gone in *amour?* Jackie Kennedy could have said that word in a way that would make you want to be in love, pronto. Once, Grandfather North told me my mother's political opinions put Uncle Judd off because she always voted a straight Democratic ticket and Uncle Judd was a staunch Republican. They usually fought during at least one holiday dinner over the results of the November elections.

Sometimes I thought my mother voted for President Kennedy partly because he was such a fast reader. He consumed whole books in one afternoon, his eyes flitting over pages like that little white ball bouncing over song words on T.V. Kids at school signed up for Evelyn Woods speed reading courses so they could model themselves after him. He had written a book called *Profiles in Courage* during his recovery from back surgery and it won the Pulitzer Prize. My mother told me in her expansive voice the story of President Kennedy's bravery in *the War*. She said, "Just look at him, a hero. *Noblesse oblige* is alive and well in the Democratic Party." Then she laughed, enjoying her opinion. Such proclamations always brought her moments of brief and exalted happiness. I was supposed to applaud as if for Eleanor Roosevelt then.

Nat King Cole sang, "Those Lazy-Hazy-Crazy Days of Summer." Then a disc jockey spoke in a fuzzy voice above the white noise and static until a man's voice boomed: "Sunday at Motor City Speedway, the racing capital of mid-America. All the great cars and drivers will be there." As I listened to that hammering voice I wanted to be there, too, on Sunday or any day, to be there at the speedway where I had never before been, where the car engine sounds would spin a corona of noise around my head while the best drivers in America turned back death at every turn.

The announcer began talking about an accident they'd had the year before at the speedway where Connie Kalitta spun out on a curve, wrecking three other cars. I imagined the cars crushed like metal accordions, webs of broken glass in the windshields.

"Turn here," Queen Mom commanded. We veered into the Diehls' long driveway with the white brick markers. Sunlight flashed through the windows of the Mercury, milky on my arms. The Shirelles sang "Dedicated to the One I Love" on the radio. I thought I would sing this song to my first boy of the summer. I'd chant it at night to call him to me from across the quiet of Glass Lake, raising him up like a spirit, a phantom boy made real.

• • •

Aunt Joan loped up the back lawn to meet us dressed in a French blue shift. Like a coach my mother quizzed her about her plans for the summer. We huddled in the center of the back lawn. Dad slipped off to the Mercury and leaned like an auto mechanic on break against the hood. Aunt Joan stared blankly, her eyes shifting up, then down. Her streaked hair was pulled back in a French twist and her features appeared pinched like those of a child whose mother had pulled her hair into tight braids.

"So Joan, what's your summer look like?" Queen Mom asked, "Besides babysitting North?" She laughed a conspiratorial laugh.

"I'm in a play reading group," Aunt Joan said ethereally. "We're doing the *Glass Menagerie*. I play Amanda, with a Southern accent." She smiled and I almost laughed when I pictured Aunt Joan speaking in a drawl. But then I saw resolve in her face and caught my grin behind my hand.

"I hadn't expected you till after lunch," Aunt Joan said to me. "Dee's out skiing. But she'll come in soon, hungry and cold. The lake's chilly this year." Aunt Joan looked into my face. I imagined she was sizing me up to see how much trouble I would be for the summer, but then I noticed her eyes looking beyond me at the tea roses climbing the white fence that ran along the boundary of their estate.

"North needs eight hours of sleep," my mother told Aunt Joan. "If you want the good North. Without rest she's a monster. Right, honey?" I stood zombielike, Miss Statue. "She listens to rock and roll nonstop. Tell her when you can't stand it. Just tell her to turn it off," Queen Mom said. Aunt Joan nodded. "And remind her to eat fruits and vegetables." My mother smoothed the curls that spun like excelsior on top of my head as if I were her pet. I felt like growling.

"An apple a day," Aunt Joan said, coming to life suddenly, laughing and pulling at the sash on her shift.

"When's Judd coming down?" My mother dipped her shoe into the gravel and drew a line.

"On some weekends. He works way too much." Aunt Joan fingered her sash.

"You've got it made, spending his money. Work, work, work. Wish somebody I know would do the same," my mother shouted my father's way while throwing him a sharp glance. He slumped down further against the Mercury's hood. The sun went under a cloud. Shadows pooled around us. I felt cold and separated from everyone, though I had not moved an inch.

"Queen bee Joanie. You're the queen bee," my mother said, shaking Aunt Joan's forearm. Look who's queening whom, I thought.

"Oh, Mary. Really. Bees? You've always been so creative with words." Aunt Joan tossed her head. Queen Mom shrugged her off.

I phased out the rest of their conversation and stared at the lake. Flocks of motor boats zoomed in zig-zag patterns, the white churning water trailing behind them like jet streams. Some of the trails left scripted letters in the blue surface. I saw an L and an O where a boat circled around to pick up a downed skier.

"Mary, go see the world while you can. North—" Aunt Joan took my hand in hers, "you'll be happy here." Her voice softened. She walked between us up to the Mercury stroking my neck, but I recoiled from her icy fingers.

I pulled on Dad's hand when we reached the car. "One last picture of you two!" I said. He handed me the camera and I shot my mother and him beside the Mercury. Queen Mom towered by the driver's door, her head turned toward Dad and her eyes uplifted. The suit she wore looked white, almost shining. Dad bent over to kiss my mother on the lips, his back curving like a movie star's. I could have counted on my hand the times I had seen him kiss her on the lips. Racy kisses. I loved seeing them like this. I hoped their kiss promised new happiness in their marriage, a return to true love in Europe.

Their trip would be, in Queen Mom's words, "our first honeymoon." They had postponed a honeymoon because Grandfather North held back my mother's inheritance for years. He didn't like it when she married an artist who, in his words, "would spend every penny he gave her." But when I had my eleventh birthday he gave in, and established her trust fund. He said I would need to go to college one day. He didn't want me to be punished for her choice of a husband. I always hoped that my father had never heard this story told so coldly. Once she had received her money my mother asked Uncle Judd to invest it for her, and now that his wise choices had paid off, my parents could afford this trip and still send me to an Ivy League school.

I watched as they slid into the Mercury and slammed the doors. Click. It seemed momentous, like the closing of a space capsule door. Then their good-byes erupted as fast as the quick light of my dad's camera flash igniting the darkness. The wheels of the Mercury kicked up gravel from the drive as Dad drove them away.

"North, we'll write you!" my mother called, leaning out her window. She waved, and blew me a kiss the way she had once blown kisses when she left me with the babysitter. But her thrown kisses had always disappointed me because I never felt them land anywhere on my body no matter how patiently I waited, teetering on my clumsy legs. I'd once tried to catch them as if they were soap bubbles on my hand.

The Mercury rattled up the driveway, a gray cloud of steel. Somewhere down the road, my parents would lean toward one another like teenage lovers in a car, the words *I love you, I love you, too,* flowing from their lips. I saw their words encased in balloon captions like conversations in the Archie cartoons. The empty place where the car had been parked looked huge now beside the garage.

"Let's go inside," Aunt Joan said. But I gripped the itinerary my mother had hurled into my hand. It flapped in the wind like a little paper sail. I opened it and scanned the list of all the places my parents would visit, the addresses of American Express offices where I could write them.

"Lots of cities there for you to write to." Aunt Joan meant to comfort me. She smiled a drifty smile and walked toward the house. "Leave your suitcase here. I'll get Mr. Robertson to carry it," she called back to me. When she was out of earshot, I tried to read through the names of the cities in France and Italy and Germany but the letters blurred. I couldn't focus through my tears. The print looked like weird hieroglyphics on the white page. If only I could say the names of those cities with the correct foreign accents I thought I would somehow be connected to my parents. Already I wanted them, though my escape had been my main desire for weeks. Now I tried to say Paris, to say the name of the city of lovers. *Paree, Paree,* I said. But I sounded like a farm girl calling a hog. I wished the words would work like the ruby slippers Dorothy wore in Oz, but instead of going home I'd go to Paris! "Ah, gay *Paree*," I said, and I sounded like Pépé Le Pew. I couldn't speak foreign languages like Jackie Kennedy. It seemed that everyone: Aunt Joan, my parents, even Dee—though I hadn't yet seen her—had vanished into the shadow of my bad pronunciations. A chill climbed my backbone then, even though it was almost the middle of summer.

Aunt Joan emerged from the back door to the house with Mr. Robertson, her houseman and gardener, following. His silver hair glinted in the sun. I folded up the itinerary and stuffed it into my pocket as they approached. Mr. Robertson took my suitcase in a shaky hand.

"Thanks," I said, as I was very glad to have someone waiting on me. But I hoped he wouldn't have a heart attack which I'd then feel I had caused. Queen Mom's influence. Mr. Robertson carried my suitcase to my room, a suite with a bathroom adjoining Dee's room. He brought me pink towels embossed with roses, laying them on the bed. He told me to call him if I needed anything.

"O.K." I whispered, feeling somewhat ashamed now to notice his humpback shuffle toward the door. I watched him bow slightly as he turned to leave my room, his black pants dusty at the cuffs. He shuffled down the hall. Rustle, Scrape. Shuffle. *C'mon, Mr. Robertson, you can make it;* I rooted for him, because he seemed even more alone than I was then.

I closed my door and in the quiet of my room I opened my suitcase and unwrapped Jackie Kennedy's picture. Her tiara nearly glistened when the sunlight rushing through my windows hit the jewels. Beside her the President flashed his wide smile. *Paree. City of lovers. Paree.* I could almost say it now, when alone with her picture. I danced a step with her in my hand, picturing myself in a ball gown, dancing all night with a prince of a boy—not a boy turned from a frog to a prince, but a princely boy from the beginning. Looking at Jackie Kennedy made me feel I was not alone at Glass Lake. She was with me, another, nicer mother. Beautiful and elegant. *Be like me,* she seemed to say to me from her picture.

I looked for a place to keep the picture. I couldn't leave it out in the open in the house of an avowed Republican. A colonial-style bed with a white eyelet bedspread and canopy stood in the far corner of the room between two sets of windows. One window had a built-in window seat with huge sunflowers printed on the cushions. Beside each of the windows two panels of chintz curtain fell, the pattern of goldfinches ascending like ivy, twisting vertically. Through the windows I saw the north cove of Glass Lake where lily pads grew and blossomed with yellow magnolia-like flowers in mid-July.

There was an antique bureau made of burled walnut. The mirror on top swiveled inside an oval frame. I turned it around and around, first to my reflection. I saw my gnarled hair, dark, chin length, curly and full from the humidity; my hazel eyes, half Dad's brown and half my mother's green; my lips, curved and thick. My mouth looked so much like my mother's I almost cried out, *Is my mouth sexy? Am I as sexy as Queen Mom?*

Sweat beaded my palms, wetting Jackie Kennedy's picture. But I said to myself, *Jackie Kennedy is sexy. She's sexy and she's pretty and she's smart.* I didn't have to be like my mother, who screamed her unhappiness like some Queen for the Day loser gone rogue. I wiped my hand on my shorts and turned the mirror around. The back side showed a silvery black glaze. I tucked the picture of Jackie Kennedy and the President in the corner between the mirror back and the dark wood frame.

I placed the picture of Queen Mom and Dad in the opposite corner, their heads turned toward one another, the dark of the mirror back pooled behind. I slipped their itinerary into the top drawer of my bureau, burying it beneath mounds of underwear. Just as I slid the drawer shut Dee padded into my room, barefoot.

"God, North. Hi," she said, hugging me so close I smelled her Coppertone lotion. We sat down on my bed and talked, at first bashful, then faster and faster. Like a speeded-up recording.

"Best news first?" Dee asked me. I nodded. "I've got a new boyfriend," she said, grinning.

"What's his name?" *Tell me, tell me,* I thought.

"Shrimp." She laughed.

"What is he, a midget?" I rolled my eyes, Jerry Lewislike.

"No, he's real strong. Just shorter than me." Dee fingered the elastic along the leg of her bikini. "You'll see when I take you to the Club. The boys hang out there." I hoped they'd be dream boys like the phantom boy in my fantasy, boys with arms full of muscle and with sweet, unsaid words running through their minds, romantic messages which one of them would one day deliver to me. Just me.

Dream Boys

At breakfast Dee described the boys I would be meeting at the Club, trailing their names together: *Bill Frank George Don.* "Frank's a card," Dee said, smoothing her auburn hair at the crown where it was teased. "And Bill's Mr. Perfection."

"What's so perfect about him?" I asked.

"Everything. Too much, really. He's almost a nerd. He wins all the boat races and the car races and makes straight As." Dee laughed. "I should've picked him instead of Shrimp. But, God, Shrimp can ski."

"Car races?" I knocked my cereal bowl with my arm, sending the Cheerios spinning on top of the milk like tiny wheels.

"They drag race behind the Club. But don't go, North. It's real dusty." Dee grimaced, and faked a cough until I nodded. Still, despite her description I wanted to watch the boys race the first chance I had.

"North, eat up. It's almost ten-thirty," Dee said.

"I'm done." I felt the Cheerios and my stomach collide.

She bolted upright and lifted my wrist, pulling me halfway across the living room as if on her leash. She let go in front of the sofa. I saw Jess and me, naked, hanging there just as Queen Mom had said.

The day Dad took the picture rushed back to me. July, very hot. I had just turned ten. The smell of newly mown grass hung in the air. In the middle of the meadow behind our house I shed all my clothes, including my pink Carter's underpants. Wrapping a sheer white curtain around my head and shoulders I fashioned a Sari-like dress. Dad twined blue tassels from an old curtain valance around Jess's head.

Then I danced in circles around Jess as if he were a primeval fire. The curtain unwound as I ran. Dad snapped pictures as it fell away. The last shot was this one. Me with my arms flung up, my breasts, two bee sting marks on my chest, and my outward belly button like the tied end of a balloon.

"My dad loves that picture," Dee said, rolling her eyes.

"No way he could," I said.

"He stares at it all the time."

"Don't say that." My body looked so gangling my cheeks flushed. I felt a rush of energy like Superman in the phone booth and I imagined yanking the picture down. The ways my Uncle Judd could change women's bodies flew through my mind. Sometimes I wondered if he had worked on Dee, because she seemed perfect with her two white-domed breasts the same generous size and her nipples cake-icing rosettes. Perhaps he'd even pulled her waist in tight and firmed her thighs with muscle. My mother said he performed miraculous surgical feats: nose jobs, face lifts, eyelid tucks, and new chins. Like a sculptor of flesh she once told me. But, no, I thought. More like God making a person in his desired image.

"I look so stupid," I said, my knees, weakening. "I'd never do that again."

"Run around with a pony?" Dee teased.

"Run naked in a field," I said.

"I bet it felt good," Dee giggled, blushing.

"I wouldn't know," I said in quite a mean voice suddenly, although I did recall feeling pleasure running in the field. And freedom. The wind on my bare shoulders. Weeds brushing between my thighs. But seeing the photograph didn't make me feel good. Any pervert who came to visit could look at me naked, not to mention what the boys I might meet at the Club would think.

"Let's take it down," I said. "It looks stained on the matting under the glass. Get your mom to get it fixed." I stood very close to the picture and peered, grimacing.

"No way we're touching it." Dee ran out the door to the dock, calling, "Last one to the boat's a rotten egg."

I followed Dee. She let the speedboat down off its lift, the white

released wheel spinning fast circles, like my own thoughts of my naked image in that house behind me going around. Aunt Joan walked
out after us to the dock's end.

"Off so early?" she asked, her hair styled in a beehive that caught
the sunlight like spun sugar icing.

"Yep." Dee lowered herself into the boat and started the motor.
I crawled through the back seat into the front seat beside her. Aunt
Joan stood mute watching us. No interrogation, not one word. I wondered if she could really be Queen Mom's sister. Dee backed us up,
then turned around and motored out. Aunt Joan waved good-bye for
a long time as if she had nowhere else to go, as if she might stay there
forever, gazing out after us as the boats passed, as the skiers fell and
rose. I waved back as she shrunk in the distance.

Then Dee opened the throttle on the Johnson motor, and the
thrust of the boat threw me back into the white-cushioned seat. The
bow of the G-3 rose like a space rocket on a launch pad, then leveled
into a plane. Dee drove at full speed toward the channel that split the
sandbar between the north and south ends of the lake. When we hit
a wake from another boat the floor of the G-3 banged against the
white crests of water. I bounced up, then down. Each time I landed
my brain jarred inside my skull. I worried that if I suffered brain
damage from boat riding I'd have to go to a junior college and endure
Queen Mom's wrath on top of a disability.

All around us the sun burned down so fiercely that everything
seemed glazed with a white icing of light and heat. The boats, the
lake, the skiers, and the sails hung suspended as if in a hazy island
that floated in air. White sprays of water flew on both sides of us like
fins. In the distance the buoys of the channel bobbed, little dwarfs
drowning, then reviving again and again. The south shore grew visible, a green horizon smudged with the colored shapes of cottages.

"North, look!" Dee shouted, but I could barely hear above the
turbulence. She pointed to a wooden Chris Craft with a boy skiing
behind it, zipping in and out of the boat's wake way out to one side
then back through, his head almost touching the water. He let some
slack into his ski rope and snapped forward as the rope tightened.

"That's Shrimp," Dee shouted. "It's him." She grabbed a silver cylinder from the glove compartment between us and spread light pink lipstick on her lips. Two arcs of powder blue eye shadow fanned above her eyes so that she looked years over fifteen.

"He's the best skier around!" Dee shouted, waving her arms in Shrimp's direction. When he saw her he dropped his ski and skied barefooted. Dee clapped with both hands and waved wildly. The speedboat veered toward a red sailboat off to our left. An old man and woman crouched inside it, glaring. I pointed to the sailboat and grabbed Dee's forearm.

"Jesus!" she screamed.

"Turn the steering wheel!" I pressed her fingers around it. My voice sounded mechanical, but Dee obeyed me. She spun the wheel and we just missed the red sailboat.

"Idiots," the old woman screamed at us.

"God, North, I've never come so close to hitting somebody." Dee's face paled. "It was seeing Shrimp. I'm crazy about him." She looked as swept away as Elizabeth Taylor had looked whenever Richard Burton approached her in the movie *Cleopatra*. I imagined Dee would obey Shrimp even if he told her to have an asp brought to her bedroom in a basket.

"I've missed him so much," Dee said, settling down in her seat and driving carefully. For hours last night she told me how much she had missed Shrimp while he was away at the Dare Devil Ski Meet in Petoskey. This was the first time Dee had seen him in two weeks and I knew she felt overwhelmed. Still, the near crash terrified me. *So that's what happens when you find your dream boy,* I thought, *you lose touch with reality.* You're driving in your car and he puts his hand on your thigh; you drive over the yellow line and there's a Mack truck barreling toward you. Even though you see it, you freeze because all you can feel is that *one place* where his hand touches you and it's everything.

The apron on Dee's pink polka dot bikini flapped in the wind as we drove closer to the Club, the lines of the big white wooden building sharpening. At full throttle Dee steered us straight in, and for these last few minutes of high speed I closed my eyes and felt the wind flatten my hair. I listened to the motor whir, letting the air pour in through my opened mouth. The sense of speed hurled me outside myself like a satellite, like Sputnik. And I wished that Dee and I could speed like this always, that we could circle the world through canals that ran like the longitude lines on a globe. And as we raced my right breast would grow larger, so that by the time we returned to Glass Lake my two breasts would be identical. I would emerge from the G-3 looking like Dee: perfect.

Inside the Yacht Club the rooms were vast with twelve-foot high ceilings. Oak floors glistened with the sunlight that poured in through the door-sized windows. Heading toward the snack bar Dee and I walked through the ballroom where a thin girl our age slipped a coin into the juke box in the far corner of the room. Her bleached blond hair hung limp and straight to her shoulders. I thought she had tried for the surfer girl look. Because it was a fad that started a year or so ago in California and was just now catching on in Michigan.

"Don't Say Nothin' Bad (About My Baby)" by the Cookies rang out. The poor grammar the lead singer used would have provoked a lecture from my mother. I was relieved she was far away in Austria where Mozart was played daily in parlors on authentic instruments. I envisioned my dad holding her hand while the violins performed a fancy slide that sent her insides up and down the way your stomach flies around when you're on a Ferris wheel. When you're up so high and it feels like the look in your boy's face could hold the sky up around you. And you are the stars, all of them glinting in the sapphire night.

"North, you hungry?" Dee asked as she stepped into the snack bar line.

"Always." I put my hand on my stomach and read the day's menu scrawled in chalk across a black board. Back along the white Formica counters a silver malted milk machine stood ready to whir.

"Order anything," Dee said. She spent money so easily, and my dad and mother never charged things.

I deliberated between a malted and French fries, wanting both but fearing gluttony, which was a sin. The starving children in China would thrust their bony hands out to me the way Queen Mom predicted, if only in dreams. Madeline Spears had warned that the battle of the bulge could begin any day now. Dee seemed to prove Madeline's theory true, having just ordered a Diet Rite Cola and an orange popsicle.

"Is that all you're getting?" I asked.

"They're my favorite things." Dee flipped her hair behind her ears. The waitress stared at me.

"Sorry. I'll hurry." I thought about the way girls starved themselves, hoping to resemble the models in *Vogue*, wanting to be tall and thin as Barbies.

"I'd like a chocolate malted," I said. Starvation was something I could not abide. For two weeks in the seventh grade I had gone on a crash diet, not because I was really fat, but to learn discipline. I ate one can of Campbell's vegetable soup a day and four soda crackers. One Tuesday I fainted at the drinking fountain next to science class. John Easton, who was a football star, caught me in his arms the way Rhett Butler caught Scarlet O'Hara in *Gone With The Wind*. Then Judy Tuttle ran for our homeroom teacher while John carried me to the principal's office. I always wished I could better remember John's arms around me.

Madeline Spears, who watched the whole thing, said John had pressed my head close against his chest as he carried me. I always wished I had been more conscious of how that felt. In the principal's office I lay on a cot that, as I revived, began to smell musty. When the guidance counselor asked what was wrong, I confessed my plan to become a woman reduced to bones and muscle. But then one of the secretaries brought me a cheeseburger and French fries on a tray. The grease smell wafted up to my nose. Within minutes I devoured everything. Now I saw my knee bones like funny door knobs in my thin legs. I was already called *skinny* by the older boys at school. I told myself, *Jackie Kennedy's favorite lunch is a hamburger with French fries.*

"Let's sit on the porch. Watch for the boys," Dee said, signing the bill after the waitress handed me my malted. "I can't believe nobody's here," she lamented.

We walked through the ballroom, heading out to the glassed-in porch. Above us a crystal chandelier hung with its many pendant-shaped pieces dangling in the wind. Clinking, a sound cold and white. Two leather-covered doors off to our left opened to a long bar shaped like a giant C. Behind the bar was a room-length mirror with rows of liquor bottles like little skyscrapers shelved in front. A wooden ship's wheel and two stuffed fish hung above it. At the far end of the bar a young woman who looked to be in her early twenties sat smoking a cigarette as if it were her last one. Her neck muscles pulled with each drag.

"That's Linda Turner." Dee veered into the barroom toward Linda. Sipping my malted, I followed her. "She manages parties for the Club." Dee said *hi* to Linda, who lifted her chin revealing an aristocratic face with high cheekbones and a long, pretty nose.

"Oh. Dee," Linda said, waving her hand slowly, as if through water. Dee stopped by Linda. I smelled what must have been her cheap, dime store perfume.

"Linda—meet my cousin, North," Dee said. Linda Turner studied me with her eyes aglow like miniature suns. I cleared my throat, managing to say *hi*. Linda answered with a stilted *hello* while staring deeper. If her eyes had been X-rays, I'd have been another Madame Curie by the end of her look.

"Linda, we want a reservation for North's birthday," Dee said, "next Monday, July first. A table for ten."

"I'll take care of it." Linda pulled another drag from her cigarette, the muscles in her neck bulging like purse straps. She smoked Camels. I suddenly believed the advertisement that said a person would walk a mile for one of them.

"But I don't know anybody," I said.

"This way you will. Soon." Dee smiled, but Linda didn't smile back. She shifted her weight on the stool and her feet hit the bar in front of her making a strange wooden sound. I saw she wore pants and strange thick white socks that were too hot, I thought, for the summer.

Dee walked toward the porch. I said, *nice to meet you* to Linda Turner and followed Dee. I had learned to be polite from my mother's etiquette drills. Queen Mom was my Henry Higgins who said I'd been born a little barbarian in need of shaping up.

Dee and I sat down at a small table by the front windows where I watched Linda Turner rise too slowly for her pertness. When she walked she dragged her left foot. Had she had polio? I stared after her.

"Earth to North. Earth to North," Dee teased.

"What's with Linda Turner?" I asked.

"She's always in a bad mood." Dee's face tightened like a mask.

"Did she sprain her ankle?"

"No." Dee looked out the window to the lake where the water looked smooth and shimmery like glass that would break all around you if you dove through it. "She lost her foot in an accident." Dee's words flew past my face. The malted milk stuck in my throat as if meat. "She has a fake foot, North. But she learned to walk real well, so don't sit around feeling sorry for her like she's pathetic." My stomach turned suddenly.

"How'd it happen?" I asked.

"She was swimming and a motor boat propeller cut her foot off. In an accident about eight years ago."

I couldn't say anything. In the ballroom the chandelier crystals beat together, a high-pitched icy noise, brittle and white.

"Don't think about it, North." Dee hit her palm against the table, her pink fingernails gleaming. "Let's go down to the gazebo. That's where the boys must be."

As Dee stood, she smiled alluringly. I thought she was fantasizing finding Shrimp there. Once outside we arranged our sandals along the Yacht Club's field stone foundation. Tiptoeing across the lawn, Dee pressed a finger to her lips. "Shh," she said, "down there." She pointed to the flat roof jutting aboveground next to cement stairs. "That's the gazebo. Not a word from now on." Dee's eyes glittered, mischief in the little flecks of gold.

We squatted along the roof of the gazebo in front of a line of clerestory windows filled with screen. Five boys gathered inside, most dressed in shorts and T-shirts, some standing and others sitting on crude wooden deck chairs. Each boy held a piece of rope in his hand. A few of them were tying boat knots.

"Try the bowline," the most handsome boy said. He looked as if he could enroll at Princeton any day. After one look at him, the admissions department people would have admitted him on sight. He wore his dark hair combed to the side. Yet his hair seemed thick, so if the wind blew through it, it would surely toss wildly. I imagined him standing on a windswept beach, looking as irresistible as Frank Sinatra in *From Here to Eternity*. He wore black Buddy Holly–style glasses, too.

"The rabbit goes 'round the tree and up through the hole. Back 'round the tree again, and down through the hole," he said, moving the rope with the story. When he finished, he pulled the end of the loop to test the knot and it stayed.

"Big deal," a stocky boy next to him said.

"That's George Parker, G. P. He's a dip," Dee whispered. *I thought we couldn't talk*, I lip-synced, my eyes popping.

"You can whisper." Dee grinned, scrunching up her nose. Elfish.

"Tied up in knots. That's how Bill feels around Sally Fry," a boy wearing chinos and green-framed sunglasses teased.

"Tongue-tied. Have you tried to kiss her with your tongue tied, Bill?" George Parker taunted.

"Have you felt her big tits, Hamilton? They're handfuls aren't they? They're jugs." The tall boy with acne said *tits* so loudly the word burned my ears. By now most of the boys were laughing.

"I never felt her tits," Bill said, and I believed him. I pictured him taking a lie detector test, passing no matter what the charge.

"That's Bill Hamilton," Dee said. "See what I mean about him being handsome?" She elbowed me.

"Yes," I whispered. He was handsome right out of the Ivy League, like President Kennedy. I imagined myself walking arm in arm across Harvard Yard with Bill Hamilton. He wore a gray Harris tweed suit and I wore a blue wool dress with bell sleeves that the wind lifted open. I whirled in his arms like Ginger Rogers and everybody in the Yard stared. My eyes were pure green like Jackie Kennedy's.

"Who's Sally Fry?" I asked.

"She's a party girl. Not pretty. But she's got a great bod. Frank says she's 34-22-36," Dee said. Those three numbers hit me like stones.

"Bill wants to get into Sally's pants," G. P. said in a sing-song voice. He strutted after Bill Hamilton, who swung the knotted rope in his hand like a whip. "You want a piece. A piece of pie. Cherry pie would be all right, too. Wouldn't it?" G. P. almost stepped on Bill's heels.

"Damn it, G. P., shut up." Bill Hamilton pivoted and faced G. P.

"You're whipped. You want some of Sally Fry so bad." G. P. flexed his knees, tightened his thigh muscles, and pushed Bill backwards.

"Up yours, G. P. All you want to do is talk dirty. I don't give one goddamn about Sally Fry." Bill regained his balance and twirled his rope beside his hip. "I wouldn't have her if she lay down on the floor naked with her legs spread open." Bill turned and walked toward the front of the gazebo.

"You lie, Hamilton. How about you and I race? The winner gets first dibs on Sally," the tall boy with acne said, laughing wildly.

"Shit," G. P. said. "I'll race you, Frank."

"No, I challenge Bill." Frank set his hand on his hip, looking to Bill.

"I'll race you, Frank, but I'm just racing to race. That's all. Not for Sally." Bill tossed his knotted rope on the table, then stood brooding, gazing out at the lake. I admired his face in profile, and the way he said no to making a girl his prize, a girl he didn't seem to want to win, ever. Then I envisioned the race, the cars with their engines churning, their tires spinning over the ground. And right then I promised myself, *North, you will go to that drag race if it's the last thing you do.*

"Bill, what if we tell Sally you couldn't care less," Frank sparred.

"Frank, go ahead. Try me. Do it."

I felt my body loosen when I realized that Bill Hamilton really wasn't in love with Sally Fry. But my face felt flushed and my ears rang with the word *piece*. Like in an echo chamber. I, too, could be called a piece by some boy. Any girl could be. I focused on Bill, tall Ivy League Bill. I closed my eyes to daydream of him. "Don't call me a piece," I shouted at him back at Harvard Yard. The sleeves on my dress rippled in the wind. "You're not a piece," Bill answered me. Then I pictured myself taking my clothes off the way I had for Dad's photography sessions. I lay down naked in the middle of the Yard like I did when Jess and I frolicked. Bill Hamilton came to me, stroking with his thin hands, cool on my thighs, my breasts, my face. *Don't call me a piece, I said. And he said, You're not a piece. You're North.*

But Queen Mom told me that boys dropped girls who gave into their advances. *North*, I told myself then, *just don't go all the way. Let Bill Hamilton kiss you on the lips, and even let the tip of his tongue play in your mouth.*

Bill, try my limits. Try me. Come around the Diehls' house calling my name.

"Do you want to meet him?" Dee asked, and my cheeks felt fiery. I thought Dee had read the sex scene in my mind.

"Yes, yes," I stammered.

"C'mon then. They'll be coming up the stairs." Inside the gazebo the boys gathered their belongings. "We'll run up to the Club, put on our sandals and walk toward the gazebo like we've just come outside." Dee's voice was breathy. "I'll introduce you to Bill. Oh, I wish Shrimp was around. This is so exciting." My stomach tied itself into knots as tight as Bill Hamilton's bowline.

Dee and I slipped into our sandals and walked, just as she planned, down the concrete walk toward the gazebo. I tried to picture my face the way Bill Hamilton might see me, whether I looked homely or attractive. Finally I asked Dee: "How do I look?"

Pretty, she said, but my hair felt wiry and the tip of my nose, when I touched it, seemed chiseled and thick.

We stood at the top of the stairs while the boys ascended, Bill coming first, with his skin a deep bronze color like the little girl's skin in the Coppertone ads, the little girl who pulled down her underpants to show her tan. His eyes were dark brown like my dad's eyes. But his eyes looked fierce, like Stirling Moss's eyes when the TV announcer had asked about his last accident and he said, "It was a bloody good crash, old boy." I envisioned Bill driving a fast car that I would ride in. Soon.

"Hi, Bill," Dee said. All the boys stopped in their tracks to stare at us. "This is my cousin, North. She's here for the summer. North, this is Bill Hamilton, and George Parker, and Larry Meeker, and Don Richardson. And Frank Boyd." Frank Boyd was the tall boy who had said *tits* so often. Bill Hamilton looked in my face for what seemed hours and I felt like a balloon in the Macy's Thanksgiving Day Parade, as if I needed ropes tied on my hands and people below to hold me or I would float off. *Hello, North.* His words rushed my ears. He waved his long hand, so tan and as brown as wood. I wanted him to touch me softly, to brush his fingers over my cheek.

"Hi, Bill," I said in a croaky voice. His name caught in my throat as if I'd already consumed him. Buddy Holly songs ran through my mind. I knew then why Dee almost hit the red sailboat. If I'd been driving a vehicle at the moment I met Bill I would have crashed. Gone through the splintering glass, dumb and eager. Dee pulled me by the wrist along the sidewalk. Bill Hamilton towered above us, at least six feet tall. His face was a classical face like the one Michelangelo had sculpted on the *David*. I saw him naked like the *David* and my toe caught in the dockboard. I stumbled forward.

"North's falling for you." Dee laughed, taking my hand in hers to steady me. "So why don't you visit us, Bill?" Dee said. "Why don't you come to North's birthday party Monday. Here at the Club. You'd like that, wouldn't you, North?"

"Yes," I said. *Yes. Yes. Yes.* I didn't stop saying the word until Dee stepped on the toes of my uninjured foot. The sun seared down but I wasn't sure if the heat spreading across my arms and chest was sunburn or from meeting Bill. Dee pulled me along the dock to the G-3, where I flopped in like a bean bag toy.

All the way home the waves crashed in a rock and roll rhythm. Bill Hamilton's name was every other word and his face every other vision in my mind. I sang the words to the Crystals song, "Da Doo Ron Ron." At the channel we slowed down and I looked into the deep cobalt blue water. I envisioned Linda Turner's foot there, bloody and shriveled, floating in a murky layer of the lake. Would our propeller reach down to slice through her flesh again? My backbone sparked shivers, as Dee opened the throttle again.

Back at Dee's house I ran to my bedroom and turned the mirror around. I looked into the black glaze and saw the blurred image of my own face floating in darkness. I imagined Bill Hamilton's face swimming alongside mine, picturing our two faces together. Everywhere. Then I looked at my picture of Jackie Kennedy and the President. The mirrors on her dress radiated light. Together they looked like royalty. I wondered if Jackie Kennedy had met the President one day when she least expected to meet someone and if, after she did, she had difficulty concentrating. I believed in fairy tales suddenly. I believed that princes could slay dragons and witches burned in ovens they'd hoped to cook others in. And evil kings died violent, early deaths. My mind played little films of Bill and I growing up to live together as romantically and elegantly as I believed Jackie and the President lived. I felt the floating sensation I had felt when Bill said, *Hello, North.*

After dinner Dee and I watched *Bonanza* in color, with Aunt Joan reading her *Glass Menagerie* play book while perched alongside us in a Charles Eames lounge chair. In the T.V. story Little Joe had a sudden argument with another rancher over a group of lost cattle. When the other rancher threatened violence, Pa asked Hoss to help Little Joe work things out. The episode ended happily since Hoss could intimidate people without drawing a gun. I felt grateful to Hoss that no blood had been shed.

"Time to fade," Dee said, clicking off the television. She acted peevish from having missed Shrimp at the Club today. Shadows fell over Jess and me in the picture. My lanky body lurched in spastic motion across the field. I wished I'd been the pony. I wished. I wished. I'd have reared up and broken the picture with a flailing hoof.

After my bath I said my prayers early and sheepishly asked God an unusual favor. "God," I said, "you don't have to answer this kind of trivial question. I know you've got lots to do. But if tonight's a light night, would you please put in some complimentary words for me with Bill Hamilton. God bless you, God! Oh, I'm sorry. You *are* God! Bless the starving children in China, then. Amen." I should have promised I wouldn't act like Eve in the Garden of Eden, that I'd leave the apple uneaten and ignore talking snakes. I should have asked if stripping in a meadow for art's sake was a sin.

Next door Dee's salon-style hair dryer *whooshed* and the smell of nail polish remover drifted through the bathroom into my room along with the heat as she prepared herself for seeing Shrimp tomorrow. He had finally phoned to say he missed her. She told me he had said he loved her so many times she forgave him for not coming by the Club during the day. Dee said she thought of Shrimp constantly, and I couldn't stop thinking of Bill. I heard his voice repeating, *Hello, North* like a stuck record. Except I liked his voice stuck. Just that way. I replayed images of his tall tanned body as he had walked up the dock beside me. I'd smelled his suntan lotion, the coconut scent hanging in the air magnified by the sun's heat.

Rolling over onto my back on the bed, I pretended Bill was lying down on top of me, kissing me deep with his tongue. *French kissing. Oooo la la.* He touched me everywhere and I let him. *Bill.* I imagined it all so clearly. Bill was the first real boy I had completely envisioned making out with.

I slid my hand inside my pajama bottoms and felt the lips between my thighs, the nub of my occasional pleasure between. There I moved two fused fingers in circles, as if drawing tiny Os to go with the sounds of the sighs flying through my head. The perfume smell from Dee's room thickened in the air. I circled my hand like a record player arm going around on the disc faster and faster until my spine arced, my thighs tensed and let go. Tensed and let go. And my arms and legs and the place deep inside me all contracted around my fantasy Bill. I lost track of myself for a few minutes.

An orgasm? But no one had ever told me my muscles would twitch and how much I'd want it to happen. The word orgasm sounded like the word for oriental paper folding, but all I could see was the paper shredded to colorful confetti, flying through the air. What would my mother say if she knew? She had told me that being too free with sex could ruin a girl's reputation. But I said to myself,

What you do in your real life is a different story. And I realized, too, that sex was what had made Jackie Kennedy pregnant; I hoped that she had felt as wonderful as I had felt just now when she and the President had made love. Sex was probably better when you had someone real holding you and kissing you and doing all those things you did yourself, just right. And that was why Queen Mom worried about me this summer.

Exhilarated still, I began reading an article in *Newsweek* about two Russian cosmonauts who would travel in space at the same time. The man's name was Bykovsky, and after he orbited the earth for a few days a woman cosmonaut named Valentina would fly into space in a separate rocket that would hook up with his ship. I pictured them in their rendezvous. Bykovsky would look out the window of the capsule into a sky domed with stars and feel suddenly romantic; then moving his arms toward Valentina's arms he might touch her hand, his fingers locking into the spaces between her fingers. If he pulled Valentina close they would float in the space capsule like two balloons with their arms entwined. And then if the world blew up below them from an atomic bomb, Bykovsky and Valentina could make love in space and begin mankind all over again. For a moment I felt our future rested with them and I wished they would remain above us forever going around and around. I imagined traveling in a space capsule with Bill Hamilton, our hands clasped together and floating between us. Bill pulled my arm and I moved as softly as a silk scarf toward him. He wrapped his arms around me but I felt no pressure, just a drifting warm feeling that carried me off to sleep.

Glass Lake

Monday morning my G.E. clock radio alarm woke me at eight. The news announcer quoted President Kennedy's space race speech. I imagined a rocket hurtling upward with a shawl of white fuel spewing beneath it, the astronaut huddled inside with his stomach in knots, as glints of silver sun sparked off the rocket-skin. I imagined myself lifting up with the spaceship into weightlessness, a feeling like what I'd felt when I met Bill.

President Kennedy sounded so confident in his speech. He asked the United States to back a twenty-billion-dollar space program with a goal of a manned flight to the moon. Some critics called it *moon madness*, but most ordinary people like me were excited about the astronauts. Every time an astronaut soared skyward in a space rocket, he seemed to be reaching for the stars for all of us down below. Space missions. Rocket men. Danger and glory, every bit of it lay within my comprehension because of President Kennedy's strong beliefs.

I remembered the flight of Gordon Cooper in his capsule, *Faith*, the way his auto pilot system had failed late in the flight, placing him in great danger. But with the help of John Glenn, who talked Cooper through all the checks of the systems from his command post on the ship *Coastal Sentry*, Cooper set the flight in order manually and came hurtling back through the atmosphere to land his parachute in a perfect bull's-eye. Their escape from death comforted me. *Maybe it took something like faith when you faced a bad situation. Faith and some help from your friends.* If another space emergency occurred I believed the astronauts would fix the problem in the same calm way.

President Kennedy's promise would come true: the American astronauts would one day reach the moon before the Russian cosmonauts.

The radio played "Little Deuce Coupe," a new song by the Beach Boys. I recalled the drag races the boys had mentioned. I told myself, *You're going to go over to the Club to watch them. ASAP.* The music blared as a car roared up the gravel driveway. Tires squealed in the asphalt parking lot and, because it was humid, I thought whoever it was drove too fast and slid on wet pavement. A car door slammed and I walked to the window. Mr. Robertson's soft voice floated up to me, then Uncle Judd's baritone from the back yard. Uncle Judd wore a blue blazer like an English schoolboy, his red tie wound tightly around his neck. Up in the asphalt lot the Stingray glistened, more beautiful than I had remembered, its red space age body beckoning to me. My arms lifted up at my sides automatically as if in a dumb attempt to touch it from so far. It would be hot on the hood, with erratic engine sounds clicking beneath, the black interior holding the sun's heat. I threw my clothes on.

Downstairs Aunt Joan cooked breakfast, a surprise to me as usually Dee and I fixed cereal or toast. She had dressed in an ankle-length Hawaiian print shift. Her hair was pulled back in a chignon, her lips coated with fuchsia lipstick. When she cracked an egg into the sink instead of a bowl Dee and I made eyes at one another over the dining room table.

"She's doing all this for your birthday," Dee whispered, rapping her fingers on the table.

"I wish she wouldn't," I said behind my hand.

"Happy Birthday, North," Aunt Joan said in a chirpy voice I'd never heard before. She served the eggs, her white arm landing the plates on the table like giant skeet. Uncle Judd walked in from the screen porch and seated himself across from me. His foot nudged mine under the table as if by accident.

"There's the birthday girl," he said pressing his toe on top of mine. I pulled my foot back under my chair and fingered the edge of the tablecloth, a dark blue and orange floral print. I pulled it a little bit so that Uncle Judd's plate moved toward me.

He looked straight my way. He was handsome, though his sandy brown hair had grayed at the temples in patches like steel wool. He parted his hair on the left and combed it to the right, in a hair style like President Kennedy's. Except his hair was thinner and lay close to his head. He wore rounded tortoise shell glasses shaped like Mc-George Bundy's glasses, and the smooth skin on his face reminded me of Egyptian sculptures. The madras shorts and white knit shirt he wore seemed like clothes a well-to-do surfer might wear to a dance. A gold watch circled his wrist. Lifting his fork, he stared at his plate, saw the rock hard yolk. His face turned blotchy red, then grape purple.

"What's this, Joan. Garbage? For Christ sakes." Uncle Judd stood and marched into the kitchen, tossing his egg into the sink. Moving like an exotic bird, Aunt Joan flitted out the back door as if toward a luxury hotel Spa, as if no one had rebuked her. Dee planted a yellow candle into the yolk of my egg, lighting it.

"Make a wish," she told me. I looked down to blow out the candle, breathed deep and wished that Bill Hamilton would come to my birthday party. Suddenly everything was too yellow: the bright egg yolk, the hollandaise sauce, even the candle flame. My stomach ship-rolled. I held myself still, put a hand on my waist like Napoleon and closed my eyes, then blew out the candle, all the while wishing to be anywhere where Bill would appear.

"It's great," Dee said, eating rapturously while I picked at my food. When Dee finished Aunt Joan came back inside and brought me a package wrapped in brown paper, with the postmark *Zurich, Switzerland,* stamped across it in black ink. She sat back down in her chair, but stared out the front windows to the lake. I wanted to tear the gift open until I saw the wrapping paper wrinkled around my name. Suddenly my parents seemed universes away.

"Open it," Dee said. When I tried, the brown tape wouldn't budge.

"Need help?" Uncle Judd asked. He stood beside me holding a kitchen knife, offering it to me by the handle the way a nurse hands a surgeon a scalpel. I pictured him operating on women, changing their lips, their breasts, their noses. My lips quivered as I sliced through the wrapping. Inside I found four giant Swiss chocolate bars wrapped in gold foil and slick blue paper with the brand name *Lindt* scripted in gold across the top. As I unwrapped one bar, melted chocolate oozed over my fingers. I licked the drips like someone in *Tom Jones*. The deep rich smell rose around me. I imagined the entire country of Switzerland smelling like chocolates.

"Gross," Dee said as King, Uncle Judd's German shepherd, licked my hands; he had just licked himself seconds before. "Stop that, King," Dee admonished while stomping her foot on the floor until he slumped away. I washed my hands at the kitchen sink, returning to the table, squeezing my eyes partially shut to stop my tears. The Swiss chocolates seemed to have melted into the miles separating me and my parents.

"North," Uncle Judd spoke softly from beside me. "We can put the chocolate bars into the freezer. O.K.?"

"O.K.," I said, feeling oddly soothed by the way he spoke gently. Using a spatula, he lifted the chocolate bars like little bent car roofs off an assembly line, one by one to a stainless steel sheet-cake pan.

"We'll serve them after your party." He smiled at me over the kitchen counter. I managed to nod.

"There's a letter." Dee handed me a folded white sheet of onion-skin paper. I opened it. Dee pushed her feet against King's ribs. He rolled on the floor beside her, flipping over on his back and pushing out his penis that looked like a tube of opened red lipstick.

My Dad said he missed me, especially when he saw a girl my age walking across a stone bridge in Salzburg. My mother wrote a paragraph about the birds and the bees and the advent of menstruation. She said I should ask Aunt Joan if I had any questions about female matters; I shouldn't worry if I experienced stomach cramps one day suddenly. *Head up. Best foot forward. Take it in stride, North.* After all, she said, I had packed my Kotex. And I should be in bed each night by nine-thirty to do my reading. But—going to bed so early was out of the question as Dee stayed up until eleven-thirty without ever asking permission.

"My head's pounding," Aunt Joan said, standing up. "I'm going upstairs." She pressed the back of her hand to her forehead and looked to Uncle Judd as if for permission.

"Take something for your head." His voice sharpened, his eyes like laser beams following her, rays I imagined were like the rays from Godzilla's eyes slanting against her back. Aunt Joan moved away from the table sideways like a hermit crab shuttling, her mouth finding a tilted smile.

North, my mother closed the letter, *you're fifteen but that's no reason to waste your time on boys*. I sighed aloud. Queen Mom was wrong again. Bill Hamilton wasn't a waste of time. If she had just turned fifteen she, too, would have found him attractive.

Dee placed a 45 on the RCA stereo-console player, and set the needle down. She turned the volume up loud. Side by side we sat listening to the Essex sing while Mrs. Graybill, Aunt Joan's cleaning lady, cleared the table. She rolled up the tablecloth and underneath the marble glistened like an ice rink. My mother had impressed upon me the fact that this table was a genuine Saarinen original. It looked like a piece of furniture the astronauts would install in a moon settlement. Four white-molded plastic pedestal chairs accompanied it, and each time I dropped down into one I felt I was entering the future around the time of *The Jetsons* cartoon. I felt grateful to Aunt Joan for the more traditional furniture upstairs because if I had slept in a space age bed the night after I met Bill Hamilton I might have whirled out over the edge of the universe. I might have spun into orbit along with Bykovsky and Valentina.

Mrs. Graybill bustled through the room into the kitchen, rinsing the dirty dishes, putting away the salt and peppers. "Run to him," the Essex sang.

Midmorning I dressed in my white linen dress with the pleated skirt and the princess sleeves. I wore white patent leather shoes that looked as glassy as the lake water. I even wore light plum-colored lipstick that made my face look more tanned and my eyes greener, more like Jackie Kennedy's eyes. My hair deepened to black. When I looked in the mirror before we left for the Club my brown arms and legs startled me. In two weeks at Glass Lake I had tanned more than ever in my life. For a minute I even felt glamorous when Uncle Judd passed me on the stairs.

"Lovely," he said with a sigh in his voice and his eyelids half opened. Pausing on a step like a gymnast striking a pose, he opened his eyes and what I saw in his stare took my breath away. I wanted one of those scarves Muslim women wore to fall over me. But then I told myself, *Jackie Kennedy has men of all ages telling her she looks lovely all the time, men she keeps at arms' length, men she handles with a smile.*

On the way to the station wagon, I took one long look inside the Stingray. The bucket seats were covered in black leather. There was a black gear shift on the floor; all the dials for the speedometer and the oil pressure and the clock, its second hand ticking, looked like the control panels I had seen in the cars in racing magazines. I couldn't stop watching the clock hands jolt forward in precision rhythm.

I heard steps behind me, then someone covered my eyes with hands. "Guess who?" She said in a faked man's voice.

"Count Dracula?"

"Wery vunny." She faked German now.

"Oh, I know. It's Topo Gigio." I said, laughing. We always quoted Ed Sullivan introducing him and cracked up.

"That's a mouse, stupid." Dee slitted her hands open some so I could see.

"Dee. Good mouse. I know it's you." I pet her head.

"Time to go. C'mon, North." She lifted her hands away, giving me a shove. "Ask Shrimp. He'll tell you I'm no mouse." The Stingray glowed. I couldn't move an inch. "North, don't go catatonic on me," Dee said, "just because it's your birthday."

"It's the Stingray. I want to ride in it. I want to sleep in it. I want to . . . God, Dee, I almost said *die* in it."

"Don't ever say stuff like that," Dee said sharply. "You'll probably get to drive it. So don't pine . . . Topo Gigio? North, that was a crazy guess. You just like saying his name, don't you? Cause it's Italian." I shook my head yes. She took my hand in hers and I felt like I had a sister.

• • •

My party began at noon, but by a quarter after only half of the guests had arrived; we ordered despite the empty chairs. Uncle Judd sat at the head of the table next to me. Dee sat on my other side. Uncle Judd ordered a club sandwich and flirted with the waitress while he spoke. He called her by the name on her name tag, Wendy.

"Where you from, Wendy?"

"Albion," she said, pulling her waitress pencil from behind her ear.

"Nice college there." Uncle Judd smiled.

"Yeah. Anything else?" Wendy held her notepad breast height.

"Bring the Manhattan right away," he said. Empty chairs surrounded us like a set up for musical chairs.

"I bet people went away for July fourth." Dee touched my forearm. "Some kids will come for cake and ice cream."

I doubted people would come to the birthday party of someone they didn't know. But Bill had met me and he had not yet arrived. I felt my chin drop. Dee rested her fingers on my wrist.

"Tell me what's the matter, North." Dee nudged me with her knee under the table. I'd stared at my silverware so long it must have seemed I believed it could tell my fortune by the way it lay on the table.

"Nothing, really," I white lied.

"It's Bill," Dee said.

I nodded while shrugging my shoulders; I thought I might cry. Dee must have possessed telepathy to know why I felt so miserable.

"He left for camp in Traverse City." Dee said. "His sister Debbie told me this morning. I should've told you, North."

"Hey, Deedee, did I hear you say Bill. As in Hamilton?" Frank Boyd shouted from the opposite head of the table. He sat down. "I heard he's out looking for Sally Fry." Hearing Sally's name caused the hairs on my arms to stand erect and all I wanted to do was swear, but I couldn't swear because of my mother's instructions to stop myself from swearing no matter how angry I might become. If you swore you cheapened yourself, she told me. No boy would want you then.

I dabbed my French fries into a hill of ketchup while Uncle Judd told stories about the go cart he had raced down country roads when he was a teenager. He held his sandwich toothpick between two fingers like a tiny spear.

"The cart didn't have a gas gauge. I ran out of gas all the time. Hitched a ride back once from a farmer on horseback. What irony, coming home on real horse power." Uncle Judd looked at Dee and me for a laugh like he'd turned into Johnny Carson. Dee laughed automatically, and I sat quietly beside her thinking, *Ha, ha, very funny,* watching him drain another drink.

When our waitress cleared the plates for dessert Uncle Judd moved his chair around the corner of the table so close it touched my chair. Wendy set the white frosted cake in front of me. Uncle Judd wrapped his arms around Dee and me, singing a sloppy version of "Happy Birthday." I pressed my thighs together; Uncle Judd perspired on my neck and shoulders, the odor of his skin mixing with Mennen deodorant and his English Leather aftershave.

As the glow from the candles dazed me, he smelled as exotic as a gardenia flower. I thought about my mother turning her face to kiss him once, years ago. Strange how I sat similarly beside him now. Why couldn't he have been Bill Hamilton? I looked over the cake hoping to see Bill walk through the front doors of the Club. Instead, Linda Turner stared daggers and Uncle Judd faced her, his eyes spitting back knives.

"Hurry up, North, blow out the candles," Dee said. "Make a wish."

I almost wished that Uncle Judd and Linda Turner would leave the room. But I didn't want to waste a whole year's wish on vanishing them. So first I brought to mind Jackie Kennedy's face in my picture; I saw happiness, her night in Paris. I knew there were cities across the world far from Glass Lake. Jackie Kennedy traveled through them, radiant as a day star. I felt a smile like her smile erupt on my face. I held it there. Then I wished my one wish for the year. I wished that Bill Hamilton would fall in love with me, and blew out all fifteen candles. Dee cut the cake and I sucked the icing off the candles.

"She's staring at me," I whispered to Dee because Linda Turner's eyes fixed on my face like the eyes of a movie zombie. I tried not to look at her false foot but I couldn't help it. The skin of that leg was too glossy, like plastic, like the leg of a doll. She wore those same heavy socks. She sat at a barstool smoking, blowing smoke from her nose, with her eyes slits of yellow light like cat's eye marbles following Uncle Judd everywhere. Kids began leaving all at once after cake, some embarrassed that they hadn't brought presents.

"My mom couldn't take me shopping," Marge Blakely, a short girl with blue plastic glasses, stammered.

"At least you came," I said too brightly, stroking my fork across my empty plate. The fork made a harsh metallic sound I hoped would scatter my guests further. Marge and Frank sauntered away.

I looked down at my lap where the present Dee had given me before the cake came lay, wrapped inside a small square box with ballet-pink bows printed on the white wrapping paper. I loosened the scotch tape from one end, but when I turned to find Dee she no longer sat beside me. Shrimp was gone too. Everyone had left except Uncle Judd, who sat so close I smelled the liquor on his breath.

"Whatcha got there?" He leaned his shoulders into mine, then twisted in his chair, placing his face in front of my face. I saw him so close, the air filled with the smell of bourbon. That smell seemed to pull his face and distort it so that he looked like someone in the Excedrin headache ad on T.V. A melting mask of a face, as if viewed through my Grandfather North's reading glasses. The liquor smell burned my nose. All of Uncle Judd's smells swirled around me. His lowing voice echoed in my ears: *Honey. Honey. Whatcha got there. Honey.*

Was I some strange confection that would attract bees? Queen Mom once read Kafka's *Metamorphosis* to me. Maybe I'd turn into an insect after so many found me sweet.

I sensed Uncle Judd's sweat pooling on my arms, his breath a hot mist on my cheeks. The hairs on his legs brushed my shaved legs under the table. What would Queen Mom have done if she'd been me at this moment? Turned to kiss him? I forgot where I was suddenly and then I told myself, *North, you're here at Glass Lake. For the summer.*

"Why dontcha open it?" Uncle Judd reached over, his fingers

crawling into my lap where the present lay, for a moment, hidden under the table. He wiggled his fingers like worms and I felt stunned.

"You ticklish?" he asked.

I filled with a rush of pure physical power. I bolted upright. Hearing the present thud against the floor I ran, thoughtless, out the front doors to the side yard of the Club where a privet hedge grew, spindly and wild.

I sat down beside the hedge, my lungs heaving and the sun beating on my shoulders. I huddled there until I felt so thirsty I ran to the drinking fountain between the flagpole and the gazebo. Gulping water, I looked around before each drink to make sure Uncle Judd wasn't approaching, feeling a sudden empathy for the Negroes in Alabama who, if driven by thirst to a white person's fountain, would have to drink this same furtive way. Then in the distance I heard Dee and her voice seemed to be a bright light I could run to, so I ran until I reached the gazebo where the sound of a boy's voice stopped me.

"Dee, please." It was Shrimp. I could tell by the high squeak in his voice.

Crouching down behind a lilac bush beside the gazebo, I looked inside. Dee lay on her back on the concrete floor, her bikini top circling her waist and the bottoms hanging loosely around one ankle. Her breasts swelled, her nipples pointed on each, as she rolled from side to side, moaning, "No, please, somebody might come down here. Oh, Shrimp, stop." But her voice didn't sound like she wanted anything she felt then to stop for her, ever. I told myself, *North, run back up the steps.* But when I tried to move my feet felt like concrete, so I stood there watching everything.

Shrimp rubbed his fingers through Dee's pubic hair and kissed her body all over. He sucked her nipples until they stood up like bullets. Dee spread her legs, then Shrimp pulled his baggies down around his knees. I pressed my face close enough to the screen to see his blond pubic hairs and his penis horizontally erect from his body. His penis was the first penis I had seen for more than a second or two. I had once glimpsed my dad's when his towel fell off after he took a bath, but I'd turned away from him. Seeing Shrimp naked was different because I wanted to look. His swollen penis was so exotic and huge I couldn't imagine it fitting inside Dee. And yet he wrapped his hand around it then lunged inside Dee, thrusting in and out as Dee's cries surrounded him with clouds of sound. He moved faster and faster until suddenly he shouted, "Oh, God, Dee. I love you, Deedee."

Dee rolled back and forth wildly as if she could have gone on longer; when she writhed I felt a part of myself rolling on the floor. It took her a while to stop and sit up and when she did; tiny catlike whimpers caught in my throat. I was huddled over by this time, my breathing shallow as if I'd just vaulted up the steps. Then Shrimp held Dee's hand, stroking her fingers. Like persons recovering from hypnosis they slowly awoke to their surroundings, their heads popping up like two jack-in-the-boxes opening side by side.

I ducked close to the ground and ran up the stairs. At the deck of the terrace, I collapsed into a lounge chair and twisted a hair curl on my finger, pretending I hadn't watched my cousin make love. Or *copulate*; I considered the word Mrs. Linfield, our eighth grade health teacher had used for having sex, a word too formal for something so wild.

Dee and Shrimp walked to me across the terrace deck, both of their faces flushed and healthy, looking like the faces of people from Scotland I had seen pictured in travel magazines. Dee wore Shrimp's school ring on her thumb, its blue stone emitting star-shaped reflections as she came closer. Shrimp walked beside her, his eyes on her derriere (as Queen Mom called behinds), his short cropped hair platinum blond and the muscles in his legs and arms resembling the roots of trees. Wrapped in her nubby terry cloth cover-up, Dee's voluptuous shape still showed beneath, her thick auburn hair fell softly to her shoulders. She had to have combed it after what happened at the bottom of those stairs.

"Where's my dad?" she asked, her voice all lungs.

"I don't know. Last I saw him was at the table." I played with the woven plastic thong of the chair.

"I'll go get him." She shrugged her shoulders, turning like a figure inside a jewelry box that turns when the box is opened, and walked toward the Club.

"What've you been up to?" Shrimp asked me. *A lot less than you have*, I thought.

"Nothing much." I hid my knowing behind my Polaroid wrap-around sunglasses.

"Hey, it's your birthday. Of all the people in the world you should be up to something." Shrimp pinched his big toes around the metal tubing of the lounge chair beside me. "I've got to tell you something," Shrimp said softly then. Some dirt lodged under his big toe-nail.

"You've probably heard it a hundred times."

"No. Tell me." I'd never seen a boy Shrimp's age act so urgent about talking to a girl.

"You look like Jackie Kennedy. Around the eyes." Shrimp's cheeks flushed scarlet. "That's a compliment." His eyes rested on my face. Was I really like Jackie Kennedy? For a moment I felt older than I was; I felt I might possess a strange knowledge of things that would happen in the future if I ever gave into it. My stomach knotted up.

"Thanks, Shrimp," I said in a near whisper, as if I were saying amen in church. "That's the best birthday present."

Dee retrieved Uncle Judd from inside the Club. She walked toward us with her hand cuffed around his wrist, towing him like a pull toy on a string. He lumbered apelike, staggering. I wondered how he could perform operations without maiming people.

A few feet away Dee stopped and shouted to me to hurry up and come on. "Make yourself scarce, Shrimp," she snarled, as if he had been the drunk one, as if she hadn't rolled on the floor with him.

"You O.K.?" he asked her.

"Oh, just beat it." Dee turned Uncle Judd toward the parking lot. Shrimp bounced down the big concrete steps toward the dock like a puppy let off a leash.

Dee led Uncle Judd to the car. I stayed a body length behind them all the way, even while Dee helped him into the back seat. He rested his head on the seat back, closing his eyes.

"Get in, North. Act like everything's normal," Dee instructed me, and I did what she said. She slid behind the wheel of the station wagon and started the engine. Uncle Judd was already snoring.

"This happens when he first takes a vacation," Dee said calmly.

"Do you get to drive a lot?" I asked. She drove us out of the driveway onto the hot macadam of the main road. Tar, softened by the sun, gave under the tires. Smell of tar filled my nostrils, Detroit smell. I remembered the time my father let me drive the Mercury around the parking lot at his office, how the steering wheel had twirled inside my hand. Haloing. I'd skidded on hot tar, but he said I'd be a good driver one day. He even took photos of me behind the wheel. I'd thought I was Mario Andretti then, for an afternoon.

"I get to, sometimes." Dee drove the curves of the coves well under the speed limit.

"Can I put my hand on the wheel?"

"North, that's stupid," Dee hissed. She glanced around at Uncle Judd. "He's out of it."

"So you won't get in trouble. Just two fingers?"

"Oh, all right."

I lay my fingers on the pure white steering wheel. When she turned the wheel I let the shiny plastic whirl through my hooked fingers. I turned the radio on. Dee and I sang along with "Blue Velvet."

Before dinner I lay on my bed. I could hear the rasp of Uncle Judd's snores traveling down the hallway. Dee slept, like him, and I guessed her fatigue resulted from copulation. Aunt Joan played the player piano out in the little guest house, sending the tinny sound of "Beautiful Dreamer" through the hot afternoon air.

I lay on my stomach on my bed and the canopy arched like a white tent overhead. I checked my parent's itinerary. They would be in Italy by the time a letter I wrote today might reach them. I decided to write but couldn't begin, even though there were so many puzzling things I wanted clarified. I wanted to ask my mother what she saw in Uncle Judd, if she liked the way he smelled or his storytelling. Or was it his grooming, his haircut, and his clothes that attracted her? When he kissed her, had he smelled of liquor?

I also wanted to ask how to tell if a man or a boy likes you for yourself or just for your body. Was there some test you could put him through, hoops of fire to jump before he touched you? And did pure love make you feel like you were traveling in a space rocket? Could you tell the boy was the right boy if, when he looked into your eyes, you felt as if your body floated out into the stratosphere? If so, I was falling in love with Bill Hamilton. But every time I picked up my pen to write, the words stopped coming to mind.

I described the weather: *Dear Mom and Dad: It was so hot this past week. When the wind blew, Dee and I felt like we were sitting under a giant hair dryer.* I thanked them for the chocolate bars but didn't mention they'd melted. The finished letter was less than one side of my airmail stationery, which I could see my fingers through. I sealed it inside an envelope and placed it on top of my bureau, nestling their itinerary back in the underwear drawer.

Standing in front of the mirror, I saw my brown face reflected. Tiny creases formed in the skin at the outer corners of my eyes. Traces of plum lipstick streaked my lips in a marbleized pattern. My hair gnarled itself into tight, cherubic curls around my face. I tried to smooth them with my hairbrush but the bristles caught. My eyebrows seemed thicker than ever and as black as asphalt. Madeline Spears had once showed me how I could pluck them underneath to accentuate the natural arch, but every time I had tried it hurt so much I stopped.

I turned the mirror to the backside and Jackie Kennedy's eyes greeted me with incredible empathy, as if she knew that a man's strange behavior could be upsetting and that watching someone you knew make love could leave you confused. Her bright smile and confidence, when looking so attractive, seemed to tell me to go ahead and let myself feel what a girl feels for a boy. Maybe Uncle Judd was just too drunk to know what he was doing, leaning so close beside me at lunch. She seemed to prove that my feet could stay on the ground like hers did, and one day my chosen boy might stand beside me, smiling like the President.

Turning the mirror around I yawned, then looked out my back window to see the Stingray, glistening scarlet in the sunlight. I told myself, *North, you have to ride in that car.* Lying down on top of my bed, I stared up at the canopy while I listened to the sound of motors whirring out on the lake. Although our rooms were centrally air conditioned, my room was hot so I pretended the canopy was a blanket of snow poised above me. When I closed my eyes I dreamed that snow fell over me in slanting wet dashes.

I slept for an hour and then awoke when a shadow fell over me. I opened my eyes to slits and saw a dark shape looming next to my bed. Uncle Judd stood holding a mug of steaming coffee in hand, with a black lumpy bag slung on his shoulder. His hair lay wet and slicked back close to his head, as if he had just showered. He wore a shiny maroon bathrobe with the monogram JDG scripted in white thread on the lapel. I tossed and turned as if in sleep, clearing my throat a few times, thinking he would leave but he stood beside my bed, the filtered light falling gauzy on his arms and legs.

"North, you awake?" Gray patches flecked his hair like splashes of mercury. I recalled a thermometer I had broken once with a high fever.

"Yes," I said, rolling onto my side and facing him.

"I hope I didn't spoil your party." He shifted his weight from one bare foot to the other. Uncle Judd's eyes, as they raced over me, were as blue as peepholes cut from a cloudless summer sky. My skin felt hot and irritated, as if erupting with a rash.

"You forgot this," he said, handing me Dee's gift from the party. The wrapping was torn and the ballet-pink bows smudged with dirt. "Open it while it's still your birthday."

I sat up and began to open the gift, acting the way people who join religious cults act when they perform on command. Inside the square box under a layer of white pressed cotton I found an oval-shaped gold locket with a place inside for a picture. Inside the card with the violets printed on the cover, Dee's note read: *I hope you find the right boy who can fill this space for you. Love, Deedee.*

"I have something for you, too." Uncle Judd's voice sounded smooth, like more than a voice, like soft fabric. He sipped his coffee and sat down on the edge of my bed, cradling a large box wrapped in shiny cobalt blue paper in his lap. I imagined him dressed in a white doctor's jacket, his handsome face and bronze arms clarified.

With his McGeorge Bundy glasses he looked intelligent enough to diagnose anyone's troubles in one glance.

"You shouldn't have." I said something I had heard my mother say when she was put on the spot.

"I wanted to. Open it," he said. I accepted the gift, although I had second thoughts about it. Somehow when he told me to open it, I felt I had to do as he said. I tore through the paper, and Uncle Judd's English Leather swirled in the air, thickening. Inside, under three layers of tissue paper, I found a pure white, lace-trimmed bikini. At first I thought it was underpants and a bra, but the tag said *Victoria Swimwear*. It came with a lace cover-up with pearled buttons and puff sleeves.

"I saw it advertised in *The New York Times Magazine*. Do you like it?" Uncle Judd's breath smelled of coffee mixed with mouth wash, the bourbon beneath.

"It's beautiful," I stammered. I *did* love it as I held the soft white lace trim in my hand.

"Try it on." Uncle Judd slid closer to me. His bathrobe made a slippery sound.

"Now?"

"Make sure it fits."

I stood to walk toward the bathroom to change privately. He cupped my shoulder in his hand, lowering me back onto the bed.

"I've seen you naked since you were a baby. There's no need to be shy." The word *shy* sounded like a hiss, not soft the way it usually sounded. "Go ahead, put it on." He bolted to his feet in front of me.

I stared through the lenses of Uncle Judd's glasses to the blue of his eyes. Glassy like marbles. The eyes of a sculpture, not a person. I started undressing in front of him. I told myself I would move quickly, like Charlie Chaplin in a silent movie, so he would hardly see anything. What he did see would seem ordinary since he was a doctor and he had already seen every kind of human body naked. But Uncle Judd could change women's bodies: Dee's, my mother's, Aunt Joan's, or mine. My legs shook as I pulled off my underwear.

Uncle Judd pushed his coffee mug under the bed with his foot, and grabbed his camera out of the black bag. He began snapping pictures of me. Flashbulbs exploded like flares. I hunched my body, holding the bikini against my chest as if so little cloth could shield me. In the bursts of light I pulled the new suit bottoms on. The shutter snapped. Click. Click.

"I've got the photo of you and the pony in the meadow downstairs," he said. "I want a new picture to go with it. You're such a good model." He raised the camera. More flashes pulsed the air. I hooked the bikini bra in front of my chest and began to turn it around.

"It's normal, North. Believe me, I'm a doctor. I've seen this kind of development. One breast's smaller than the other one early on. It's your age." Uncle Judd stopped shooting pictures and put the camera and the bag down on the bed. He cupped my chin in his hand.

I didn't speak a word. I didn't say, *Oh, yes, thank you for enlightening me as to my imbalanced breasts.* He leaned down to align his face with mine, his features looking flat like a reflection in a funhouse mirror. As if in slow motion he cupped his fingers under my breast.

"You'll fill out soon enough," he said. "If you ever need to talk about it, what with your mother away, I'm here." He moved his face close up like in a movie. He fingered my nipple.

"Like that?" he asked. I stiffened my neck. The smell of English Leather swirled in the air, so thick I thought of rain. I closed my eyes and tried to imagine Bill Hamilton's face, to fantasize that it was Bill who touched me then. Because I wanted him. But each time I thought of Bill and opened my eyes, his face turned into Uncle Judd's face. Back and forth my mind spliced images of Uncle Judd and Bill. I held Bill's face as long as I could. Bill, my magic boy, then *poof,* he'd vanished. No rabbit in the hat. No scarf up the sleeve. I closed my eyes tight to total darkness. Counted to ten. When I opened my eyes Uncle Judd had left the room. Clusters of used flash bulbs lay strewn on the floor, the glass cubes milky white as if with cataracts.

From Dee's room I heard a radio playing "You Really Got a Hold on Me." Dee sang along in a peppy voice. The buttery smells of fresh bread and roasting meat drifted up from downstairs, making my stomach growl. Milky, thick saliva formed in my mouth, and I felt like one of Pavlov's dogs.

I pulled the bikini bra cups over my breasts. In the mirror I saw my tanned body, and felt a wetness inside my bikini bottom. *That's from the heat,* I thought, *from the heat wave, it's so hot you sweat everywhere.* But my breast, where Uncle Judd had touched me, burned ashen hot, as if his hand stayed there delivering some primitive form of electricity. As I watched the curtains on the west window the gold birds in the fabric seemed to take flight. I felt as if their wings beat inside of me. Dee's radio played louder and louder a "hold on me."

Cosmic Love

Wednesday after dinner I sat in my bedroom, thinking about the drag race Frank Boyd had mentioned, about seeing Bill there. I heard Uncle Judd downstairs fixing himself a cocktail, then ice chinking in his glass as he climbed the stairs. Thump. Chink. Thump. Chink. I remembered the movie *The Mummy,* the sound of the mummy dragging his foot. "Can I Get A Witness" by Marvin Gaye played softly on my radio. A newscaster broke in to give a report on the President's trip to Germany, Ireland, and Italy. He was traveling without Jackie Kennedy because of her pregnancy.

She was probably listening to the same news reports of his travels, lying on a bed in a New England summer home with an ocean view. She heard the speech he gave in West Berlin where he spoke in German, calling himself a Berliner. He said no one was free until all men and women were free, and that all the free peoples of the world were symbolic citizens of Berlin; one day when everyone was free, the cities of East and West Berlin would be joined together again. Then the West Berliners would be proud that they had stood for freedom for all the years they had lived in the shadow of the Berlin Wall. The Berliners cheered for him, like he was their president for the day. Jackie Kennedy must have heard the applause on her radio. Because of her talent with languages she could have said even more to the Berliners in German than the President did, had she been there.

I wondered if President Kennedy carried a picture of Jackie Kennedy in his wallet, so that once he was far across the Atlantic and he missed her he could look inside to admire her face. I walked to my mirror, turned it around, and pulled the photograph of Jackie and the President from behind the wood frame. Uncle Judd thudded down the hallway outside my room, ice alone left in the glass now by the sound of the clinking. With shaking hands I began carefully folding the picture. I folded the President behind Jackie and then folded her image at the waist so that she was wrapped around him. My hands steadied some. Then I folded her over so that just her face showed on top. It was this face that I pressed against my chest over my breast, where Uncle Judd had touched me.

I wondered what Jackie Kennedy would think of me wearing her picture inside my clothes. Would she think of me as strange? Oh, but she must have gotten used to being idolized, and I thought if she ever knew what was happening to me here at Glass Lake she would want to help me in any way she could. Her picture folded against my breast calmed me, just as seeing her face smile from the covers of magazines had calmed me before now. Just as once, with my gaze focused on her features, I'd believed the world was round and whole and full of promise. Now, with her picture damp with sweat on my flesh, I believed Russia would not bury us and neither country would drop nuclear bombs on the other country. Ever. When she was with me, Uncle Judd couldn't take my body from me by coming into my bedroom and touching me when I was asleep. He couldn't change my breasts, shaping me into a pin-up girl, even if it was his everyday job. I'd be thin like Jackie Kennedy with breasts that fit into champagne glasses, which Queen Mom said was a sign of class in a girl. "Big boobs, small brain," Queen Mom said whenever Jane Mansfield made a movie entrance.

"Let's Go Steady Again" played on the radio and I turned up the volume. Jutting my arms out as if to hold a boy's hand, I tried to dance a few steps across the room. I stopped and crouched the way Shrimp stood on skis, imagining myself driving in a drag race, pushing my foot to the floor.

"God, North, what are you doing?" Dee said, walking into my room from the bathroom. She wore the top of her madras bikini and shorts.

"Just messing around," I answered, opening my eyes and standing up straight.

"You look bored. Listen, as soon as Mom goes to her play group I'm leaving in the G-3. Shrimp says to meet him in the south cove." Dee smoothed the waistband of her blue short-shorts.

"Will you drop me off at the Club?" I asked.

"I know what you're planning. You want to watch the drag race. I'm warning you, the dust'll make you cough. If you have any sense you'll wait at the end of the dock till it's over like I do. Except I told Shrimp I wouldn't even meet him tonight unless he skipped the whole thing." Dee stomped her bare foot on the floor like a horse in a stall.

"Dee, I want to watch the races. Take me." I pivoted on my toes across the floor.

"O.K., and I'll pick you up afterwards, too. Unless you think you'll be riding home with Mr. Romantic." Dee ran over, poked my shoulder and laughed, then rushed off to her room.

Dropping me off at the end of the dock, Dee sped off to find Shrimp, the G-3's wake humping white. A black boat with an Evinrude motor shot by behind her with a rooster tail wake that I could see rainbow colors in. I made a beeline for the straightaway, rushing by kids taking Red Cross swimming tests and Linda Turner, who stood by the flag-pole staring at me. I waved to her but she pretended she didn't see me though she looked me down the legs. I sensed her eyes drawing lines over my skin.

Out behind the Club house on the dirt straightaway, two cars were parked, engines idling, at the starting line—a Ford Fairlane and a Lincoln Coupe. I crouched behind the hedge that hid the Club's giant trash containers, squinting to make out the drivers. G. P. drove the white Ford and Frank Boyd drove the Lincoln. I wondered if Bill had already raced or if, because he had refused to fight over Sally Fry, they had disqualified him.

They revved their engines, and when Larry Meeker raised a green flag each car lurched forward. Dust whirled above the raceway so that I could barely see cars. Clouds of dust rose as if in a storm in Death Valley. A car emerged from the dust cloud, then two. At the finish line a boy in beige baggies waved a checkered flag. A red and white Chevy BelAir stood parked behind him. His glasses and his slender figure told me it was Bill. My heart beat fast in my chest. His arms moved the flag up and down. The drivers raced toward the finish line, G. P. leading. But his white Ford spun out suddenly in three lateral circles, whirling wildly like a water bug turned over then coming to a stop on the bumped lawn beside the straightaway. Gas spurted over the ground as a clanking sounded from the engine and smoke poured from the exhaust pipe. Dropping the flag, Bill ran over to the car, pulling out G. P. who careened until Bill steadied him. Blood oozed from a gash like a second red eyebrow above G. P.'s eye, proving that driving so fast was *very dangerous*. Still I couldn't stop myself from wanting to.

Larry Meeker brought a first-aid kit over to Bill's car and they bandaged G. P.'s cut, as if they had done so a thousand times. Frank spun his Lincoln back to the starting line, where he lit the wrong end of a cigarette. He tossed it out and lit a new one. Maybe the sight of blood had jangled his nerves.

"Is G. P. all right?" Frank yelled.

"Yeah," Bill shouted. "But it's a warning. I'm calling it quits."

"What about Sally? Hey, was she worth it, G. P.?" Frank lit another cigarette. G. P. frowned, the bandage wrinkling on his forehead a little bit.

"You win her, Frank," Larry Meeker shouted, closing the first-aid box and handing it to Bill. He helped G. P. over to his Fairlane.

"I'll have to get her to give up Bill. Hey, Bill, why don't you tell her I'm a great guy." Frank Boyd exhaled a plume of smoke out his window. I wished I could have walked over to Bill, who stood so thoughtfully in the still dust of evening, settling now under the pink and blue swirled clouds. He seemed to see some solution stretched out in the horizon for him. Airplanes wrote messages in the sky sometimes. I saw shapes in clouds that told me my fortune. A cloud ship meant you'd go on a journey, Dee told me once. I saw a blue castle cloud drift over Bill's head now. I wanted to ask him, *Do you see the castle, too? Tell me. Tell me.* I wanted to be inside his eyes. Bill waved

Frank off with his hand, then walked over to G. P.'s car to help him start it.

Any minute one of the boys might have walked by me, so I crawled along the hedge until I reached the sidewalk where I bolted up to the Club, then past it, and out to the dock's end. I sat down with my feet dangling in the water like two fishes. I kicked them down deeper, fanning my toes. Speedboats whirred by, but it was Bill I thought of. The orange disk of the sun sank, but it was Bill's voice I heard above all the sounds of evening, saying: *Hello, North.* His face filled my daydreams, through all the time I waited for Dee to come back and pick me up.

I was slipping into my brown one-piece Jantzen when Dee zoomed into my bedroom, her feet hardly touching the floor as if she'd discovered the secret of levitation by having such a good sex life with Shrimp. At séances we'd tried to raise the dead and raised an orange crate with their ghost energy pulsing through our fingers instead. Maybe if I ever made love with Bill I'd be raised up from the dead of this strange summer. It was Independence Day, the morning of July fourth. Already firecrackers snapped in the distance.

"Hurry up and get ready. The ski show starts at eleven. We've got to find a good spot on the lake. Plus, I've got a surprise for you." Dee's eyes glittered.

"What?"

"I'm in the show. I ride on Shrimp's shoulders. We've been practicing all summer, real early in the mornings. I couldn't tell you before 'cause Mom hates daredevil skiing. She'd have had a cow if she found out. But now it's too late to stop me. Dad's going to take us over and then watch the show with you."

"Your mom's not coming?"

"She hates daredevil skiing. But, North, I'm so excited. From up on Shrimp's shoulder I can see beyond the tree tops. It's like flying." Dee held her hair back in a ponytail and gazed up, looking enlightened, as if she could see to the place where the world ended, when she rode Shrimp. She turned back toward me, looking the sexiest I had ever seen her look with her deep brown face incandescent and her voluptuous body packed into a black bikini that was as slick as a wetsuit. "Aren't you happy for me?" Dee shook my arm with both hands and I felt I should spew compliments like water.

"Sure." I tried to smile.

"Be ready in a half an hour." Dee froze in place for a minute. "Don't dawdle. It'll make me more nervous. I already feel like I'm going to wet my pants." She rushed out of my room, her laughter trailing behind her as she raced down the hall.

"Don't wet your pants, Dee," I called after her. Dee cackled but I meant it. My mother's friend, Sara Randolph, couldn't control her bladder because she had multiple sclerosis. She got the disease suddenly. Women suffered more from it than men. I felt such a sudden urge to pee now whenever Uncle Judd walked into a room. I wondered if I might be developing multiple sclerosis. By pressing my thighs together I could barely stop the urgency. If I got sick who would I tell? Uncle Judd? *He was a doctor.* But he'd insist upon a physical examination.

"Dad's ready." Dee popped her head in my doorway. "You're riding over with him. I'm going with Shrimp. We have to talk about our show." I glared at Dee as if with X-ray vision. "You're not even close to being ready," she said. "Why are you wearing that ugly one-piece suit?"

"It's a free country," I snapped.

"You look better in a bikini. Don't you want to attract boys?" *Boys would be fine,* I thought, *especially boys like Bill Hamilton, but not fully grown men who drink and whose hands wander.*

"I want to attract Bill," I said boldly.

"Make eyes at him and I bet something will happen." Dee spun on her heels and thumped down the stairs. *Something would happen, but it might not be what I wanted to have happen. That was the way the world seemed to be, as if built on stilts in a lagoon. The world was like Venice where you could sink in sludge or fall in love, depending on your fortune.*

"North, let's get going," Uncle Judd called from downstairs, his voice rasping. "North, North." His voice sounded throaty, like what I imagined a ghost's voice would be.

I turned the mirror around and grabbed Jackie Kennedy's picture, cradling it in my hand. She looked so sensual and at the same time so very happy—just seeing her calmed me. I placed the picture inside the cup of my bathing suit bra, as if my bulletproof shield, over the place Uncle Judd had touched.

With Uncle Judd in the driver's seat of the G-3, I sat pressed against the gunwale on the other side of the boat. My legs dark like ebony wood against the white cushions. "You've got Gypsy blood," my father told me that day in the meadow with Jess. "I bought you from the Gypsies." He laughed, so big. Maybe my wildness about sex and driving had come from this shadowy background.

Now and then the G-3 pulled at the anchor line. Uncle Judd set the anchor, throwing it like a giant cloven hoof into the lake. Beyond us to the north, the scaffold of the Devil's Hole diving tower rose, the water around it glowing with a blue-gray light. Peppered by wind, the water churned molten gray and then the lake surface smoothed like glass again.

A group of ski boats assembled flotillalike in front of the Club. Uncle Judd slid over to me, his arms glistening with sweat, his skin pores like a thousand little wells Alice in Wonderland could fall through. Watching his Swiss watch glitter starry glints of light, I felt hypnotized. *You'll do as I command, the hypnotist on Ed Sullivan said. You won't remember anything.* Uncle Judd slipped off his pink alligator shirt. The wiry, graying hair on his chest twisted like steel wool. Lifting his arm along my seat back, his hand behind my neck, the hair in his armpit showed long and peaked like the hair on troll doll prizes at country fairs. He rapped his knuckles on the dashboard as if to call the boats. A wooden Chris Craft zoomed toward us across the lake with red, white and blue flags waving from its flagpoles.

When I saw the colors, I thought about President Kennedy's inaugural speech when he'd said we should ask what we could do for our country. I thought of Thomas Jefferson who owned slaves. And George Washington who had wooden teeth. I recited the Declaration of Independence, what I remembered of it, knowing that what we celebrated on July fourth was independence. I had inalienable rights.

Damn it, North. Inalienable rights. I lived in America where Jackie Kennedy radiated grace. I could get as mad as the people at the Boston Tea Party. I could rip apart the white cushions in the G-3 and throw the stuffing into the lake. I could jump into the water and swim away from Uncle Judd.

But a man's voice booming over a loudspeaker stopped me from jumping: "Welcome to the fifth annual Glass Lake Ski Show. Enjoy the parade of our skiers," he said in a voice like Bert Parks.

A fleet of ten boats roared our way, each one towing two skiers on slalom skis who crossed the wake simultaneously, ducking under each other's ropes. Shrimp skied behind his Chris Craft with Dee seated inside facing backwards, her windswept hair draping her face. She waved to us in big sweeps as if cleaning a car windshield. I waved back, but my fingers felt like lead plugs passing through the hazy air.

An engine puttered beside us, then muffled to a stop. I looked over to see Bill Hamilton parking his raft a few feet away from where he stood behind the big steering wheel. He looked into my face.

"Didn't expect to see you," he said. I felt a soaring inside as I gazed into his brown eyes that seemed as vast as space. He wore blue baggies and huarache sandals. The swirl of light brown hair in the middle of his chest spread out like a galaxy—or an explosion. It could have been an explosion. Some Italian men had hair on their backs, Dee told me. God, I wished she wouldn't have divulged this. She said their wives combed their back hair with their fingers like apes. Now I believed her, because I would have gladly combed Bill's chest hair like a monkey or whatever animal he asked me to be.

"How do you know Bill?" Uncle Judd asked in a whisper.

"From the Club," was all I could say to him. "I didn't expect to see you either," I said to Bill, my voice catching on *you.*

Bill said *hi* to Uncle Judd, calling him Dr. Diehl, and Uncle Judd answered curtly before he looked back to the show.

"Well, aren't you going to say *hi* to me, too, North," George Parker teased, walking over to Bill. He wore a brown Band-Aid over his cut now.

"Hi, George," I said. Frank, Don and Debbie sat at the front of the raft out of range of my greetings. "Shrimp's really a good skier,"

I added suddenly. Although it was like saying the world was round, I felt compelled to say or do something because Uncle Judd had scooted halfway across the seat closer to me.

Dee sped by again, this time perched on Shrimp's shoulders as a man announced their event as a water ballet. Up high on Shrimp's shoulders she looked like the top of a rocket, and I imagined she *did* feel like she was flying while seated there.

"Psst, East. Uh, I mean, North. Got my directions mixed up," Frank Boyd said quietly. "Have to get a compass, I guess." He stood along the railing of the raft, the lenses of his blue plastic sunglasses reflecting the puffed shapes of clouds. "Anyway, Bill's been talking about asking you to the fireworks show. I keep saying, well, you better do it 'cause if you don't I will." Frank Boyd chucked boyishly like Johnny Carson. "Would you go out with Bill?"

"Yes," I said too quickly. I should have held myself back, said, *I don't know, maybe. What did you say. Repitame, por favor.* Now I stared at an open space on the wind-creased water. "God's breath," was what my father called the wind. When I looked up, Frank wasn't beside me; he stood huddled in a conversation with Bill. Then Bill sauntered toward me, his long arms swinging at his sides. When he reached the railing, Uncle Judd cleared his throat.

"North." The way Bill said my name sounded exotic. I looked right at him. North, south, east, and west converged. The compass spun inside me as if I'd landed on Mars. "Do you like the show?"

"Yes," I said. "Shrimp can really ski."

"Like a professional."

"I've never seen anything like him." The palms of my hands stuck to my thighs. Bill leaned over the railing. I envied boys that. They didn't have cleavage, so they could lean without being measured up by the other sex.

"There's this fireworks show, and I wondered if maybe you'd like to watch it with me, on the raft. Tonight. Round nine-thirty." Bill's tan face gleamed with sweat and light as he pushed his glasses up farther on his nose.

"O.K. Yes," I said. Uncle Judd started coughing like he was about to die in this moment when I could start to live.

"Shrimp and Dee are coming too," Bill said. "I'll pick you up around eight-thirty."

"O.K." I said, *A O.K.* I was counting to lift-off when I'd soar higher than Tarzan in the tree tops if Bill ever held me close.

"Hey, West," Frank said, "You said yes to Hamilton. Broke my heart." Uncle Judd cleared his throat and stood up.

"Hey, Dick, Dave." Uncle Judd flagged his arms at his friends in a cruise boat. "Come over tomorrow. Have a drink." They gave him an O.K. sign. He sat again and scuttled close so his thigh pressed my thigh, his skin hot against my skin. Frank walked away. "North, honey," Uncle Judd said. "What does Dee see in that Shrimp character?" He slid a finger down my thigh. I looked over toward Bill, but he was totally absorbed by the ski show.

"You're not answering me. Where's the bikini I gave you?" Uncle Judd whispered.

"At home. I might get it dirty if I wear it," I stammered.

"You look beautiful in it," Uncle Judd said. "Modesty." He sighed, throwing a towel over our legs, laying his hand on my thigh and stroking up to the edge of my Jantzen, then down to the bone of my knee. I closed my eyes and tried to pretend that Uncle Judd's hand was Bill Hamilton's hand, but when I opened my eyes the towel had fallen off my thighs; I saw the coarse black hairs popping out of Uncle Judd's hand that covered my knee bone. I clamped my legs together and Uncle Judd's hand fell from my knee down my smooth, shaved leg. His hand in hot avalanche. He turned his face toward me, his thick lips open so I could see the round bud of his tongue. Jackie Kennedy's picture nested against my breast.

"Cat got your tongue?" he asked. I looked at his cheeks shining under his black sunglasses that made him look like a giant fly. His breath smelled faintly of liquor.

"No," I said, meaning *Yes. Cat's got my tongue but not my mind. Not yet, because in my mind I am cutting you to pieces with the kind of knife you use.* I felt as if a rag were stuffed in my mouth.

Uncle Judd slid over behind the steering wheel. I smelled gas spurting and heard the Johnson motor whir. All around us, tandem skiers flew over dual jumps so fast my eyes could barely focus on them. Bill shot me a confused look and I lifted my face up.

"Leavin' already?" G. P. called.

"Guess so," I answered. "But, Bill. See you tonight. I can't wait." I couldn't believe so many words meant for Bill had come from me. Bill smiled and Uncle Judd reeled in our anchor just as Linda Turner drove our way in a sleek, black speedboat. The closer she got the meaner she looked, her mouth set in a straight line like a cartoon character's mouth. She wore a green bikini that shimmered like a mermaid's skin, but her stomach hung so loosely above the elastic I thought she *must* have had a child. Pregnancy was in fashion this summer. Not only did Jackie Kennedy expect a child, but so did the wives of both of the President's brothers. Still, I didn't think motherhood suited Linda Turner. So I began to worry about her child. Did she keep it upstairs in one of the private rooms at the Yacht Club where it wailed away the daylight hours alone? Who was the father of the baby? Linda Turner idled her boat nearby as Uncle Judd settled down in the driver's seat. He glanced sideways at her once, then opened the G-3 to full throttle and we sped away.

After dinner I dressed for the fireworks show, the smell of English Leather lingering on my skin even though I'd taken a bath. I drew two lavender fans of eye shadow over my eyes. I thought I might steal the Stingray keys from Uncle Judd's pants' pocket while he napped. I'd take off, the wind pouring in through the windows, whipping my hair out around my face. I imagined finding Bill along the road. Then I looked as closely at my face in the mirror as I thought Bill Hamilton would look at me during the fireworks, and the arcs of eye shadow over my eyes looked dusty like a moth's wings.

I chose my hot pink shift with the white swirls like bull's-eyes. The vivid color set my black hair off and complimented my eyes. On my feet I wore white thong sandals that clumped against the wood of the dock board as Dee and I walked out to meet Shrimp and Bill. The four of us huddled on the raft, moored at the dock. We watched the sun drop in the west where cumulus clouds glowed above the horizon like pink cotton candy.

"Red skies at night. Sailors' delight," Bill said, standing beside me. Dee and Shrimp leaned against the steel railing that turned the corner a few feet away.

"Red skies in morning. Sailors take warning," Shrimp answered Bill.

"That means tomorrow's going to be nice weather. Let's teach North to water ski." Dee looked at me, her blue eyes teasing. I imagined I would rise out of the water, like the Loch Ness monster rising up from the deep. Suddenly my bikini top would slip down, revealing my tiny white breast which, from Bill Hamilton's viewpoint in the ski boat, would look like a chicken dumpling. Fortunately Bill and Shrimp didn't respond to Dee as twilight fell over us.

The lights in the house blinked on. I saw Aunt Joan passing through the living room, moving stiffly as if half asleep. I remembered glimpsing her after dinner when I walked in on her in the bathroom. She stood in front of the medicine cabinet, her hand cupping a bottle of pills.

Uncle Judd stared out the front window, pressing his nose against the glass like a child straining to see a forbidden adult party. I remembered what he had said to me when I walked out the door: *North, you're my good girl, my beautiful, North. That's why I've got your picture on the wall right here. I can look at it when you're away and still see you.* I wondered if he'd developed the pictures he shot on my birthday, those of me naked, with one breast a dinner roll, the other a snow cone. If so, he could sell them to a magazine that handled lewd pictures of children. Or hang them in his home or office or have a show. Or use them for lectures in plastic surgery as the *before breast implant* pictures.

Bill drove the raft and I stood at the back of the raft behind him, holding onto one of the steel poles that supported the red and white striped canopy where tiny white lights hung. By their dim illumination I could see Shrimp and Dee standing up front, entwining their bodies to kiss, fondle, and kiss again. Like a ship's figurehead coming to life, they moved.

The sky passed overhead, a giant planetarium show. The first of the night stars pulsed so brightly I felt sure they were sending us messages in a visual Morse code. Anything seemed possible as Bill parked the raft in the deep water in front of the Yacht Club where we drifted, water gently licking the pontoons.

The pontoons resembled the nuclear missiles Khrushchev had placed on military bases in Cuba until President Kennedy forced him to take them out. Back then we thought there might be a nuclear war. The threats of war between Russia and America flew so wildly about that some people even built bomb shelters. Dad and Queen Mom made our basement into one, including sandbags on the windows. They stocked it with canned foods you wouldn't think of eating unless starved for several days. But President Kennedy stayed his ground and Khrushchev backed off. I had felt so sure then about the future of the world, just knowing President Kennedy could handle a big crisis and win it without losing any lives.

"North, how do you like living at the Lake?" Bill asked me, smiling so I saw his line of perfect white teeth. He must have had braces.

"Lots." I lost my vocabulary in his presence. If Bill kissed me tonight the heat shooting through my body might set the pontoons off like bombs.

Fountains of color burst above us in the dark sky, spraying arcs of blue, purple, red, pink. Booms like cannon fire rumbled in the distance. White arms of ash flowed through the sky as streamers, shattering to swirled pieces like whirly maple seeds turned to jewels. A red firework domed a fountain above and the pink swirls on my dress lit up like sparklers. Bill moved closer. I heard his breathing. I smelled the scent of coconut butter suntan lotion. His biceps bulged under the sleeves of his white tennis shirt, the hairs on his arms curving downy soft. We drifted farther on the lake as if a current were taking us out. Bill pointed to a purple blast of color.

"Sure's the prettiest I've ever seen," he said. I smiled at him, admiring his face, sensitive and strong-featured; his chin with the Kirk Douglas cleft I imagined his tears would run down. But maybe he didn't cry, ever, because the firm tone of his voice reminded me of Stirling Moss when he had talked in his T.V. interview about crashing.

"Do you have a car?" I asked, although I knew he did. We both faced the bow of the raft. Shrimp moved his hand in circles under Dee's pink blouse and the zipper head on her shorts dangled halfway down.

"Yeah. I do." Bill cleared his throat, turning from Shrimp and Dee. "It's my dad's old car. After I learned to drive he bought a Riviera. He gave the BelAir to me."

"It's a Chevy?" I wanted to impress him with my car knowledge.

"A 1957 Chevy BelAir."

"A convertible?"

Bill nodded. I looked into his eyes through the lenses of his glasses and found them deep. Very deep. I thought about his thoughts zooming through the white hills of his brain now. *Were they thoughts of me? Could he picture me in the front seat, what Queen Mom called the death seat, of his Chevy? Could he see my dark hair flying up around my face and my blouse rippling? Did he have visions of my erect breasts beneath the cotton fabric?*

A powder blue firework exploded above us like beads bursting off of a giant glass necklace.

"What's the inside like?" I looked into Bill's face, tinted blue.

"Want to see for yourself? Go for a ride tomorrow." Bill walked to the molded plastic chair behind the steering wheel with me at his heels. "I Will Follow Him" by Little Peggy March filled my mind. Bill started the motor as the finale of red, white and blue fireworks exploded above. I felt as if the whole sky caught fire then. The world burst open like a mysterious fruit sliced in half, and my heart flew in the red ash that sprayed the darkness.

A smell of gasoline spurted in the air as Bill turned over the sputtering motor. Dee and Shrimp rolled on the raft floor in front of us. Bill clasped my hand in his hand, pulling me close. My arm collapsed like a scarf. He lifted my chin until I stared into his face, the lights from the fireworks reflecting a rainbow of colors in his glasses, his lips parting slightly. I glanced at the whorl of hair on his chest showing inside the neck of his shirt. He pursed his lips, moving closer until his lips pressed mine open, his tongue playing in and out. My lips opened more widely. His tongue touched the inside of my cheeks and the roof of my mouth and flitted along the top of my tongue.

When Bill drove up the driveway, the BelAir shone like Aunt Joan's tile floors when Mrs. Graybill cleaned them. The glint from the car caught my eye. I walked into his path to stop him, so he'd have to hit me if he wanted to park by the garage. I didn't know why I'd done such a rash thing. It was like standing in front of a bull at a bullfight. But I smiled at Bill with my head tilted then. I'd dressed in my white short-shorts and my lime green sleeveless blouse that was the color of sherbet.

Bill idled the engine so that the pistons made a purring sound. I noticed the V insignia and the word *Chevrolet* scripted in chrome on the hood, the writing loopy like writing in icing on a birthday cake. Up high on each fender two symmetrical chrome ornaments resembled the tips of arrows made large. I imagined these arrows fired by a remote control switch in the car, as in a James Bond movie, one whizzing toward my right breast. I turned to run back into the house. But then I looked around to the car, seeing Bill, his hands curled around the steering wheel.

"C'mon." He motioned to me to get in the car. I walked to his voice, to the Chevy, and slid onto the red and white seat covers inside next to Bill. He had the top down, neatly hidden under a red canvas snap-on cover behind the back seat. "Whelp, here goes," he said, revving the motor, popping the clutch.

Bill drove us out the driveway. Scooting toward him, I settled so close I could have placed my hand on the steering wheel, the way my mother did when my dad asked her to drive while he put his wallet into his pants' pocket. Bill smiled at me, as if amused by my affection, while I wished over and over that he would let me drive.

We parked along the dirt straightaway behind the Yacht Club where the boys had raced, our hair blown every which way from the fast ride. Queen Anne's lace and loosestrife bloomed in the surrounding fields. Bill laid his right hand, palm down, on my forearm. I closed my eyes as we listened to moldy oldies on the radio, "Earth Angel" and "(I wanna be your) Teddy Bear."

. . .

"*I'm going to* marry Bill Hamilton," I told Dee after lunch. We sat at the moon settlement table eating strawberries.

"How can you be so sure, North?" Dee challenged, her fist full. She ate her berries from her palm like a dog or a horse.

"I just know it. That's all." I bit down slowly; the rough skins broke and juices sprayed inside my mouth.

"You're getting weird, North," Dee said. But she asked what I would wear on my wedding day. I described a silver organdy wedding gown with feet and arms in it like a space suit. I said I'd wear a matching helmet with diamonds set into the silver plastic above the face shield.

"That's too much," Dee groaned. But I continued. I said Bill and I would be the first couple married in space. A famous minister, like the Archbishop of Canterbury, would officiate. We would be chosen from millions of applicants by President Kennedy, who'd call us *Teen Angels* because we would be sent soaring so high.

Our wedding would be a television event. Everyone would watch our rings floating above us until the Archbishop snatched one from its spiral and began the exchange of the rings portion of the ceremony. After we said our vows Bill and I would float and take Communion. The blessed wine would flow up to our mouths, defying gravity. As we slept together for the first time, my hair would float beside my head and Bill's glasses might levitate. Once we were married, even my mother would have to accept our lovemaking while weightless. I'd float away from Bill but he'd scoop his hands after me through air grappling to bring me closer.

Jackie Kennedy would open the newspaper and see the photograph of our wedding. She would think back on her wedding because, despite the space helmet, I'd remind her of some aspect of her younger self. Maybe, just maybe then Shrimp's impression of my resemblance to her would occur to her, in a private moment.

The Ring of Fire

Saturday morning I awoke to the sounds of Dee sobbing. Stumbling out of bed, I crossed my bedroom and approached the bathroom where her cries rose more distinctly as whimpers and cascading sobs.

"Dee?" I knocked on the bathroom door. She didn't answer but she coughed and retched again. "It's North. What's wrong, Dee?"

"Go away," Dee whimpered.

"Shouldn't I get your mom. Or a doctor?" *A doctor, Uncle Judd was a doctor. But I couldn't volunteer to wake him up.*

"Don't do that," Dee pleaded. When she opened the door a crack, the smell of vomit enveloped me. I pushed the door halfway open and found Dee sitting on the white tile floor in front of the toilet, her right arm lying across the back of the toilet seat, her left arm curled in her lap. "I'll be O.K. Don't mention it to anyone. I don't want to worry Mom and Dad." Her face looked gaunt and whitish green.

"You're pale. You must have the flu or something." I touched the wet, cool skin of her forehead. "I heard you crying, Dee. Has something bad happened between Shrimp and you?"

"I always cry when I'm sick," Dee said. "But I'm better now. I just want to lie down."

"You sure?" I asked. Dee nodded.

"Then you call me if you need me." I touched her forearm.

"I will," Dee said, standing up. She held her stomach with her hand and walked slowly toward her bedroom, the sleeves of her ice blue pajamas flecked with vomit. "Not a word, North, promise." She turned back to me and hissed.

"Don't worry." I walked back into my room.

My G.E. clock radio said 6:45, early enough to go back to sleep, so I tried lying down on my bed. But then I desired Bill and felt achy, alone, and too excited when I recalled the way his arms tightened around me as we kissed on the raft, the night sky pulsing with stars and fireworks embers drifting overhead.

I dove my hand into my underpants and stroked, my hand moving in tiny arcs. *Bill*. But then I smelled Uncle Judd's English Leather as if he had spilled it on my bedroom floor. I moved my hand faster. Uncle Judd's face came to mind, huge as a billboard poster of Khrushchev or the devil himself. I stopped moving my hand. Squeezing my eyes shut, I tried to bring back Bill's image. My mind filled with bursting abstract colors, as if the fireworks show played again inside my head. Dee coughed and I opened my eyes. A dim light filled my room. The dresser, the bed frame, all the furniture sharpened at the edges.

I dressed in my maroon and black sleeveless shift with the vertical stripes that accentuated my thin figure. I saw my reflection in the full-length mirror inside my closet door. I'd grown taller since I came to Glass Lake, the hem of my shift hitting my legs mid-thigh. My chin dropped a longer line and my cheekbones stuck up like two miniature tents pitched under my skin. Dark, slivered crescent moons arced under my eyes though I'd tried to hide them with Cover Girl. With my tongue I traced the crests of my twelve-year molars halfway risen in the back of my mouth. How strange to have fallen in love while teething.

Turning the mirror on my bureau around, I lifted Jackie Kennedy's picture from its place behind the frame and slid it inside my bra where it fit naturally. My breasts had grown larger, the right breast becoming cone shaped; the left larger, more full. The sky grayed. Muted light laid a shawl of molten steel on the lake. In the north cove the lily pads spread a shimmering cloak spotted with cupped yellow flowers echoing the color of Linda Turner's eyes.

I tiptoed downstairs, through the kitchen to the back door with King trotting at my heels, though I'd pushed him away with my leg in the living room. He came right back, whining and scratching at the door until I let him outside where he ran to the first fledgling pine tree and peed. I coaxed him back inside with a dog biscuit; I couldn't stand him brushing his damp fur against my legs.

At the green out-cottage I looked through the window at the chairs with cushions covered in art deco-style fabrics, the emerald green player piano pushed to one corner of the room, and the small weavings in neutral colors hanging on the walls. They were Aunt Joan's creations—birds wove nests of such colors. Queen Mom told me Aunt Joan wanted to be a textile designer. She'd graduated from Cranbrook, but when Dee was born she stopped weaving.

In the asphalt lot the Stingray reflected the sun so mystically I felt drawn to it. Before I knew it I was sliding inside. A chrome T rested inside the steering wheel; the crossed racing flag emblem was set inside a smaller metal circle like a bull's-eye there. I laid my hands on the wheel, rocking it back and forth. *All* the dials circled—the speed-ometer, the fuel gauge, the oil pressure gauge, and there was a clock at the top of the console above the four on the floor. If I'd released the parking brake and put the car in neutral it would have rolled backwards, but not far, so I laced my hands around the wheel.

I closed my eyes fantasizing driving the Stingray in a drag race. I pushed the accelerator to the floor. Clouds of exhaust fumes rose like fetid breath. I felt a tickle in my neck as if a fly had landed there. I brushed it with my hand and touched a finger. I opened my eyes and saw Uncle Judd, his arm through the opened window. Now he kneaded my neck, as if it were dough.

"Relax," he said. I leaned forward, as if to pick up something I'd dropped. His hand fell to the seat back behind my head.

"Your muscles are all tight," he said in a voice thick with honey. I saw the car keys dangling from his hand and decided to act civil. "What're you doing in the car?" he asked me.

"Daydreaming about driving," I said, smiling into his alabaster face, his skin glistening like wet tile.

"How about a ride?" he asked, and I felt the place where the picture of Jackie rested. I thought of her beauty as a bandage but still my breast burned, as if pierced by arrows.

"O.K.," I said, crawling across the console into the black bucket seat. Uncle Judd stashed his camera on the floor by my feet and got in the Stingray behind the wheel. He wore madras shorts and a white Oxford cloth shirt and leather sandals without socks. With a wrist flick he started the engine and then popped the clutch, backing us swiftly around, spewing comets of gravel for show. We rode out the driveway, stones clicking under the wheels.

"You like fast cars?" Uncle Judd asked.

"Yes." I pressed the camera against the floor mat with my feet.

"You're riding in one of the fastest cars made." Uncle Judd slipped off his McGeorge Bundy glasses. "Put these in that case," he said, looking at the Coach leather glasses case on the console which would exactly fit a bowie knife. He pushed his square-shaped black sunglasses on. "I've had it up to one twenty on the road."

"That's fast," I said. I wanted to say that I aspired to drive race cars. Instead I put my black wraparound sunglasses on, even though the sun wasn't bright. That both of us should wear sunglasses seemed to suit riding in an exotic sports car. Or maybe I didn't want to be recognized, as if I committed a crime by going with him. I slouched down in my seat then and rested my head back, feeling the speed of the car.

Uncle Judd drove us around the lake, along the west cove by the water. The water changed colors with each depth as light scooped across the lake. Wind wrinkled the water as if silk.

"You ever been to the straightaway behind the Club?" I asked.

"Straightaway? Sounds like a drag racing place."

"Yeah, the boys race there," I said. Inside I trembled, fearing how bold I had become.

"Which boys, North?"

"Frank Boyd and George Parker."

"And the Hamilton boy, too?"

"I suppose." I cleared my throat and felt the trapped wings beating inside my chest.

"That's childish. Against the law, too. They drive old wrecks." Uncle Judd rounded the inside curve at the cove by Ramsey's Marina so fast my shoulder pressed against his arm. He gripped the steering wheel, his knuckles white as marshmallow nuggets as he drove us to the dirt straightaway, stretched out deserted in the afternoon light.

"This the place?" he asked me. "No boys around here."

In the fields around us Queen Anne's lace bowed as if miniature doilies. White hosannas in the breeze. Uncle Judd floored the Stingray, braking hard at the end of the road. My forehead hit the windshield. He took off his sunglasses and turned toward me, his eyes blue as sky, and his nose as regal as a hawk's beak.

"You're too lovely," he whispered. Eyes, nose, face came closer. "Hold it in gear," he said, placing my hand over the top of the gear shift. He laid his hand on my thigh on top of my shift and rubbed up and down. The striped fabric moved in his hand. *Like candy*. It looked like a candy cane. He raised his hand, stroking with his index finger along my lower lip as if he could wipe Bill Hamilton's kiss away. I turned my head from him.

"Hand me the camera. Just one picture. You in the car with your sunglasses on. Like a movie star." His voice was like an ointment. I stared out the windshield, pressed the camera with my toes.

"Give me the camera," he said. I shook my head no. "What's the matter?" he asked.

"My face's broken out," I said in a whisper, pointing to the blemishes on my chin.

"I could touch that up. In the picture," he said.

"No," I said. "Let's just listen to the radio." The smell of English Leather hung in the car. I rolled my window down to keep from coughing up breakfast like Dee. First he turned the radio to a station that played Glenn Miller songs. I stared out the windshield, until he changed the station to WDT where the disc jockey played "One Fine Day (you're gonna want me for your girl)."

"You like rock and roll music?"

"Yeah."

"Sounds noisy to me." Uncle Judd laughed deep down in his chest. "The way you kids dance without touching seems like no fun at all." He raised his hand, the flat of his palm pinkish white arcing slowly through the air toward me. He rubbed my left breast up, then down. Inside my underwear I felt a wetness that could have been my first period. I had no pads with me, no place to change. Uncle Judd stroked the nub of my breast like a button on a machine he turned on and off. *North*, I told myself, *this isn't really happening*. Then I smelled English Leather and looked at my breast where Uncle Judd's fingers appeared huge.

The radio played Johnny Cash's song "Ring of Fire," and I went down to a place as fiery hot as hell. A dark place where orange flames licked the darkness. Uncle Judd could take me there anytime he wanted to, and once he had me there he could do anything he wanted to to me. My bladder tensed up. I shoved my knees together, hunching over in the seat. Uncle Judd's hand fell into my lap where he moved his fingers, tickling. I jiggled my knees so his hands jumped in the trampoline of my skirt.

"You're high strung," he said, laughing. I stomped my foot; the camera rocked on the floor mat. I doubled over head pressed to the windshield.

"What's wrong?" he asked me then. *Everything happening here is wrong*, I wanted to say.

"I have to go to the bathroom." A warm blush spread over my cheeks.

"Go behind that big oak tree. Crouch in the weeds. I'll honk the horn if I see anyone coming." He pointed to a wide oak that stood a few feet away.

I slipped out of the car, slammed the door and walked into the grass behind the oak tree, believing that Uncle Judd could see through the tree trunk to where I squatted in the Queen Anne's lace and pulled my yellow underpants down. Inside them a wet coin shone, not blood, but something like saliva. It took forever for me to go.

While I waited I read the initials of lovers carved into the tree trunk, some resembling scars. *T. B. loves K. S.* The letters were like love's branding. I looked for Bill Hamilton's initials. But they had been pressed into the muscle of my heart the first time I laid eyes on him.

A tiny stream of urine trickled to the ground, another sign of *multiple sclerosis*. A sign of the disease that would send me directly to the first doctor in sight once I started stumbling around the house.

I decided I wouldn't tell anyone, no matter how sick I became. I would hide all the clues to my demise. I'd clean up after myself and blame the wet spots on King.

Gray cumulus clouds spread steamy towers up to the heavens. A white light glowed at the edges of the clouds. I wished I could rise into the clouds to float with a silver-white light shining around me. *Oh, ride me in a space rocket straight to the moon*, I asked God then. *Send me into an orbit that will last for a very long time.*

"A storm's coming," Uncle Judd called. Thunder rumbled from far off and the field flowers stilled in the sulfurous light, a green light like the color of the sky before tornadoes. I walked through this light toward the car.

"Get in." Uncle Judd motioned to me with his hand, a glint of light flashing from his gold wedding band. But I walked to the driver's side.

"Let me drive," I said, smiling a little.

"You ever driven before?"

"Yes," I lied. But it wasn't exactly me who spoke. It was some temporary inhabitant of my body. "You let Dee drive."

"Because of the situation it was safer." Uncle Judd stared at me as if memorizing some map to my soul that he could read on my skin. *It was safer that way because you were drunk*, I wanted to shout. *You couldn't even walk, damn it.*

"I'll be careful." That strange sure voice rose up again from me.

"If I tell you to pull over, you listen." Uncle Judd scowled.

"I will." My lips opened so that I smiled as Uncle Judd got out and slid into the rider's side. I started the engine and backed up, letting the clutch out hesitantly. Shifting into second, I ground the gears. Uncle Judd cupped his hand over mine on the gear shift. "Like this." He moved the knob back and to the side, his fingers hairy like a tarantula's legs.

"Push the clutch in. Again." I did what he said. "Accelerate." I pressed the pedal and his hand guided mine, pushing the gear shift into third. We sped toward the darkening sky. Thunderheads billowed like ink spills above the southwest shore. Wind slammed the lake, hurling white-capped waves across the water.

"It's going to pour," Uncle Judd said, lighting his hand on my thigh. "Might hail, too." He drew a finger over my skin. I couldn't feel the line he drew if I concentrated on driving. Like one of those Buddhist monks I saw once on television I could have walked on hot coals then, not feeling pain. I only knew his hand was there if I glanced down, and even then his hand seemed to separate from the rest of his body. All my fear focused on the storm. Forked lightning pitched overhead. My hands sweated on the wheel.

When I looked at the black road stretched out ahead of us, I became another North, the North who loved to move forward, who watched the trees, the lake, and the dark sky go by. A cadmium yellow fork of lightning set a hairline crack in the sky. I snaked the Stingray close to the road along the curves at the coves.

"You're a good driver." Uncle Judd pushed his sunglasses up on his head, lifting the front of his hair; the untanned skin of his forehead shone like a white half moon. I downshifted, pulling into the Diehls' drive. "Like that?" he asked me. I stared ahead.

"It's gonna soak us if we don't hurry up," I said, parking beside the garage.

"Want to drive again?" he asked me.

"Maybe."

"Wear your white bikini next time."

"I don't know." My leg hit the bottom of the steering wheel. Uncle Judd brushed the nipple of my breast. The cloth of my shift caught and then smoothed. I felt as if a chemical sprayed inside me then, something radioactive with a half-life that glowed beneath my skin. I looked at my hands. Yellow light rimmed my fingers with a menacing radiance. Thunder crashed through the sky, the sound synchronized with the chemical shooting through my body.

"Your figure's in fashion. Small breasts, slim hips." Uncle Judd held his hand on my breast as if he owned it. "I want us to be special friends. We'll take more drives. But they must be kept secret." He stroked my thigh, up and down. I tried to imagine myself driving again, tried to forget about Uncle Judd, but the smell of English Leather filled the car, affecting me like anesthesia. I drifted, feeling his hand stroke me down the shoulders as if I were a sculpture of clay he fashioned then. Eve out of God's hand, Eve who fell by the apple. Then I envisioned myself behind the wheel of the Stingray, floored, running over him, back and forth. In forward and in reverse. He collapsed the way the Resusci-Annie doll had fallen limp on our laps in babysitting class.

Then Uncle Judd touched me inside my thighs, beneath my knee caps, tickling along the curve of my neck. I smelled English Leather and lost track of what was happening. His hand became a hand disconnected from his body. My body disconnected from my mind. And my mind launched a rocket emergency flair of sentences, all silent, inside, pleading. *Don't. Stop it. Please. Get your dirty hands off.*

Raindrops fell like bullets on the roof, slanting in sheets against the windshield. I watched as in the air the silky threads of cottonwood fruit, thick and white as snow, hung draped from the rustling branches, like the hair of angels turned silver in an instant by fright as they fell through the arms of those trees on their way toward Johnny Cash's fiery hell.

Dee and I watched the play unfold from the screen porch. Aunt Joan read the part of Amanda, her shoulder-length hair hanging free and full like Sandra Dee's hair. Entering the living room, she carried a tray of lemonade in hand but stumbled on a bump in the rug and barely kept the glasses upright.

"Well, well, well," she spoke her lines in her studied drawl, and I heard her slur some words. I remembered her in the afternoon inside the downstairs bathroom, taking more yellow pills. In the play Amanda has walked in on Laura and Jim, the gentleman caller, who accidentally broke Laura's glass unicorn, part of her treasured collection. *Poor Laura*, I thought, *the poor crippled thing*. The threat of multiple sclerosis crippling me flew through my mind. To distract myself from horror thoughts, I began thumbing through the magazines that lay on the wicker tea cart beside me.

One was *Glamour*, from May. In it I found an article about Jackie Kennedy's pregnancy, which included a discussion on cesarean sections. Jackie Kennedy had to have them with Caroline and JohnJohn, and they expected her to have one for the birth of this baby, too. They said the operation was safe but it sounded gruesome; the mother was left scarred. I pictured the way Uncle Judd could fix the scar and make a woman appear perfect again. My hands trembled when I showed the article to Dee, who sat on the floor next to me looking at the open pages. Her face blanched white. With her eyes fixed on the corner of the room, she shoved the magazine away.

Through the screen of the porch I saw the world as if through black gauze. Rain pelted the lake with the big drops that bounced back up into the air like Mexican jumping beans. Searching the stack of magazines once more, I opened an *American Journal of Plastic Surgery*. Even though the mailing sticker on the front read *Dr. Judson Diehl*, I made myself open it. The very first article in the issue was titled. "Reconstruction of the Penis In a Twelve-Year-Old Boy."

"Did you know plastic surgeons can make penises?" I held up the journal to show Dee.

"My dad does stuff like that all the time." She sighed deeply and turned to look out at the lake. Aunt Joan's drawl sounded like it came from a radio now instead of the next room.

"It's like being God," I said. "Dee, look at this one." I held up one of the pictures of the nude boy.

"Medical stuff bores me." Dee glared at me, then opened a *Vogue* with Jean Shrimpton's picture on the cover.

"Do you think your Dad could make a girl into a boy?" I couldn't stop myself from asking this question. If he made me a boy maybe he'd stop touching me.

"That's moronic, North," Dee snarled at me.

The pictures of the nude boy showed close-ups of his penis—or what was left of it, because his penis had been partially shot off in a hunting accident. To make a new penis the doctors used skin from the boy's abdomen and some cartilage from a rib. *It's like God making Eve from Adam*, I thought; *Eve was a piece, a piece of a man.* Or maybe Adam was actually made from Eve, the boy after the accident looked more like a girl. Maybe Adam was a piece of a woman. Whichever it was, it took several operations to make a new penis for the boy, and this new penis had to be sewn onto the boy's belly so it could heal there. Later the doctors cut it free.

At the end of the article, the doctors said that only time would tell whether the new penis would ever function as a sex organ. In the last photograph they showed the boy sitting at his desk, dressed in a checked shirt and khakis with his blond hair combed neatly to one side. I thought they should have put black slat marks over his eyes because they told far too many details about his private parts. The next article was about artificial breasts and one of the authors listed was *Judson Diehl*. I told myself there must be another Judson Diehl, but his credentials said he went to the University of Michigan and worked in private practice in Grosse Pointe Farms.

The woman who wanted new breasts in the article had breasts that looked just like my defective right breast, with teeny nipples on top of fat pads the size of *petits fours*. During the operation, the underside of each breast was opened and Teflon-silicone implants were slipped inside, then glued and sewn into place. The authors said all the women studied had pleaded with them for new breasts, most asking for huge, pendulous ones so that the doctors had to act as the forces of moderation, suggesting breasts of a normal size.

Knowing how Uncle Judd created breasts haunted me. *Maybe he could do that to me once I fell through that ring of fire.* I turned to show Dee the article but she was asleep, her head lying in a nest of flowered pillows she had pulled to the floor, her legs frozen, knees up.

"Deedee, the telephone's for you," Mrs. Graybill spoke softly from inside the doorway to the porch. I watched as beyond her in the living room the play group moved into the kitchen for refreshments.

"I'll take a message for her," I said, standing up.

As I walked to the phone, Mrs. Graybill handed me a postcard from my parents. The picture side showed Michelangelo's painting of God making Adam on the ceiling of the Sistine Chapel. I thought Eve should have been painted on the ceiling too, flowering out of God's hand. I tripped over King, who lay in the living room. He whined as if I had kicked him on purpose.

"Shrimp, Dee's asleep," I said. I asked if I could take a message. Shrimp said he wanted Dee to go with him to the Pavilion that night to hear Dale Driver and the Motor City Wheels. "And Bill wants to meet you there." My fingers felt light as I envisioned Bill Hamilton dancing with me.

"O.K.," I said. "I'll tell her. And tell Bill I'll be there."

"I'll pick you both up at nine." Shrimp's voice sounded high-pitched, like a Columbus Choir boy's voice. I wanted to say something more, to say, *Shrimp, Dee is sick*, but to do so felt like a betrayal so I said good-bye quietly.

I read the postcard from my parents. My mother said, *North, we haven't heard a word from you. Dad and I checked in Rome and there was nothing.* I wondered what had happened to the letter I had sent, picturing it lying on the floor of a post office in Rome. *North, try to make use of your free time this summer. Read your books and improve your mind and please don't cause trouble. Do whatever Aunt Joan and Uncle Judd say; follow the rules of their family. . . .*

Follow the rules of the Diehl family and I will wind up a drug addict or a prostitute, I thought. *Do as Uncle Judd says and I'll fall through that ring of fire and never come back up again.*

My blue and white striped sleeveless dress with the bell skirt swirled brightly in the flashing lights as I danced with Frank Boyd to Dale Driver and the Motor City Wheels. Dale Driver wore a black leather motorcycle jacket as, to the fast beat of music, he danced across the stage. "Around. Up, down." They were playing "The Peppermint Twist" and Frank Boyd crouched close to the dance floor as he twisted. My hips slipped back and forth, rhythmically.

Dee had shown me how to do the Twist one evening the week before. "You pretend that you're shining your rear end with a bath towel and putting a cigarette out with your front foot at the same time," she had said, demonstrating after she'd taken a bath. I read in *Newsweek* that Jackie Kennedy and the President danced the Twist at White House parties. I supposed that now that Jackie Kennedy's activities had been limited she probably wouldn't be twisting anymore. Still, she did once, and she would approve of my gyrations; somehow I knew this.

Beneath my dress the gold locket swung like a pendulum against my chest, still empty inside. I wanted a picture of Bill there, but when I dressed for the evening I opened the locket and imagined Uncle Judd's face leering there, haunting me, until I snapped it shut.

"Great dance, North," Frank Boyd said. "It's been real." He lit a cigarette, then sauntered away to join G. P. and Larry Meeker, slouched like hoods against the wall near the stage. I stood in the middle of the dance floor where Frank Boyd had left me, looking up at the ceiling of the Pavilion. In the rough beam rafters the flood lights burned like stars. I listened to the Motor City Wheels play their song "Strange Nights."

It was a song about a boy and girl who went out for a drive in the boy's father's Ford Fairlane late one night. They drove by the factory where the boy's father worked on the Ford assembly lines. Through the tall factory windows they saw the car bodies hanging in air as they were passed from man to man. The girl tells the boy she is pregnant and the boy doesn't know what to do. If he marries her he'll have to work in a factory like his father does. If he doesn't marry her she says she'll try to lose the baby.

When the boy considers working in the factory his whole life, he decides they will run away to a town that has a different dream, where men aren't caged inside steel buildings making steel machines. So he accelerates and they roll the windows down. The air that blows in feels like freedom, but the girl is crying because they are leaving their friends. Then the boy makes a wrong turn and misses the exit out of Detroit. He ends up parking the car down by the Detroit River where he notices his gas tank is almost empty. If he drives forward he'll drive into the water, killing both of them and the baby. If he turns around he'll drive back toward the factory.

"North," Bill Hamilton stood beside me. "What're you doing out here by yourself?"

"Listening to the words of that song," I said.

"How about dancing with me?" Bill seemed so tall as he pulled me in. The lights dimmed and the Wheels played a slow song called "Hello Stranger." I could never give words to how smoothly Bill led me across the floor inside his arms. He leaned over to reach me and I stood tall, feeling his thick hair mingling with mine as we touched faces. Images of our space age wedding flew through my mind, our twin silver helmets adorned with jewels, the way we would kiss as we floated in weightlessness, my breasts pressed against Bill's body.

"Want to go outside?" Bill held my hand as if he wanted everyone to see I was his girlfriend. Sally Fry stared at us as we walked by her in front of the stage.

We must have floated outside; I had so little memory of how we arrived there, except that Bill pulled me along and I followed. The humid air formed halos around the lamp lights in the dirt parking lot. When my eyes adjusted to the darkness, I saw Shrimp and Dee leaning side by side against the hood of Shrimp's Corvair. Shrimp squeezed Dee's forearm as we walked closer. Fireflies pulsed in the air above their heads like moving diadems.

"Stop touching me," Dee shouted, her ponytail bouncing behind her head.

"I just want to kiss you. Like always." Shrimp faced her, grabbing both her arms at the elbows.

"Leave me alone." Dee lifted her face toward the place in the sky where the moon should have hung but because of the haze a big white fuzzy circle glowed.

"Don't you love me?"

"I don't know anymore." Dee dropped her chin and I saw Shrimp's ring with the bottom side wrapped in white mohair gleaming on her ring finger. Bill veered between two parked cars, steering me away from them. We reached his Chevy and slid inside, where my thighs stuck to the vinyl seats because of the humidity. He pushed the key into the ignition and turned the radio on. WDT played "Don't Make Me Over," Dionne Warwick's song.

Bill turned toward me, pressed his lips against mine then pushed his tongue between my lips until my mouth opened. He panted a little and started rubbing my back with his hands moving in fast circles. He reached around my back to finger my breast and I felt my heart race. I pulled my face away from Bill's face in the middle of a kiss. He looked at me, his mouth dropping open. The street lamps reflected a dim light across the lenses of his glasses. Bill's eyes are brown, I told myself, *brown eyes, brown brown brown*, but I couldn't see through his glasses, and in my mind I saw Bill's eyes gleaming blue like Uncle Judd's eyes. Then Bill's slender hands thickened. *Please say your name. Say: I'm Bill Hamilton*, I thought. *Say who you are and you can kiss me again.* Bill pulled back and stared at me.

"What's the matter?" he said.

I remembered Uncle Judd lecturing us before we left for the Pavilion. He said we should be home by eleven o'clock, that we should not go joyriding around the lake. He knew all about the places where boys took girls to park so if we stayed out too late he would come looking for us. I thought maybe he had already started searching and if I looked out my window now I might find his huge loathsome face glaring there. Bill's fingers brushed my cheekbone. My stomach felt twisted as if in somersaults. Bill touched my arms but I couldn't respond.

"I'm sorry, Bill. I feel sick. Where's the bathroom?" I was lying, borrowing Dee's illness.

"It's O.K." He took my hand in his hand. "I'll walk you back inside." Bill led me in the way he had led me out. I felt prickly sensations in my hands and feet. *Multiple sclerosis, the disease that makes you turn into Snow White, asleep before you're really asleep. The disease that makes your whole body feel like it's sleeping. And you lie inside a glass case for someone to touch whenever he wants to touch you.*

The Diving Tower

I skied on two skis and stayed inside the wake like an old lady skiing for the first time. Bill must have thought me prematurely feeble. I fell four times, and every time I waited for Shrimp to circle the Chris Craft around for me, I thought about Linda Turner, my body growing colder and colder, especially my legs and feet. I began to believe she had lost her foot in a skiing accident instead of while swimming. I could lose my foot now, if Shrimp wasn't careful, and sometimes he drove toward me at full throttle until he put the motor in neutral all of a sudden, the boat surging into a languid drift.

After I told Shrimp and Bill and Dee I'd had enough humiliation, we came into the Club where Dee and I changed bathing suits in the basement. Dee told me we would go to the Devil's Hole diving tower for our afternoon swimming date.

"Heights are so exhilarating," she said.

"What's it like on top of the tower?" I asked, pulling my canary yellow bikini on. My right breast nearly filled the bra cup.

"You can see over the tree tops, out to the Irish Hills," Dee said. "At night you can even see the screen at the Drive Inn. Once Shrimp and I watched parts of *Splendor in the Grass* from up there."

"Was there a lot of kissing in it?" I felt my cheeks flush hot.

"Oh, yes. Kissing and necking on the grass, that's how they came up with the title." Dee tensed her thighs as she pulled on her rose-colored bikini.

I thought about the word *splendor*, how beautiful it was, how it described the first kiss Bill Hamilton gave me. But there needed to be another word for the way I felt when he kissed me now, a word like a fraction in math class. *Splendor* divided by alarm.

"Shrimp and I used to go to the diving tower to talk about our future. About him becoming an advertising executive and me . . ." Dee stared at the ceiling.

"You doing what?" I pulled on my bikini bottoms and, when Dee wasn't looking, I lifted my picture of Jackie Kennedy from my canvas swim bag. I placed it inside the bra of my bikini along with a shoe string I planned to use to tie the back straps of my bathing suit together.

"Nothing, just dumb stuff like having a house and children. But right now I'd rather go to the moon."

"President Kennedy wants us to beat the Russians there." I said something trite because Dee looked so unhappy. I wanted to change the subject.

"My dad hates President Kennedy." Dee sat down on the wood bench beside the rock wall. "I don't see why it has to stink so much down here." Everything in the Yacht Club basement smelled musty like my great-grandmother's old clothes. It was so wet moss grew on the stone walls and mosquitoes buzzed all around.

"Because it's a basement," I said. I tried to ignore the mention of Uncle Judd, who left me a gift when he returned to Grosse Pointe last Sunday. He hid it under my pillow like money from the tooth fairy, but I hadn't opened it. I had only opened the card with the scribbled note that said, "To my beautiful dreamer, more secret rides, you driving. Love, Uncle Judd." I'd thrown the present under my bed, hoping it would break before I laid eyes on it.

"Ready?" Dee slipped into her pink terry cloth cover-up. "Let's sneak down by the gazebo and see if the boys are there." As we walked along the front sidewalk, Linda Turner approached us from the deck by the flagpole. She wore a beige turtleneck and Levi's with those same heavy socks. Her black shoes were like the shoes that nuns and old maid schoolteachers wore. She stared at the sidewalk until we reached her, then lifted her head. "Hello, Dee," she said sharply.

"Hi," Dee said, walking faster as we moved closer.

Since I had not heard my name mentioned I gazed up at the silver aspen leaves shuttling above us like silver coins. When I glanced at Linda again I saw her breasts hanging like melons under her clingy shirt, like the breasts of a new mother filled with milk. Maybe she was going upstairs now to breastfeed her lonely baby.

"Now be real quiet, North," Dee said. "I've never been caught spying on the boys." Dee laid her sandals on the grass by the stone foundation.

"O.K. It's not like I haven't done this before." I placed my white thongs along side her shoes. As I followed Dee across the lawn I remembered my first glimpse of Bill, when he had tied a bowline knot. I saw that knot like a noose of rope swinging from his long thin fingers.

At the gazebo we crouched down along the high clerestory windows, pressing our faces close to the screens. The whole gang of boys had gathered there, most dressed in baggies, except for Frank Boyd who wore a skimpy green swimsuit.

"I'm taking Sally Fry to the Pavilion Saturday." G. P. strutted like a rooster before a fight.

"How could you stoop so low?" Shrimp asked, standing with his knees flexed, the way he stood when he skied.

"She's got those jugs, Shrimp. Big watermelon tits. G. P. got horny Saturday night when he watched her dancing and her tits bounced around. He wished his hands were her triple D bra cups. Didn't you, G. P.?" Frank Boyd leaned against the wall, the way Arab men lean in doorways. "I bet when she dances the weight of her jugs breaks her bra straps. She probably has to carry an extra bra in her purse."

"Shit," G. P. said, but Shrimp was laughing. With his white teeth and white hair he could have been an albino, except his skin was so tan.

"Sally used to have her eyes on you, Bill," Frank Boyd said. "But now that you've got a girlfriend she's on the make."

"Yeah, Billie boy, how's North? Does she let you French kiss her?" G. P. asked. Hearing my name mentioned made my skin burn.

"Sometimes." Bill dragged the heel of his shoe across the concrete. I felt as if the line he pulled through the dirt cut into my skin. I think I gasped because Dee elbowed me, signaling me to be quiet.

"Bet she's kind of cold, though. You haven't really gotten much, have you?" Frank Boyd said.

"It's cold up North," G. P. laughed, and everybody except Bill joined in, cackling.

"Making it with her would be like fucking an iceberg," Frank Boyd roared.

"You could get pneumonia standing next to the North Pole." G. P. cracked up laughing.

"She is a pole," Larry Meeker said. "She's as skinny as a bean pole." The whole gang roared except for Bill who walked out of the gazebo as if he could stay above it all. I wanted to scream: *Stop it, stop it, damn you.* But something closed my throat off and the swear words whirled around deep inside me.

The Devil's Hole diving tower loomed in the north cove of the lake like a scaffold, its wood weathered to driftwood gray. As we motored closer, it seemed to possess an untouched beauty as if it were a relic that the lake had heaved up. The wind shifted from south to west, crosswise gusts rippling the water. Bill and I sat side by side in the back seat on the blue cushions that doubled as life preservers. I studied him, his dark hair tossed by the wind and his chin dimpled with the cleft.

Shrimp had teased Dee before we left the Club, saying he would look straight at the solar eclipse, expected at four-thirty. Dee hadn't laughed. On the ride over she gripped the gunwale of the Chris Craft so tightly her knuckles turned as white as after-dinner mints.

Near shore Shrimp threw the bronze anchor down. I watched it fall through the water where tiny white stones tumbled like confetti. Shrimp handed the anchor line to Bill who wound it around the bow cleat, then knelt on the deck staring up at the tower.

"How dark will it get?" I asked Shrimp, who was pulling off his yellow T-shirt that said *Glass Lake Daredevils*.

"Dark as midnight. Bats will be flying through the air. You won't be able to see anything." He spoke in a false Dracula voice.

"Let's go up on top of the tower and tell ghost stories while the sky goes black." Dee's eyes widened. But her face sagged, and I thought maybe the sunlight exaggerated the bags under her eyes, the red, beginning blemishes on her chin.

"It won't be as dark as night," Bill said. "It will be more like dusk or the sky before a storm." He hurled his navy blue sweatshirt onto the seat beside me. The whorl of hair at the top of his chest seemed to move in a circle, the way water moves around a dropped stone. "C'mon, let's get in." Bill looked at me, then slipped off his glasses and handed them to Dee.

"In a minute. I want to warm up first." I wanted to say, *I can't warm up if I'm as cold as you boys say I am; but then, what is this one burning spot on my breast?* Bill dove in, swimming toward the tower. Shrimp followed with a cannon ball. Dee dove with her toes pointed ballerinalike, and when she surfaced she called to me, "Last one in's a rotten egg."

"It's not cold." Bill treaded water while waving.

"Goddamn horsefly!" Shrimp ducked down under the water as a horsefly buzzed his head, then flew toward Dee, landing on her forehead. She wrinkled her face and swatted with her hands, darting down under the water. I watched Bill swim surface dives toward the tower until the horsefly bit my back in all the places I couldn't reach and I jumped into the lake with my blouse on.

"Need some help?" Bill popped up beside me, his head rising above water like the bust of someone famous.

I rolled my wet blouse up and placed it in his hand. He swam it to the Chris Craft, throwing it into the back. I swam the side stroke, and Bill did the breast stroke with more surface dives as we approached the tower. Shrimp began climbing the rough wooden ladder, the muscles in his legs rippling with each step. Dee followed him.

When I reached the ladder, Bill coaxed me, saying the world looked beautiful from the top of the tower. I watched the sky turn wintry gray and the water darken around us. When I glanced back at the Chris Craft, the wide shadow the boat usually cast was replaced by a curved, diminished darkness.

"It's the eclipse!" Dee shouted. Suddenly I wanted to look at the sun glowing behind the blackened moon. I wanted to look at something bright enough to burn my eyes. I turned my face and lifted my eyes to see it, but Bill grasped my arms, stopping me. Underwater his hands felt like silk brushing my skin.

"Let's go up." He pulled my arm.

I could barely feel the wood slats underfoot as I climbed. Bill followed me. I thought my legs must have looked as long and thin as a pair of stilts from behind. My head swirled with thoughts that ran together like two radio stations tuned in at once. *Was Bill my dream boy or just a boy who wanted a piece of me?* My thoughts whirled until Shrimp shot his hand over the top of the ladder and pulled me up.

Dee was right; you could see over the treetops, and all the different depths of the lake possessed sharp edges like the colored areas on game boards. Bill joined us, and we huddled in the middle of the platform.

"Well, Hamilton," Shrimp said. "How's your summer reading? You read *The Wet Bed Sheets* by I. P. Knightly yet?"

"No, but I read *The Yellow River* by I. P. Daily," Bill joked back, and I couldn't help but laugh.

"What about *The Open Kimono* by Seymore Hare? Or *Curing the Scourge of Masturbation* by Dr. I. Kutchercockoff!" Shrimp roared. I laughed, too, even though I felt sad, remembering the little boy who had lost his penis. Still, I felt a camaraderie with everyone, sitting there in a circle.

"Do you ever go to the speedway?" I asked. I stared at my feet lying dark against the gray wood.

"Sunday, Sunday," Shrimp imitated a sports announcer's voice, "Sunday at Motor City Speedway, the Racing Capital of Mid-America. See Connie Kalitta and Rickie Deans drive their hearts out. Sunday. Sunday."

"I'm serious," I said. *This girl you boys say is cold wants to feel the heat of the raceway.*

"I've never been, North. They don't take dates there. It's too dirty." Dee brushed wisps of hair off her forehead.

"We do go sometimes," Bill said. "To Raceway Park Speedway near Jackson. It's a two-mile paved oval track."

"I'd like to go." *With you, Bill, even if you think I'm like ice. Even if you told the other boys you French kissed me.*

"I'll take you," Bill said, "some weekend in July. I'll check the schedule. I think they're going to have a big race then."

"Don't count on me," Dee said while grimacing. "Who wants to go smell oil burning and exhaust fumes?"

"Who wants to go over the edge?" Shrimp asked, bolting upright.

"Why do they call this the Devil's Hole?" I asked. Thinking about the edge made my stomach go around. *I'm not going down until I know what's there,* I thought. *I'm not going down until I know I will come back up again.*

"It's just an old wives' tale," Bill said, squinting.

"No, it's not," Dee said. "Somebody drowned here. A boy named Tony Bradford. He was a good swimmer. He dove here all the time. But once on a real nice summer day he came to the tower alone and never returned. They dredged the lake for his body, but the hole was too deep. People say Tony's still down there where the devil took him. They say the devil pulled him down with his voice. *Tony, Tony,* the devil called, and he got a cramp in his leg and went under just like that." Dee snapped her fingers.

Suddenly I had to go to the bathroom so badly I crossed my legs and stared up at the sky. *North, just don't look down at that black water,* I thought.

"That's not a true story," Bill said.

"How do *you* know?" Dee hit her heel against the platform.

"It's a ghost story, made up to scare girls." Bill rolled his eyes.

"Well, I heard another story," Shrimp offered. "I heard that during the summer when the sun rises, a red torch burns across this deep water, makes it look like the lake here is made of fire. And since the devil lives in Hell where everything's burning, people say the torch marks the Devil's Hole."

"Hope he doesn't come up with his pitchfork raised when I jump over." Bill laughed.

"Might poke you in the ass, huh, Hamilton? Oh, sorry about the language, North, Dee," Shrimp said, nodding to us.

Don't apologize, I thought. I was beginning to like swearing. I wanted to try it myself. Saying *Damn. Damn it. God damn you.*

"Let's go, girls." Shrimp grabbed Dee's arm, pulling her upright. She kicked and tore at his back with her light pink polished fingernails. "No, Shrimp, don't. Stop it." I heard the thuds of her feet as Shrimp dragged her to the edge of the platform and pushed her off. "Shrimp, I'm gonna kill you, Shrimp!" she screamed.

"O.K., North," Shrimp grabbed my hand as I locked my free hand over Bill's arm, my grip tightening like handcuffs so that Shrimp pulled both of us then, his dark legs bulging. I leaned more toward Bill, and the strap of my bikini fell over my shoulder.

"No, Shrimp, don't!" I screamed. I flew over the side of tower, pulling Bill with me, our hands unclasping as we fell. I wished over and over that we could rise up into a weightless world, a world without gravity. When I saw Bill's face above me, he was smiling, "See you down there, North!" he yelled.

Below us the black water spread out as dark as India ink. I reached for Bill again, but he fell above me. *I must be heavier,* I thought, *like a stone.* My arm dropped to my side. I felt the top of my bikini loosen. The white shoestring dropped out of my bra cup, falling through the air like a streamer swirling off a cheerleader's pom-pom. Down down down. Curling like a white diving snake, it fell through the ring of fire toward that spot in the lake that led straight to Hell.

Feet first I plunged into the lake. The bra of my bikini billowed away from my breasts. I opened my eyes under water and saw tiers of yellow ruffles waving in the water, my right breast floating, a white fuzzy curve of flesh. *Where's my picture?* I wondered. I searched inside my bra cup, but I couldn't feel it. I looked through the water for Jackie Kennedy's image, for the tiny mirrored moons and stars glimmering on her dress. My arms arced through emptiness, white scuttling shapes. The last breath I held inside my lungs oozed from my mouth, forcing me to the surface, bubbles of spent air flowing from my mouth like bubbles escaping an aqua lung.

I dove down once again, eyes wider open. I grasped at the black water as if to catch fish. The cold lake gave itself to my fisting. Again and again, I dove as if Jackie herself had been lost from me then.

"North, get your butt back in the Chris Craft!" Dee shouted from the boat.

I lost Jackie Kennedy. My bandage. My bulletproof shield, I wanted to tell her. But I thought she'd laugh at me.

"Jesus Christ, North, we're freezing." Dee slapped the gunwale of the Chris Craft in a rhythm as if playing a bongo drum.

I sat on top of my bed, fashioning a gum chain from green Doublemint wrappers. I wove in Juicy Fruit and Spearmint wrappers for color changes. I laid the gum chain, which was about three feet long, across my bedspread and thought, *Maybe I should send it to President Kennedy.* It would be a peace symbol. If all the girls my age in America fashioned gum chains, we could join them together and stretch them across America "from sea to shining sea," wrapping the world up into one world. The girls in Russia could make gum chains, too, and we'd join their chains to ours. But maybe they weren't allowed to make symbolic gestures in a totalitarian state.

"North, the phone's for you." Uncle Judd walked into my bedroom. At first I didn't believe him. "Your mom's calling from Athens." He walked within inches of me, stood hunkered over, and lifted the gum chain by a finger, holding it like a baby snake of folded paper. I smelled whiskey on his breath. His dark purple swim suit and yellow tennis shirt together resembled a bruise. "North," he said, "do you hear me?" I bolted to my feet and into the hall. Downstairs I lunged by Mrs. Graybill, who wiped off the table and set fruit salad out for lunch.

"Hello." I took the phone in hand, spoke into the receiver.

"It's Mom." I noted the familiar crispness in Queen Mom's voice and breathed deep. I tightened my fist on a crumpled Spearmint wrapper.

"You didn't write us," she said. I couldn't defend myself. I could only think of all the bad things that had happened. I wanted to list them out loud. But when I tried I remembered Uncle Judd's instructions to keep our rides secret. All the things that had happened formed a woolly ball in my mind. I struggled to unwind the strands. *I have fallen through a ring of fire,* I wanted to say. *And I'm not sure of all that happened there. But I know I don't want Uncle Judd touching me anymore.* Yet Uncle Judd stood next to me, leaning over the table, scooping fruit salad into a bowl.

"North? You still there?" My mother sighed.

"Yes." *Part of me is here,* I thought, *but part of me isn't.*

"What have you been doing that's so much fun you couldn't write?" A lump caught in my throat.

"I did write. A letter to Rome." My voice was a whisper.

"It wasn't there when we went by American Express," she cut me off. "Write us another. Write what it's like to live in luxury all summer." My mother laughed enviously.

If this is luxury, I thought, *I'll take poverty. I would prefer to be raised in the wild by something non-human, some animal like the wolf who raised Romulus and Remus.*

"North, how's your reading? What do you think of *The Waste Land?*"

"I haven't finished it. But I liked the beginning," I only half lied. Out of curiosity I had read the first page one night before I left home.

"Get back to it. You apply yourself this summer and you'll improve your mind," she said. I breathed deeply. "Well, what *have* you been up to?"

"Dee taught me to water ski. And I jumped off the diving tower," I said, the words strung together like an add-a-pearl necklace. I should have said I was pushed off the tower by Shrimp into the Devil's Hole where a boy had recently drowned. It was a horrible feeling, falling so far. I lost Jackie Kennedy's picture in tar-black water.

"Then you can teach me this year. Judd likes to get everyone up on skis once a summer." His name softened her tone, and the distance swelled between us. The world didn't seem round anymore; it seemed as flat as Columbus had feared, flat like a road. And my mother's voice traveled to me through a dark damp tunnel burrowed under that flat world.

"Where's Dad? Can I talk to Dad?" I shredded the Spearmint wrapper, let it fall on the floor, confetti to my toes.

"He's taking some pictures up on the Acropolis. I hiked down to the street to call you while he started tripod work. He says hello." I pictured my dad on the Acropolis shooting pictures of the Parthenon and other temple buildings that were now falling down.

"Tell Dad hi," I said. The phone connection crackled electrically. I could barely hear my mother say, "North, something's wrong with the phone. I've got to go. Write. Behave yourself." Her voice withdrew into the tunnel. She would walk back to the ruins. My father would take pictures of vestal virgins whose stone heads supported the weight of temples for centuries. My mother would tell my father I sounded fine.

All afternoon I stayed in my room, wearing my white terrycloth bathrobe. I refused to put any makeup on. When I heard laughter from out on the lake I wanted to go outside, but when I tried to dress, my shorts felt heavy, like a body rather than cloth. I remembered Uncle Judd's finger tracing under the cuffs. Dee locked herself in her bedroom like a famous person in seclusion. I'd heard her in the bathroom that morning throwing up, and asked again if I could help her.

"Get lost, North!" she screamed. She said she didn't want to see anybody, not even Shrimp. She said she wanted to be alone. And the word *alone* cast so urgently from her lips sounded haunting. *Alone. Alone.* It was like a strange bird's call heard at night.

Finally I felt so hungry I went downstairs and ate an apple. Uncle Judd materialized out of nowhere like Houdini.

"You want to swim?" he asked me.

You want to drown? I should have said, but I just said I didn't want to swim. *No, thank you.* He hung around me like a bee buzzing a hive, then went outside and swam by himself. Afterwards he came inside shirtless and sat in the living room with me. King followed on his heels, his silver dog tags chiming. I watched a rerun of *Leave it to Beaver.* Whenever Wally said, "Hey, it's the Beaver," I laughed nervously, because boys used the word *beaver* to describe a woman's pubic hair. I didn't like being compared to an animal.

"What's the story about?" Uncle Judd asked me, standing near the center of the room, staring at the T.V. I said that Beaver had brought his school's pet mouse home to care for it during summer vacation. It got out of its cage the first day. June, Beaver's mother, started shrieking and then hauled out the vacuum. She vacuumed the house wildly all the while saying the mouse would ruin her perfect house in one day if they didn't catch it. Ward Cleaver thought about using a mouse trap, and Wally said, "Hey, that's a neat idea." Beaver started crying then.

I walked upstairs when my eyes teared up over Beaver's soon-to-be-dead pet mouse. Uncle Judd followed me. Chink, chink, chink. King tagged along. I slipped into my room. Uncle Judd walked toward his bedroom.

I checked the date on my calendar. It was Friday, July 19th, the night the boys planned to drag race. I wanted to be sealed inside a speeding car with a boy; I wanted to drive so fast the world would blur all around me and I would only need to focus on the road ahead. I began changing into my white lace bikini. I was pulling the white cover-up on when Uncle Judd walked into my room, the hair at his temples glistening like stainless steel.

"You're wearing your bikini," he said. "How about wearing your other present?"

"I'm kind of in a hurry." I slipped my white thongs onto my feet.

"Wear it for me." His blue eyes misted up like a movie star's eyes.

"I'll wear it. If . . ." My voice snagged the rest of the sentence.

"Go on." He touched my forearm.

"If you'll let me drive. Tonight." I pressed my thighs together.

His eyes moved over my body like a camera. My stomach tied itself into bowlines.

"Put on your other present." Uncle Judd played footsy with my foot; he wore newly polished white duck shoes. I pulled my foot away.

"It's under the bed." I knelt down, reaching under the bed, fishing out the gift, now covered with fine dust.

"Open it," he coaxed.

I ripped off the glossy paper, revealing a square, white gift box. "You give it to me," I said.

Uncle Judd opened the box. A gold bracelet circled inside. He pressed a tiny lever, opening it. I extended both arms, and he slipped the bracelet on my right wrist, snapping the circle shut. I felt the odd impulse to say thank you to Uncle Judd but swallowed the words. When Mrs. Graybill called us to dinner, I shot down the stairs.

She served us ribeye steaks barbecued on the grill and green beans and boiled early sweet corn. The tiny white kernels melted in my mouth like little buttery pearls. Dee had her dinner served in her room on a tray. Aunt Joan sat across from me, her streaked hair styled in a bouffant. She poked a finger into the highest teased hair absent-mindedly while Uncle Judd told stories about daredevil skiing.

"I jump once every year. Keeps me in shape." Uncle Judd laughed boisterously. Aunt Joan gazed out the picture window toward the empty ski jump floating in the east cove like a ramp to the sky of another world.

I fantasized Uncle Judd, fallen on his jump attempt, his arms tangling in the ski rope, the boat dragging him to the ramp's end, edged in jagged metal that sliced into his face. I devoured the steak although it was cooked more rare than I liked it. I even ate strawberry shortcake for dessert with two spoons of whipped cream. Every time I laid my spoon on my plate I heard the gold bracelet chink against the marble tabletop.

"Excuse me. I'm going to lie down," Aunt Joan said, looking at Uncle Judd and then me, her eyes dewy and distant. She rose from the table, leaving her dessert uneaten. Queen Mom's starving children in China thronged my fantasy. I felt as if I'd somehow caused Aunt Joan's waste.

I ran upstairs through her perfume, and in my room I stashed my plum lipstick into the pocket of my cover-up. I ran back downstairs to wait for Uncle Judd. I peed three times, and while in the bathroom I opened the medicine cabinet. Pills in huge bottles stood like minia-ture sky scrapers in a row. The labels were names like *Valium, Chloral hydrate* and *Methyl Quaaludes*. I recalled the easy way Aunt Joan chunked her pills into her hand.

Uncle Judd's keys jingled in his pocket as he entered the living room. *Give them to me,* I thought. Once a policeman in school had showed us how to gouge a robber's eyes out with your car keys when you were attacked. I remembered how quickly he'd said you would have to act. I was alone with Uncle Judd downstairs except for Mrs. Graybill, who clanked pots and pans in the kitchen.

"You ready?" Uncle Judd asked me, I looked into his eyes that appeared so laboratory cool and calculating. I felt he could quickly measure me up. He might fashion a name to describe my condition to other doctors, a name for the affliction of lopsided breasts. I wondered if he was planning to use the pictures for medical presentations, or for an article like the one about the little boy. Or maybe he'd just stare at them in private and get a hard-on. A boner, as the boys called it.

King tagged us as we walked to the Stingray, brushing his fur against my legs. "Go away!" I shouted, stomping my foot under his belly so that he skittered off sideways.

"I'll drive to the Club. Then it's your turn." Uncle Judd slid into the Stingray. I fell into the rider's side, the bucket seat curving around my hips. I let my head drop against the cool glass of my closed window. Uncle Judd drove us past the cove by the channel where Bill Hamilton's cottage stood. I pictured Bill in his bedroom at night, reading about science and the distance from star to star, about black holes that could suck stars into a whorl of darkness.

Uncle Judd drove the curves. The low-slung sun reflected sudden patches of light in his glasses. Behind the Club he veered off onto a gravel lane where sycamore branches scraped the roof of the Stingray. He stopped the car and stroked my cover-up. He drew circles around the middle pearled buttons with his fingers.

"It's warm. Why don't you take this off?" Uncle Judd's voice was a doctor's voice telling me to disrobe for an examination. I froze as he lifted the cover-up off my shoulders. Then he pressed his palms on my bare shoulders like a faith healer.

Uncle Judd removed his glasses, unveiling his stark blue chilling eyes. He puckered his lips, moving closer. I focused on the tiny creases running through the pale pink shriveled skin—like skin soaked in the bath water too long. He nuzzled my neck. I smelled whiskey. Then he kissed me, his tongue flitting inside my cheeks. I arched my head against the head rest like a girl in electroshock. But he leaned with me. He rubbed my breast. Then he raised himself off me. He began stroking my hair with one hand while with the other hand he turned on the radio. A silver thread of saliva hung like a new spider's web from his lips.

"Want to hear some rock and roll?" he asked, and I nodded *yes*, though his voice seemed to pitch stones at me. The song "Walk Right In" played on WDT. I tried to concentrate on the lyrics but I only heard, Did I want to lose my mind? And I said to myself, *No, I don't want to lose my mind. I want to lose Uncle Judd in a cloud of speedway dust. Dust to dust, like the minister said at funerals.*

"You said you'd let me drive." My voice was a whisper. "You said you'd let me drive." I repeated Uncle Judd's promise in that sure voice that came from another part of me: North, the conqueror.

"O.K. That's what I promised," he said, and we changed places.

I didn't bother with my cover-up as I slid in behind the wheel. The cool air blowing through the open windows gave my skin goose bumps as I drove over the speed limit toward the dirt straightaway. Clouds of dust sprayed like dirt fountains around the cars. At the access road I downshifted to second, but gunned the engine rounding the corner so that loose gravel clacked beneath our wheels.

Frank Boyd drove his 54 Lincoln coupe to the starting line where G. P. waved a green flag. I accelerated and pulled alongside Frank.

"I'll race you." I waved to him out my window. Frank looked at me crosseyed. Uncle Judd vice-gripped my thigh, impressing his fingernails intagliolike in my skin.

"What're you doing?" he whispered through clenched teeth.

"Just driving," I whispered back.

"Where'd you get that car, sweetheart?" Frank asked. He said hello to Uncle Judd, his face apologetic. In the dusky light his blue sunglasses glowed above his pockmarked cheeks.

"It's Dee's dad's." I smiled slightly. "He lets Dee and me drive. Sometimes."

"Evenin', Dr. Diehl," G. P. said, taking a step closer to us.

"North, I'm gonna put a dent in your dreams. See, drag racing's for boys. You probably don't even have a license." G. P. shrugged his shoulders.

"Oh, forget about the license," Bill broke in. "This road's on private property. My dad's commodore this year. I say go ahead. If it's all right with Dr. Diehl. Let her race him." Bill Hamilton faced G. P. He wore black square sunglasses and khaki hiking shorts without a shirt. "Go ahead. Let her race him."

"It's O.K. with me." Frank Boyd lit a cigarette and smiled. When he noticed Uncle Judd, he pitched his cigarette out the window. I watched it smolder in the dirt, its red tip glowing. I considered retrieving it and throwing it, still on fire, into the gas tank of the Stingray, exploding Uncle Judd in a ring of fire. But then I told myself: *If you do that you blow up the Stingray. Just drive like you are on fire, like you can't stop burning up the road.*

"I'll beat the pants off her, I mean her skirt," Frank said.

"You mean her bikini, Frankie boy," G. P. snickered. Uncle Judd pressed my thigh muscles with his nails, as if to say, *"It's not all right with me."*

Well, then, you stop me, I thought. *You stop me, and I'll tell your secrets.* I thought he knew just what I was thinking then. I thought he saw through me the way Superman saw through cement walls, because he relaxed his hand. Over the west end of the straightaway the sky turned pink with sunset. Bill drove the BelAir to the finish line. I revved the Stingray's engine. Cirrus clouds hung like swirled egg whites along the horizon's thread where an early planet pulsed blue light.

"Gentleman, *and ladies,* start your engines," G. P. imitated an announcer at the speedway. But since the Stingray was idling, I waited, sitting poised, with all my muscles tensed. The green flag jumped. I pressed the accelerator, my shift into second sounding like a disposal grinding.

"God damn it," Uncle Judd said. He gripped my hand, guiding me into third. I popped the clutch too fast, and the Stingray shuddered forward. Frank Boyd jetted ahead of me by half a car length. I approached him from behind, pulled alongside, nosing him to the shoulder.

I wanted to yell out my window, *Tits, Frank, isn't this just the tits racing me?* But I could hardly see him, the dust billowed so thickly around our cars. My mouth filled with grit that felt like the pumice cleaner dental hygienists use. The grit coated every crease in my mouth, up above my teeth, along my gums, under my tongue and inside my cheeks where Uncle Judd's tongue had touched.

The Stingray's speedometer hit eighty, then eighty-five. Dust whirled in clouds around us. The minister at church had said we'd all turn to dust one day. He said that time passed quickly, too. So this summer would someday seem smaller than a speck of dust. I thought maybe I'd turn to dust this very day of my fifteenth year. I didn't care about what might happen then. Dusky light shone through the plumed dirt surrounding the cars. The checkered flag flapped, and we crossed the finish line. In the cul-de-sac at the end of the straight-away Frank and I turned our cars around.

"Who won?" I shouted, driving back to the finish line. I waved out my window at Frank.

"You got me!" Frank yelled, his face a scowl.

At the line Bill pulled his hand through his hair. He laughed quietly. "North beat you by a couple inches, Frank. You can ask Meek here." Bill pointed to Larry Meeker who joined him on the line.

"Sorry, Frank, it's true. North won, fair and square." Larry Meeker nodded. His hair was slicked like Kookie's hair in *77 Sunset Strip*, with what I thought must be Vitalis.

"Nice race," Bill said, shaking my hand. But instead of pumping my hand, he tickled the skin of my palm with his fingers. He walked back toward the BelAir. Frank squealed his tires, accelerating for the starting line.

"Who do you think you are?" Uncle Judd spat. "You do any more racing, and I'll never let you drive again." He gripped my cheeks on either side of my mouth. "You hear me?"

I nodded that I had heard. He pressed harder, and my cheeks met inside my mouth. I pulled away from him, his nails cutting toward my lips as I did. "I have to go to the bathroom," I said, grabbing my cover-up from the back seat, throwing it on. I unlatched my door and sprang from the car. I ran for the Club, dust clouds rising like smoke signals from under my feet. *But who would see them? Who would read my SOS?* Bill and G. P. raced on the straightaway, hurling more dust that would swallow my signals. I started choking, my throat rasping. I thought I couldn't run any farther, my breaths cut short like a dog's panting. At the side door of the Club the air cleared. I leapt up the steps by twos and ran inside to the bathroom.

I looked in the mirror after I peed. I spread my plum-colored lipstick on. I fingered my hair, pulling the sides away from my neck. I brushed some dust from my cheeks, and it fell away like powder. The dust on my arms and legs, luminous in the fluorescent light. My skin shone dully the way a moth's body shines under a light. I lifted my hands to push the door open, my arms feeling heavy, especially my right arm where Uncle Judd's gold bracelet circled and glowed through the dust covering it, the way moonlight glows through the clouds.

I walked slowly to the Stingray, plodding my feet through the dirt lot. Dirt caught between my pink polished toenails. I heard a woman's voice in the distance. "You and your hot-ass car," she said. I ran behind the Dumpster where the day's trash drew a cloud of flies. "Think you can fool everybody?" It was Linda Turner leaning into the opened door of the Stingray. Uncle Judd's head was collapsed back on his seat rest. "Son of a bitch," she swore real loud at him. "Bastard." I waited for the *f* word. "Can't keep your hands to yourself. Lush." She nearly spit on him.

"I see your mouth's in the gutter now with the rest of you," Uncle Judd said, sitting up straight suddenly and reaching to pull his door shut. She stuck her false foot into the door and stopped him. Her sock was low down, showing the pink plastic skin shining in the hazy light.

"Yeah, well, you're going to listen," she said, "because Lolita's inside. I know you're waitin' for her." I hated her for saying that. Like she was jealous. Like we couldn't murder him in a dual plot for revenge.

"I'm not your patsy. I could burn your ass if I started talking again. I want two grand in hundreds. By tomorrow morning. Bring it by here in a suitcase. Or your doctor's bag. Ha! That would be funny. Put your money in your doctor bag." She slammed the door to the Stingray and hit the hood so hard it must have hurt her hand. I wished she had cracked Uncle Judd in the jaw or the nose and saved the Stingray. I wished she had broken Uncle Judd's nose so one of his plastic surgeon colleagues would have had to operate on him. Linda Turner scowled, and Uncle Judd locked the car doors as if locked doors could keep her threats out.

I envisioned Linda Turner with two or three suitcases filled with Uncle Judd's money. She would walk into the best stores in Detroit to buy herself and her baby beautiful new clothes. They would take a trip to Hawaii next winter and lie on a sand beach in the sun. Linda Turner would start to smile on occasion. The sun would make the baby's bones strong.

"Pervert," Linda yelled at Uncle Judd over her shoulder, while giving him the finger behind her back as she walked away.

The Speedway

During the drive home, Uncle Judd and I sat in silence until we passed Ramsey's Marina when he turned the radio to a station that played muzak. The songs sounded fuzzy and far off, totally different from the songs they'd been when originally performed. A deep-voiced announcer spoke of the nuclear test ban treaty the President was pursuing with Russia. He said that President Kennedy was *pressing* Khrushchev to sign. I envisioned a mushroom cloud billowing up over America, the way I had fantasized *the bomb* so many times during all the air raid drills we had gone through at school. Minutes ticked toward hours as we hid under our desks. Radiation would have seeped through the walls and windows despite our efforts, poisoning us. Still, we sat like miniature heroes quietly waiting for the world to end, knowing that if we didn't die instantly our skin would peel and our children would be born with fins like the people in Japan after Hiroshima.

By signing this treaty President Kennedy wanted to make sure all mushroom clouds remained fantasies. If we won the cold war, or at least kept it from escalating, then we wouldn't ever have to experience a *hot* war. President Kennedy knew firsthand what a hot war was like. During World War II he had fought on a P.T. boat that was split in half by a Japanese destroyer. When his boat sunk, he led his men to safety on an island. I envisioned him swimming the breaststroke, pulling an injured man by clenching his life preserver straps between his teeth.

President Kennedy had lost his brother Joe to the War, so he had personally felt the losses of combat. He didn't want any of us to go through what he had gone through, unless we absolutely had to. I felt so grateful to him. For a moment the talk of his firm leadership erased Uncle Judd from the seat next to me. But then I looked over to my left and there he was.

I told myself, *Don't look at him. Look out your window.* Yet I could hardly focus on the lights from the cottages we rushed by. *North, you just won the drag race.* I reminded myself that I had beaten Frank Boyd. If I closed my eyes and concentrated, I could still see Bill Hamilton waving the checkered flag from inside a dense cloud of dust. And then victory quickly collapsed in memory. I recalled Uncle Judd's pinching fingers, my pressed cheeks.

Uncle Judd parked us in the asphalt lot. I unlatched my door but he laid his hand on my forearm. His face curved toward mine. Dirt fine as pollen dusted my arms and legs, my cover-up.

"Don't," I pleaded. But he came closer. "Goddamn it." Swear words leapt from my mouth, but sounded nowhere as fierce as when I swore in my mind.

Kicking the car door open, I jumped from the Stingray and ran toward the lake. Where the dock met land, I dropped my cover-up, letting it fall like a giant handkerchief to the lawn. Uncle Judd called after me, "North, where're you going?" his voice sounding like cold wind.

Near the end of the dock I leapt out over the water and came splashing down, the tar-black water cool as I plunged in. I rubbed my body everywhere to remove the dirt. Diving down deep, I blew bubbles from my mouth like a fish. I gulped water and then spit it out until my mouth felt fresh and cool. I swam wildly, kicking out to the raft and back, over and over, like a swimmer in an Olympic race. When I stopped and treaded water, I pulled the bra cups of my bikini away from my breasts, letting the coolness of the dark water in. Opening the elastic at the waist, I folded gushes of water through my bikini bottom.

By the moon's light I checked my arms and legs to see if they were clean, and I found them too dark, too tan, too sleek. A layer of color coated my skin; particles of dust stayed trapped in the corners of my mouth. Exhausted, I floated on my back. Orion's belt gleamed like diamond studs. From high above the Big Dipper a shooting star streaked down.

The lake looked dark blue like art deco glass as I lunged slowly through it, reaching the shallow water and heading up toward the beach. I heard the squeaky cricket songs floating out from land and I wondered if they sang because they loved to, like Elvis Presley, or if they sang because they needed to to relieve tension.

I started to feel cold and so I picked up my pace, slicing my legs through the water. A sudden stabbing pain pierced my heel. Stopping, I raised my foot out of the water and saw a bleeding gash. I dangled my foot in the lake to rinse the blood. Then I felt a sharp object nudging my other foot. Scooping it up to the lamp light at the break-water, I recognized one of King's gnawed-down steak bones. Held higher in air it glowed like a tiny star. I looked down again. Blood spilled through the water. My foot hurt. My head grew giddy, light. The lake seemed to tip over on its side, the trees sprouting sideways. I spun. The crickets' song enveloped me as I dropped into lake water.

Next thing I knew I was scooped into Uncle Judd's arms. He carried me through the house. He yelled to Aunt Joan to bring my bathrobe but Dee brought it instead.

"Oh, God. Are you O.K.?" she whispered, her hair tangled as if she'd been asleep. My voice was a throaty croak. No real words came and I thought my voice had been clamped off by God for swearing. Stepping on the dog bone was punishment for defying Uncle Judd.

He laid me down on the leather sofa in the living room to bandage my heel. He slipped a bath towel under my foot, then placed a gauze square on my wound. Blood oozed through the gauze in seconds. He placed two more squares on top, firmly holding them down.

"I'm taking you to the hospital," he said, wrapping gauze around my heel and my ankle so that my foot looked like the foot of a mummy.

"Come with me," I said to Dee, grabbing her wrist. She stared at the bandage and held her hand over her stomach. "Please, Dee."

"O.K. North, O.K." She helped me slip my bathrobe on. Still, I was chilled by my wet bikini. Across the living room Aunt Joan stood crookedly, like an old tower that had shifted in space. She held her face averted. "We'll save you dinner, North," she said. But the thought of food revolted me. I flashed to the way ketchup was used in movies to represent blood.

After slipping me into the back seat, Uncle Judd placed my leg on a pillow and slipped another pillow that smelled of King under my head. He drove the station wagon, Dee in the front seat beside him. I could tell by the fast sound of the tires moving over the road that he was driving over the speed limit. Dee turned on the radio. WDT played "Shut Down" by the Beach Boys. I remembered that boys used that phrase to describe a night with a girl who wouldn't give them sex. *How'd your date with North go, Bill? It was a real shut down.*

At the Alston Hospital west of Glass Lake, Uncle Judd parked in the emergency zone and carried me inside. My foot dangled, a circle of blood the size of a half dollar seeping through the gauze. I felt woozy. Uncle Judd's cologne filled the night air.

Inside the emergency room Dee stood beside me, her skin more green under the bright lights. She smiled slightly, the corners of her mouth frozen apostrophes. The nurses swarmed around Uncle Judd like benevolent swans. They helped me onto a table that felt as cold as a marble slab. They gathered instruments and drugs in tiny vials, all the while asking him what he needed, what did he want. One of them unwrapped the mummy bandage, saying the cut looked jagged, and Uncle Judd told her it was because I had stepped on an irregular shaped object.

"I'm going to freeze your heel with local anesthetic." Uncle Judd looked down at me. He lifted the syringe. When the needle pierced my skin and he depressed the plunger, I felt as if the poison from a hundred bees entered me. My foot fell asleep so that when Uncle Judd scrubbed the cut with soap and a stiff brush I felt only the slightest pressure. I told myself, *this is the way your whole body will feel with multiple sclerosis.* I thought maybe I'd already contracted the disease. Maybe I was falling asleep inside my own body this minute here in the emergency room.

Dee tried not to seem squeamish, but when Uncle Judd brought out the hook with what he had called *the suture line* on it her face turned white. She cupped her hand over her mouth, coughs filling her throat, catching and rising, until she said, "I'm sorry, North," in a muffled voice and ran from the room.

As Uncle Judd sewed up my heel, I thought about Linda Turner and shivers traveled my spine. A nurse with blond hair and sexy cat-rimmed glasses placed a warm blanket over me. "Honey," she said, "you're going to be fine." I began crying.

"Oh, please stop," I begged. I imagined Uncle Judd could alter my foot as he worked so I wouldn't be able to drive again. I began to kick reflexively.

"Let me finish," Uncle Judd said. But I couldn't stop crying and kicking. Kicking. Crying. A dark-haired nurse held my leg down.

"No. Don't," I shouted, my right arm shaking, the gold bracelet spinning like a wheel around my wrist.

"You're going to have to stay still for me so I can finish," Uncle Judd's voice descended.

"He's right. Stay still, honey, you're lucky to have a plastic surgeon working on you. He'll make you a pretty scar." The nurse with the sexy glasses held my leg more firmly down.

"Damn it," I screamed.

"Stop that," Uncle Judd commanded. "If you don't stop I'll call your mother tomorrow," he threatened. "There are other people in this emergency room. There's a little girl two beds down who shouldn't be hearing you swear." *She shouldn't see you then. But if she does she better learn to swear and swear loud. Even if he is a doctor. Even if he gives her presents and says what he's doing to her is good.*

"Damn you," I shouted.

From out of nowhere the nurse with the sexy glasses brought Uncle Judd a hypodermic. He thrust the needle into the muscle of my arm. In minutes the room grew whiter so that the sheets on the bed next to me resembled a glowing snow mound. The blue curtains the nurse pulled around my stretcher became a fluttering circle of sky.

"That should calm her," Uncle Judd said, and he was right, for the more dreamy the medicine made me the less I cared what he did.

I fell asleep and he could have done anything; he could have made me new breasts, or designed a more perfect nose for my face.

Sunday night I watched the Ed Sullivan Show on the portable T.V. Mr. Robertson brought to my room. A family of acrobats from Yugoslavia performed on the tightrope and the flying trapeze. The women wore sequined swimsuits that accentuated their cleavage while the men wore loose shirts and pants that resembled pajamas. In the dual aerial act a man hung head down from a trapeze with a metal bit in his mouth from which a woman whirled in fast circles. My head spun around with them the way it had when I dropped into the lake water.

I hobbled through the house the next week, holding my leg limp like a dog with an injured paw. On Wednesday Aunt Joan drove me to the hospital to have my stitches removed.

"I'll wait out here," she said, sitting in a rounded plastic chair that was riveted to the floor through the carpeting. She fidgeted with her white beaded necklace when the nurse called me inside; it was the nurse with the sexy glasses. Aunt Joan looked down at her magazine.

In the emergency room a young doctor pulled out my stitches. The nurse told me the scar looked perfect, that Uncle Judd had done a beautiful job and there had been no reason for me to shout while he was working on me. I pretended I didn't know what she was referring to.

"Go ahead, honey. Look," she said. I studied the fine pink lines running out from a center like the points on a drawn star.

The last weekend in July arrived. Raceway Park was hosting the Champion Spark Plug 400 that was scheduled to start at half past noon. Bill had told me that Richard Petty would be racing his blue Plymouth there. I couldn't wait to see him; I couldn't wait to see the cars driving fast circles.

While I dressed for our date I listened to the radio. It was eight-thirty on Sunday morning and I had some time before Bill and Shrimp would arrive at ten. We'd convinced Dee to stop hiding in her room and come to the speedway by promising to go with her to see *Bye*

Bye Birdie in exchange. She pretended she was at the speedway choking and covering her ears, but eventually she agreed to come. All four
of us attended the movie at the downtown Alston Theater. Dee
swooned over Hugo and Conrad Birdie. I thought Conrad Birdie
seemed not at all worth the fuss the girls made over him.

Outside in the driveway Uncle Judd supervised Mr. Robertson
washing the Stingray. The spray of the garden hose hit steel like rapid
gunfire, a watery ringing. I tried to tell myself Uncle Judd wasn't really
outside. I tried to forget I had screamed swear words at him in the
emergency room. I pretended that the cut on my heel hadn't even
happened. Presto, I almost believed my lie. But when I tried to pretend
I didn't hear Uncle Judd enter the house, I heard every creak on the
stairway, every tinkle of ice dropped into a cocktail glass, every clicking of King's toenails as he followed Uncle Judd across a room. I was
developing a shark's primitive type of sonar, my sense of sound becoming so acute I knew where Uncle Judd was by listening to the
sounds that moved through my waking hours.

I heard his voice outside again telling Mr. Robertson how to wax
the Stingray. Would the spruced-up car tempt me? At dinner last
night, Uncle Judd had said he didn't like the idea of us going to the
speedway. He said car racing was the most dangerous spectator sport
in the world and innocent people were killed sometimes when cars
crashed into the stands. *Was he from another planet? Who was he to
talk about innocent people*, I thought.

I spit the peas I couldn't swallow into my napkin, then excused
myself from the table, heading to my room. I heard a rapping on my
door. I didn't answer.

"North, I want to talk to you," Uncle Judd said, rapping again.
I didn't answer. "Would you like to drive the Stingray?" Still I
wouldn't speak. I crouched on top of my bed. "If you stay home while
the others go to the speedway, I'll let you drive while they're away."
While the cat's away the mice will play, I thought. But I didn't answer.

I dressed in my white shift with the pink bull's-eye swirls. Sometimes when I touched it I felt the way I had when Bill kissed me, but
the feeling only lasted a second or two. I chose my white patten

leather flats instead of sandals. I had to force the right shoe on over my heel. I refused to wear Uncle Judd's bracelet, which I'd ripped off the morning after I stepped on King's dog bone.

Once dressed I looked at myself in the mirror. My arms and legs, so tanned, looked longer than ever in this shift, with the hem hitting me halfway up my thighs. I wondered if I should cover my legs. If I covered my legs would Uncle Judd stop advancing? But Jackie Kennedy showed her legs and men from all over the world, presidents and emperors alike, admired her beauty.

I remembered that my parents were scheduled to be in Crete, the island in Greece where the minotaur caroused. My legs felt trembly thinking of him, half beast. I pulled my stationery from my bureau and began writing.

> *Dear Mom and Dad,*
>
> *How's Greece? Beautiful I bet. The island of Crete must provide sea air which I've heard is good for sleeping and complexions. Do you look the same as when you left me? I don't look like the same North. I look taller. I know I'm taller because my skirts are so short. Is it O.K. to keep wearing them like this? Boys have become interested in me, and men too. Men with roaming hands and lots of money. I bet you can't guess who. Here're some clues then. He drives a red Stingray and acts like he owns me. He gave me a bracelet that looks like a handcuff. He treats me like his girlfriend when I could be his daughter. He touches me. He touches me. His kisses are French kisses. . . .*

I stopped writing and tried to say *Paree,* the way Jackie Kennedy would say it. I wanted to transport myself to Paris. I wanted to emit a radiance like her radiance in the photograph I lost. But the way I pronounced Paris sounded nasal, like the name of a donut, not the most glamorous city in the world. Blotting my tears with a Kleenex, I read my letter over. Uncle Judd's threats about keeping things secret flew through my mind.

My face flushed hot as I shredded the letter and ran to the bathroom to flush it down. The water swirled evacuation, the bits of paper spiraling away. My hands began shaking like leaves in a breeze. I couldn't purge my mind of Uncle Judd. I picked up a sheet of paper and began to write.

Dear Jackie Kennedy,

I've never said this to anyone before. But I'm going to say it to you now: You mean so much to me. You're beautiful and intelligent. You love your children. Somehow you managed to meet the right man and you married him. Now you're having another one of his babies right while you live in the White House. I never knew life could turn out so perfectly. But you make me believe in the possibility.

I have to tell you, I had a picture of you from a Life *magazine that I carried around. But I lost it when a boy pushed me off a diving tower. I feel sad without it. Do you remember the dinner at Versailles? You were dressed in the gown with the little moon mirrors. You wore a tiara that sparkled like a cluster of stars shining on top of your head. All the Frenchmen in Paris were waiting to see you that evening. Somehow, through all the attention, you held your head up. Where or how did you learn to do this? How does it feel to move men with your beauty? Everybody is talking about it. . . . Do people (men especially) ever touch you when you don't want them to and if so, what do you do? Please answer this.*

I think I may be attractive. Some people have said so. But something is happening to me this summer that is making me wish I didn't look good. It has to do with pictures. I read that you worked as a photographer. I saw a picture of you taking a picture. That seemed fascinating. Some people have been taking my picture with my clothes off. I know that real art has nudity in it. And that might be O.K. in a painting. But do you think it is all right in a picture of a fifteen-year-old girl? I really don't think you'd allow people to photograph your children nude and hang the pictures around the

*White House. Would you please ask Bobby Kennedy if
there's a law against this? Because he is the Attorney General.
If he says there's a law, then he can enforce it.*

*Because you're going to have a baby soon the last thing
in the world I want to do is to bother you. So, if you're too
tired to answer, or if all this doesn't make any sense, then
please excuse me for barging into your life, but I didn't know
who else to turn to.*

Sincerely,
North Wagoner
205 Spring Street,
Ypsilanti, Michigan

I read the letter over. Jackie Kennedy's face floated through my mind.
Maybe you shouldn't send it, I thought. *It might upset her.* I folded
the letter in half and placed it inside my top dresser drawer. I didn't
want to cause her distress during this delicate time of her pregnancy,
even though I longed for her help.

At *ten o'clock* we left for the speedway, Bill and I sitting in the front
seat of the BelAir and Dee and Shrimp sitting in the back.

"I can't stand the smell of oil. Does the speedway smell like oil,
Bill?" Dee asked leaning between Bill and me.

"Not really," Bill answered. "Only sometimes when it's hot you
begin to smell tar." He spoke like a scientist describing the results of
an experiment.

"Oh, great, it's going to be hot enough today. It's supposed to
get up to ninety. Shrimp, you lied. You told me it didn't stink at the
speedway. You told me it smelled fresh like the outdoors." Dee faced
Shrimp and pouted, the corners of her mouth making the shape of a
tipped over C.

"Well, we'll be sitting outdoors, honey. So don't worry about it.
There will be lots of fresh air around." Shrimp curled his arm around
Dee, but she shrugged his hand off with her shoulders. "Touchy,
touchy," Shrimp said, sliding away.

We drove by a herd of black angus cows grazing in the middle of an open field. They lifted their heads slowly and twitched their tails at flies. The smell of manure poured in through the car windows.

"P.U. barnyard perfume," Shrimp said.

"You should like it, since you like bad smells, Shrimp. I think cows smell better than cars do. I think they smell more natural." Dee slid over by the window. "Yeah. They smell more real."

"Let's leave her right here, Hamilton. Stop the goddamn car and leave Dee in the field where she belongs. Moo, moo." Shrimp giggled. I laughed with Bill in unison, not because I found Shrimp's joke funny, but because I always laughed when people imitated animal sounds.

Bill tuned the radio to WDT as we turned onto Interstate 17 heading toward the speedway. "Cast Your Fate to the Wind" played. Listening, I felt carefree, as if I were floating off, as if I were a huge balloon with arms and legs that hung in the air. But then I thought of my fate, how I couldn't cast it to the wind because it seemed to rest in Uncle Judd's hands. I could only cast my fate to the wind for the moments when I drove a car fast, with the air rushing my face and bugs squishing hard against the windshield. I wanted to drive a race car around and around on a one-thousand mile oval in a race that would never end.

Bill pulled the BelAir onto the paved road that led to the speedway. The sound of engines shifting gears whined in the distance. I turned toward Bill as he parked us near the end of a long row of cars the colors of fruit Chiclets. Studying his face in profile, I wished I could always remember the way he looked in his black sunglasses, white tennis shirt, chinos, and brown deck shoes.

"Who's racing today?" Shrimp asked as we walked through the parking lot.

"Richard Petty and Cale Yarborough and Ray Meirs, and then, I guess, all the guys on the circuit who qualified," Bill answered. I wondered if these men who risked their lives every weekend had scars marking their bodies from all the accidents they'd been in.

"Ray Meirs is from Lansing, isn't he?" Shrimp stopped to shake a piece of gravel from his tennis shoe.

"Yeah," Bill said. "This year he's been driving the Budweiser team Chevy."

"I heard he won the Charlotte 500."

"Almost. But Petty passed him on the last lap." Bill cupped my hand inside his hand. Immediately my palm began to sweat even though I wanted to feel the pure soft friction of his skin.

Dee straggled behind us and I stopped to call, "C'mon, Dee." Lifting my right foot, I stood like a flamingo. My heel throbbed and the scar on my heel felt tender. Dee ignored my calls until Shrimp walked back to her. He tried to take her hand but she jerked away. Grabbing her elbow he turned her around and she stomped her foot. Shrimp smoothed his blue and white striped T-shirt down his chest while whispering something in her ear. Finally she started walking beside him but she tossed his hand off whenever he touched her shoulders and glared at him.

I thought she knew that she should have stayed home in her room, with the bathroom close by. A sympathetic nausea rose in my own stomach then. I suspected, although I didn't want to believe it true, that Dee was pregnant, that the prediction that sex led to pregnancy—the threat all our mother's used to deter us—had come true for Dee.

Bill stopped at the concession stand to buy Cokes, hot dogs, and some popcorn, which he started eating right away. Once we found our seats in the middle of the straightaway he offered me food, but I felt too mesmerized to be hungry.

"You thinking about being a woman race car driver?" he asked.

"Maybe, maybe not," I said.

"If you drove a stock car the way you drove the other night, you wouldn't do half bad. By the way—Frank was pretty mad at us for letting you race him. Actually, *humiliate him* was what he said." Bill laughed softly as the cars swarmed the infield.

"God, this is really gross," Dee said. "It already stinks and the race hasn't even started. I should've never said I'd come here." Beside me Dee fidgeted, pulling her hand through her hair and jiggling her knees.

"Dee, you're acting crazy. No offense," I said, looking into her blue eyes that gleamed the color of Uncle Judd's eyes for one moment.

"I don't want to be here," she said. "It's smelly and dirty and there are a lot of ugly people sitting around us. I wish you'd left me in that cow pasture, I really do."

When I looked at Dee's face and at the faces of the other people in the crowd, I noticed Dee had a tan and the other people's skin was as white as cotton balls. Many had blue circles under their eyes, carved into their skin.

Shrimp bought Dee a racing program from a boy who wore a red baseball cap. As she read the advertisements she settled down. The cars filled the infield like bees swarming to the center of a hive. The sun burst through the clouds, igniting the steel and the chrome. Glints of reflected light flashed giant rectangles. The cars gained speed. Around corners with their rear ends shimmying outward they circled, the buzzing of engines filling my ears. The only glass in the cars was in the front and rear windshields. I wanted to drive a car with so little glass to break, where intense vibration and chaotic noise would engulf me.

"Want some?" Bill handed me the box of popcorn but I shook my head no.

Richard Petty rounded the corner to take the first position, as if his car emerged from the sky itself, its body the same blue color and the white of his number 43 matching the clouds.

Ray Meirs drove his red Chevy into the first row, parking beside Petty. As he stared at the track, I wondered if he'd had a terrible accident where in one moment his whole life flashed before him. Maybe now he remembered how frightened he'd been so he vowed never to let such a bad accident happen to him again.

All the drivers lined up in their appointed places, and an announcer spoke over the loudspeaker, welcoming us to Raceway Park. He said the race would be two hundred laps of the two-mile oval track. He introduced all the sponsors and the drivers, and the crowd cheered when he announced Ray Meirs. Then he introduced a minister who prayed for the safety of the drivers. The minister asked us to remember all those drivers we'd lost, leaving minutes of silence for their memories. Shrimp cleared his throat a few times during the prayer and Dee coughed. "North, this is so stupid," she said.

The announcer asked us to sing "The Star Spangled Banner" along with a Detroit nightclub singer named Darcy Lee. When I saw the flag shoot up, I thought of President Kennedy. I felt so proud to be a part of America that I sang aloud through the entire anthem. Beside me Bill droned the words in his regular speaking voice. Then the announcer said, "Gentlemen, start your engines," and we were surrounded by loud revved-up engine sounds.

A white 409 led the pace laps. The cars accelerated behind it, gradually gaining speed until the green flag rose and the first cars burst over the starting line. Larry Woodcox pulled out in front of Ray Meirs; after the first lap he had him by four car lengths.

"I'm going to walk around the concession stands," Dee shouted to me. "This is too boring. You want to come?"

I screamed *no* into the deafening roar. I watched her argue with Shrimp then walk down the stands, her yellow madras shorts bleached white by the sun.

Shrimp scooted closer to me and the three of us leaned forward to watch the race. The cars flashed by in colored streaks, the air filling with the smells of oil, tar, and engine grease. The speed of the race became hypnotic so that I hardly knew where I was, and when Bill's knee bumped my knee I looked at him to remind myself it was Bill who sat beside me.

The race became a standoff between Richard Petty and Ray Meirs. Ray Meirs pulled away on the straightaways but lost the ground he gained on every turn.

"Who's going to win it?" Shrimp screamed.

"Petty should," Bill shouted.

"Where'd Dee go?" Shrimp asked me, his hands fisted on his thighs.

"To walk around," I shouted, but I wasn't all there beside him. Part of me circled the track with the cars.

"Where?" Shrimp shook my forearm.

"Down by the concessions." I pointed to the place on the stairs where I'd last seen Dee.

"I'm going to look for her." He stood up and walked down the stands. On the one-hundredth lap Lynn Haywood threatened to pass Ray Meirs on the front straightaway, but Ray Meirs stayed ahead of him on the east turn. Again the race became a match-up between Meirs and Petty. Some people in the stands shouted, "C'mon, Ray, c'mon." The cars whirled faster and faster the farther they drove, soaring by at what seemed a comet's speed.

Bill laid his hand on my knee and at first I liked the soft pressure. But then his hand felt heavy so that I moved my leg from side to side until it dropped off.

"Who do you think will win?" Bill asked me on the fifth to the last lap.

"Richard Petty," I screamed.

"Why?"

"Because of the way he holds the turn."

On the last lap Petty and Meirs raced neck and neck as people rose to their feet. Bill and I stood up too. Bill laced his arm around my waist, cinching me as tight as a belt. I twisted away and stood on my tiptoes while two streaks, one blue and one red, headed down the last straightaway. Petty held the lead until the last half-mile when Meirs pulled away, racing his red Chevy in first under the checkered flag.

The Michigan crowd roared and Bill clapped, stomping his feet. Meirs drove to the winner's circle where a beautiful woman with a tiny waist ran out to kiss him. He drank from a huge bottle of champagne, a host of T.V. interviewers gathering around him.

"We should get going," Bill said, looking around for Dee and Shrimp. I scanned the rows of people as the crowd began leaving. I saw a thin, dark-haired girl several rows above me on the stairs. For a moment she looked like Jackie Kennedy. She was carrying a baby, and I thought of the baby Jackie Kennedy was soon to have. But I had not heard of the baby's birth. I didn't think Jackie Kennedy would come to a car race; if she did she would have had Secret Service men circling around her. I didn't think she would ever have brought a newborn baby to a place where the loud noises could damage his ears.

As the girl stepped closer I saw a mole on her left cheek. Then I noticed her eyes were dark brown. She walked closer and I saw a hollowness in her gaze that I'd never seen in Jackie Kennedy's eyes. When she smiled I saw her chipped front tooth.

Her baby raised his white arms and swept his fingers through her black hair. "Don't you fool with me like that now, boy," she said in a voice that was nasal. I hadn't found Jackie Kennedy. I wished the cars were back on the track. I wished the cars could thrum around again in mad circles. I didn't care about finding Dee and Shrimp any more. I lunged away from the girl and her baby into the crowd. I was leaping down the stairs when Bill put his body in front of mine to stop me.

"I don't want to lose you, too." He smiled at me.

I'm already lost, Bill, and you can't find me. I tried to move past him but he stopped me. *I'm lost,* I thought, *like that pitiful baby who's living his life at the mercy of his mother's decisions and moods.*

Bill guided me through the crowd by my hand, and to the people we passed I must have looked like a sleepwalker. I hobbled. The scar on my heel throbbed. I couldn't stop thinking about the girl I'd seen and how strange it had been to think that she was Jackie Kennedy. I wanted to tell Bill how sad I felt but his face looked so happy. "North, that was a fantastic race," he whispered softly into my ear.

Shrimp and Bill dropped us off at Dee's. Bill squeezed my hand tightly when he said good-bye. "See you soon, I hope," he whispered.

"Thanks for taking me to the races." I slid out of the BelAir, my thighs squeaking against the plastic of the seat.

"I'm not going to say thank you." Dee unlatched the back door. "I had a terrible time."

"So did I. You made me miss the end of the race when you ran off. Do you know how I worried? Jesus Christ, Dee." Shrimp's face turned beet red beneath his platinum hair.

"You just acted mad," Dee yelled, slamming the door. "You do horrible things to me, too, Shrimp, all the time, like taking me to the speedway." I thought Dee must have thrown up because I saw yellow flecks like splattered egg yolk on her sandals. She pulled Shrimp's ring off her finger and hurled it into his lap through the opened window.

"I'll call you, North." Bill rolled his eyes at me. Then he looked over toward the back door. Uncle Judd slumped sideways against the door frame, drinking from a cocktail glass. Bill waved to him, but Uncle Judd didn't respond except to look more deeply at me. He wore white shorts without a shirt. The hair on his chest formed the shape of a dark cloud. Dee spoke with him, while I headed out toward the dock.

"North, don't you want to see some old movies?" Ice tinkled inside of Uncle Judd's glass. He followed me. "You like pictures, don't you? I set up the projector while you were gone. Come, see some old family movies."

"I don't want to see myself," I said, walking onto the dock. The family next door was swimming. Their presence seemed to protect me. I walked further out on the dock. If I'd carried a flare like a truck driver then I would have set it off.

"You were such a darling baby," Uncle Judd told me. "I've got pictures of me holding you. There are shots of you and Dee in the playpen. Our pet peacocks come and steal your graham crackers. You both start screaming."

I'd like to scream right now, I thought. *I'd like to scream: Get away from me.* I felt the words form in my throat. I reached the dock's end and Uncle Judd's breath fell over my neck. But then Dee joined us, taking hold of Uncle Judd's hand.

"I'll watch the old movies, Dad," she said. "C'mon, North. I bet we look funny." Dee's breath smelled like mouthwash. As she led us inside I noticed she had wiped off her sandals. I dropped back from Uncle Judd and thought of ways I could hurt him. I'd stick voodoo pins into a likeness of him.

In the dining room Mrs. Graybill had laid a veritable feast on the pedestal table—turkey, ham, sweet corn, mashed potatoes, and fruit salad.

"I'll show you girls movies while you eat," Uncle Judd said, fiddling with the projector which he'd set up on a card table. He raised a movie screen in the middle of the living room. I sat down at the table, my heel throbbing. I raised my foot on one of the extra chairs. Dee ate mashed potatoes and drank a Coke while I tried the turkey that tasted like fish sticks. Uncle Judd finished threading the film reel and closed the curtains.

"Where's Mom?" Dee asked. "Maybe she'd enjoy this."

"She's upstairs resting." Uncle Judd turned the projector on. The noise of the fan inside it filled the room.

"I'll go get her," I said, sitting up, legs flexed.

"Let her go. She's a mess today." *Because you made her one,* I thought. Uncle Judd seemed to stare right through the skin on my bare legs. I dropped back into my chair as if his eyes had pushed me. I wondered if he'd given Aunt Joan a hypodermic like the one he and the sexy nurse had given me.

Pictures started appearing on the screen. The first film clip was from 1948, when Dee was one and I was a tiny baby. My body seemed lost within the pink quilted bunting Queen Mom had wrapped me in. Dee reeled like a drunk, circling the lawn with a cracker in her hand while my mother passed me from person to person. I smiled when Grandfather North held me; I guessed because he made funny faces. But when Uncle Judd's turn came my face twitched as if with pain.

A film clip of Dee, age three, and me, two, was spliced right onto the first one. We rolled in a big wooden playpen eating graham crackers while two peacocks nipped the crackers from our hands.

"Can you believe how fat I was?" Dee asked me.

"I wasn't any lightweight myself," I said, as the film showed us both hobbling on the lawn, the fat pads on our thighs rubbing inside our legs.

"You girls were gorgeous," Uncle Judd exclaimed.

Dee and I faded from the screen and the movies became shots of a naked woman with a black card covering her face. She had tiny breasts like the woman in the article Uncle Judd had written, breasts that looked the way my right breast had looked a month ago.

Then a picture showed her after her operation with twin-domed breasts, and in each a centered nipple. Beneath her breasts you could see parts of the swollen black stitches placed at regular intervals like railroad cross ties.

"God, Dad," Dee groaned. "Why do you always end up showing the before and after pictures of your patients?"

"Got the films mixed up. When I spliced them." Uncle Judd lifted one of the other reels from the table and the light from the projector illuminated his gold watch so that it glowed. He moved his arms and I watched the gold glinting.

"You always do. North," she said, "he always does this."

I stared at the lady with the breasts Uncle Judd had fashioned. The noise of the projector fan carried me toward the ring of fire. I believed that any minute the pictures Uncle Judd had taken of me, naked on my birthday, could appear on the screen.

Boat House

My *clock radio* said eleven-thirty when I woke to the sound of slippered footsteps tunneling through the hallway. Outside my room the footsteps stopped, then someone pushed my door open, slowly. I lay frozen on my back on top of the sheets. The door swung shut and the footsteps echoed down the hall.

A haze of moonlight filtered through the windows, glazing my skin. The house fell silent and then the footsteps began again, moving closer from the end of the hallway. I heard the sound of ice clinking against a glass.

I told myself, *North, that is Uncle Judd.* He stopped outside my bedroom door for a moment. My heart flew to my throat. The powder blue walls of my room glistening with moonlight shone like eye shadow flecked with silver. He walked slowly down the hall, thudding farther off. I heard another door open, then close, and I bolted upright.

My bare feet hardly touched the steps as I ran down the stairs, the shoulder of my nightgown dropping over my elbow. I looked down at my bare breast jostling. I felt like an Amazon warrior, a woman aborigine whose leaps were boundless, whose body could do amazing things. Then I was a magician, a Harry Houdini escaping from a roped casket thrown to the bottom of the sea.

Downstairs I stopped in front of the picture of Jess and me. That's *why I have your picture. So I can keep you while you're away.* I pulled the picture down, hooking it in the crook of my elbow under my arm. In the kitchen I searched the darkened counters for Uncle

Judd's car keys, the empty surfaces of Formica sliding coolly under my hand.

Footsteps descended the stairs. I ran out the front door and down the steps, the picture slipping down my thighs. The sweat from my hands loosened my grip on it. If I dropped the picture he'd see it and then follow me, so I hurled it toward the boxwoods. I heard glass exploding against the foundation of the house.

At high throttle I drove the G-3 toward the south end of Glass Lake, refusing to look back. When I reached the channel I slowed down. Passing over the deep water, I saw the Hamilton's cottage where lights still blazed in the upstairs, in the room I imagined to be Bill's room. I told myself, *North, Bill is awake where that light shines,* as I drove over to the dock at Ramsey's Marina to moor.

The night had grown cool and I felt chilled and odd-looking, too conspicious in my nightgown, so I searched inside the G-3 for a jacket. I found Uncle Judd's off-white cashmere sweater. Even though it smelled of English Leather I pulled it on. I found a pair of Dee's white sweat socks in the glove compartment and put them on. I found a quarter and a dime. I dropped the quarter inside my sock, then carried the dime to the phone booth.

My hands shook as I dialed Bill's phone number. I didn't know what time it was. It could have been two in the morning; the sky above me loomed dark except for the moon. The road that followed the lake stretched out, deserted. Maybe it was too late to call, but I didn't hang up as I heard Bill's phone ringing, a sound like that of a coin ricocheting off the inside walls of a well.

"Hello," a boy answered the phone.

"Who's this?" I whispered.

"Bill Hamilton," he said in a soft voice.

"Bill, it's North. Bill, what time is it?"

"Midnight," he told me. I looked through the dusty glass of the phone booth and I wasn't certain what season it was. Everything seemed frozen white in the moonlight, settling on the ground and the road and the lake like snow. Bill breathed lightly into the telephone.

"Bill, I ran away. I need you to help me," I stuttered on the word *help*.

"Ran away, from what?" he asked. *Affluence. I ran away from affluence and expensive presents and promises to drive a red Stingray.*

"You ran away? From what?" Bill repeated, softly.

"I can't tell you on the phone," I said. "Just meet me somewhere, now, please."

"North, it's the middle of the night." *Oh, Bill,* I thought. *Don't refuse.*

"Can't you? Please," I whispered.

"Where are you?"

"Ramsey's Marina."

"Do you have a car?"

"No, I drove the G-3 down."

"Come over to our boat house. Stop the motor a few boat lengths out from the dock and drift in. I'll catch you." I hung up the receiver, touching the black metal reverently as if the phone were a relic inside a phone booth shrine.

I grasped the steering wheel and Bill sat beside me. Stars sprinkled the sky with dots of light. Waves lapped the bottom of the G-3. Bill had tied us beside the aluminum boat house. He wore sweat pants and a gray sweat shirt under his windbreaker. He zipped the windbreaker up and down as he talked, the skin on his hands bulging with curved veins that looked like tiny snakes.

"Why don't you start from the beginning," he said.

"Bill." That was all I could say.

"North, what's going on?" Bill asked gently.

Pulling my knees to my chest, I started crying.

"North, tell me." Bill scooted toward me, curling his arm around my shoulders.

"I'm cold." Bill rubbed my arms and the friction of his hands warmed me. But at the same time the sweater released the smell of English Leather. Bill's face resembled Uncle Judd's face. I wrestled away from him.

"North, what's wrong?" *North, honey, what's wrong.* Uncle Judd's words mixed with Bill's words, his voice braiding with Bill's voice. My arms began shaking like wings.

"Your fingers are ice cold," Bill said, stilling my hand by holding it in his. *Maybe they are ice. Maybe they're ten icicles that will melt if you kiss me again like you did the first time.*

"Let's go in the boat house." Bill lassoed me with his arms, moving me toward the boat house that shone silvery white with moon. Bill slid the door up and it reminded me of the door on a space capsule.

"C'mon," he said pulling me into his speedboat. I sat down on the soft white cushions with Bill beside me behind the steering wheel. The corrugated aluminum rose over us a halfmoon arc of metal. Beyond the opening of the boat house the lake glittered like a sequined shawl.

"There, this is warmer." Bill scooted closer and touched my hand. I cried silently.

"What got you all shook up?" Bill wiped a couple of tears from my cheek. I wanted to tell him everything that had happened. But it tangled in my mind. I couldn't undo a single strand. And if I had untangled the strands and told Bill about Uncle Judd, what he did— how I sat frozen like Daphne turned to a laurel tree by a god while Uncle Judd touched me as if a consenting lover—Bill wouldn't have wanted me anymore. He'd have seen me as bruised fruit.

"Here," Bill said, pulling my shoulders forward. "You don't have to talk." He rubbed circles over my back, warming me, then heating me up. Bill wore a watch with a face that sparkled with moonlight. He slipped his glasses off and leaned toward me, his lips growing bigger and bigger. He kissed me, at first softly so that his lips felt like Kleenex, in a minute harder, so that they felt like cloth.

Bill stroked my collar bone as if it were a relic, then dropped his hand over my breast and rubbed. Up and down. The warmth of our bodies sent the English Leather from Uncle Judd's sweater swirling through the air. I watched Bill's face turn into Uncle Judd's face and back into Bill's face again.

Then Bill slid his hand up my thighs inside my nightgown, rubbing over the cotton of my underpants. His hand circled around and around. He slipped his hand inside the waist elastic of my underpants.

I wiggled in my seat, forcing his hand out. *Bill, kiss me again like you did the first time.*

Bill pressed against me from behind, his penis hard against my buttocks. I sat up and coughed, tears fell like rivulets down my face. I didn't know if I was crying from coughing or from the aching that pulsed through my heart then.

"Baby." Bill's voice was velvet. Breathing in sharp gasps, he grabbed my shoulders. I shrugged him off.

"Bill, I feel sick. I just want to lie real still until I stop crying." I faced him for a moment. "I just want to lie here and look up at the stars."

I rolled myself into a ball, pressing close beside the gunwale of the speedboat. Like a caterpillar spun inside a cocoon, I lay there searching the sky for a falling star. *All of us are like falling stars,* I thought, *Shrimp, Dee, Bill and me. We're all falling stars with one summer, like one dark sky, to flame through.*

"She drags me out in the middle of the night, then won't even talk to me." Bill said in *sotto voce* from the back seat as I closed my eyes. A part of myself I couldn't reconcile floated out on the glittering cloak of moonlight, toward the center of the lake, toward the dark mouth of water of the Devil's Hole where that boy Tony Bradford drowned.

"Bill. Psst, Bill." Someone stood just outside the boat house, rapping. "It's Debbie," Bill's sister said.

I opened my eyes slowly, almost to a dream. Light hit my pupils as if liquid, like eyedrops. I blinked. I lay on the front seat of the speedboat, my legs bent into the shape of a capital V. Bill's windbreaker was spread over me.

"Bill," Debbie repeated. I lifted my head, a rivulet of saliva from my mouth left a patch on the cushion I'd slept on.

"Bill, Billll." Debbie knocked on the door. I wondered if she knocked because she suspected Bill and I might be in the middle of copulating. "You in there?" Debbie pounded now.

"Yeah. What's your rush?" Bill said, popping his head up in the back seat, his hair tangled and the whites of his eyes filled with thready blood vessels. I wondered if he had cried last night when I cried.

"Morning." Bill smiled at me, showing his teeth. He slid the boat house door open and looked back over his shoulder, his face sad then.

"You'd better hurry." Debbie leaned through the door, her eyes bulging.

"What's the problem?" Bill pulled his hand through his hair.

"The problem's Dr. Diehl who's inside with Mom, very riled up." Debbie stopped a minute to look into my face as if she knew. "I'm not lying to you. He's talking about how boys your age don't know how to control themselves. He says he's responsible for North this summer cause her mom's gone. Bill, he saw the G-3 docked here."

"Oh." Bill's face tensed.

"He knows she's here." Debbie placed her palm on her forehead and said, "*Why* is she here, Bill?"

"None of your business," Bill answered her.

I scooted to the edge of the boat, thinking maybe a jump in the lake could free me. I'd swim away from tyranny like refugees from Communist China. But Uncle Judd stalked down the dock, clumping in his Topsiders. Mrs. Hamilton followed, apologizing aloud to him, saying she felt certain Bill's intentions were good ones, as if she were talking to someone who knew right from wrong

"Bill," I whispered, "I can't ride home with him." The corners of Bill's mouth wilted. *Why*, he lip-synced. I made a loco sign, twirling my finger at my temples. Bill's eyes bulged, his forehead wrinkled.

Uncle Judd stopped outside the boat house, his eyes finding the opened door. The quarter rolled in my sock. *A lot of good it would do me.*

"You're coming home." Uncle Judd lunged through the door, his huge black insect sunglasses first. I looked to Bill.

"I could drive her home in the G-3, Dr. Diehl," Bill said, putting himself in Uncle Judd's way. "That way you'd get the boat back home."

But you won't take me back there, will you, Bill? No, Bill, I thought. *You're lying. You will drive me farther and farther away*

from Dr. Judson Diehl. I looked straight into Bill's eyes, but he glanced away toward the cottage.

Uncle Judd glared at us, and pushed Bill toward the end of the dock. "Drive it over later for me. Give the keys to Mr. Robertson when you do." He grinned. "Thanks for the suggestion. Next time you'll know when to take a girl home, won't you?"

"I didn't bring her here. She came to visit me, Dr. Diehl." *Et tu, Bill.* I wish I'd gone deaf, blind and dumb then, or had amnesia from that moment on.

Uncle Judd pulled me through the boat house door by the arm of the sweater, not mentioning it was his. "Shall we?" he said.

I passed through the door, scraping my cheek on the metal frame. Bill stood mute, handsome and still, the morning sun lighting his body. I lifted my hand toward him, palm up. The air chilled, shadowed. Wind rippled the lake. Gooseflesh pearled my arms. Bill's eyes closed as if he were praying. I touched the cut on my cheek and sucked my finger, my blood tasting like the metal that had cut me.

Uncle Judd led me to the Stingray as if on a leash, his hand cuffed around my wrist. He drove us back to the north end of the lake fast, the cottages spinning by. I saw people I wanted to shout to, to say, *I'm in this car with someone who I'd like to see dead. It's him or me. One of us is gonna end up a goner unless you get me out of here.* People smiled at me, as if all of them would have given eye teeth to ride in this car. Uncle Judd didn't speak to me. A raw whiskey smell filled the car. His arms, lumped with tight muscle, held like concrete against the wheel.

He flicked on the blinker at the driveway but he didn't slow down. He clenched his teeth as tight as Dody Van Werk's teeth clenched when she had an epileptic seizure during eighth-grade P.E. The haunting scene of Dody's fit flashed in my mind. I saw Mrs. Linfield, our P.E. teacher, shove the wooden tongue depressor between Dody's teeth. Madeline, Sally and I huddled like geese, our necks entwined, inside the locker room door.

"Damn it," Uncle Judd hissed. A siren whined from the road behind us. Uncle Judd braked and pulled over to the berm. A blue police car with its cherry roof light flashing parked behind us. A policeman got out of the car, looking like the son of Jesus Christ to me then. He strode to the Stingray dressed in his wide Mounty hat and his blue uniform. I thought he'd know my troubles in one look and he'd arrest Uncle Judd, the way it happened in movies about someone young who was treated badly. Uncle Judd sat up straight and inhaled a deep breath. His skin nearly shone with a cartoonish radiance.

"You were doing fifty in a thirty-five-mile-an-hour zone. See your driver's license?" The policeman stood beside the car with a pistol slung inside a leather holster strapped to his hips.

Give me that gun and some quick shooting lessons. I fantasized the thick handle inside my palm. I'd forgo target practice and get right to the heart of my needs for armaments. I thought of things I might do with the gun, ways to point it and the orders I might give Uncle Judd before I fired. *Dance, you gringo. Sing for your supper. Get on your knees. Better say a prayer. Crawl, beg. Get down in the dirt where you belong. Son of a bitch,* I used Linda Turner's phrase.

The policeman's hat dropped a shadow over his shoulder as he leaned over to receive Uncle Judd's license.

"You've already been drinking. You know the penalties for driving under the influence?" he asked. Uncle Judd held up his driver's license. "Dr. Diehl, I didn't recognize you with your sunglasses on." The policeman smiled slightly. "You're pretty close to home to be driving so fast." He leaned back down to the window. Deep wrinkles squiggled across his face.

"I suppose I am, officer, but my niece here had some trouble with a boy who kept her out all night." Uncle Judd spoke as if he were a rogue pope instructing a cardinal on mortal sin. "My intention was to get her home."

"I'm sure you mean well, but drinking and driving don't mix. You're a doctor. You've seen injuries from car accidents first hand."

"I've operated on the victims. Of course," Uncle Judd said.

"You and your niece don't want to get into an accident." The officer laid a hand on his hip near his pistol. *Go ahead, draw. Aim between his eyes. Pull the trigger. You never took a Hippocratic oath.*

"Of course not," Uncle Judd said in a breezy voice. "Officer, I don't intend to get into an accident," Uncle Judd spoke emphatically.

But *I* wanted to get in a car accident in which Uncle Judd could be killed instantly.

"Today I'll take your word on that." The officer handed Uncle Judd his license. "But I'm going to issue a warning. You'd better lay low while you're vacationing up here. If you're stopped once more for DUI this summer you'll get six points and a hundred-dollar fine. People haven't stopped talking about that Turner girl's accident. Now, I'm going to get in my car and follow you home."

Uncle Judd parked the Stingray at the house and the policeman whirled his car around, heading out of the driveway. I didn't want him to leave me, to take away his gun. *Stop! Please. Give him a ticket. Give me a ticket. Arrest both of us. Talk to Linda Turner and find out the truth.* Dee said the driver of the boat hadn't seen Linda Turner and now I knew who the driver of the boat was. I wanted to sneer at him and swear the way Linda Turner had sworn. *Son of a bitch.*

"North, you listen to me and you remember every word." Uncle Judd raised a forefinger. "You tell anyone our secret and I'll tell your mother you stayed out all night with Bill. I'll say you drove our boat without permission and you destroyed property. I found the broken picture. You destroyed the frame but I plan to have the picture reframed and hung in my offices."

I opened my mouth but no words would come. Only a bubbly sigh rose from my mouth, a *whoosh* of breath. I imagined the picture of me and Jess hanging in Uncle Judd's office, balanced over the heads of all the women who begged for huge breasts. The picture would remind them of why they'd come to Uncle Judd. I'd speak from my spindly body of their original imperfections, from which he could deliver them. The new pictures Uncle Judd had shot would hang on the same office wall. But I could only envision them reversed like negatives. My hair was a ghostly white, my skin blackened, and my nipples glowed like targets in the centers of my breasts.

I must have caught Dee's sleeping sickness because all I wanted to do was sleep. I wanted to sleep all day long the way King did and I wanted to sleep all night, too. But at night I awoke every hour on the hour with my heart beating like a tom-tom. Uncle Judd had packed his bags and left the cottage the day after the policeman gave him the warning. But every time I awoke I felt, for a moment, his presence in the room.

Dee stayed in seclusion, locked in her bedroom. I could hear her radio and television playing, weaving voices from a world where people laughed too often, in unnatural rhythms. Their laughter tunneled away from me. Once her radio played "Rock Me in the Cradle of Love" with the volume so high I shouted to her to *please turn it down*. Aunt Joan asked Mrs. Graybill to wait on us; she made thick hamburgers and home fries and peach cobbler which she served to us on wicker trays. She did our laundry every morning, returning it in the evening in a single stack. My white bikini returned to me on top of one pile, the places where it had touched my skin still edged with dust.

Aunt Joan played the piano in the out-cottage day after day, the tinny music reeling up to my bedroom through still, humid air. One night a clap of thunder rocked the house around ten-thirty. I sat up startled, the room pulsing with lightning flashes. I heard Dee coughing and stumbled over to the bathroom and rapped on the door.

"Dee? Open up," I said.

"Go away," she growled.

"No. You open the door." I drew my toe along the line of light at the bottom of the door.

"Forget it."

"I can't forget it. Plus I have to go to the bathroom. Please," I pleaded. Dee cracked the door and I slipped inside the bathroom. Dee hobbled into her room.

"You need help," I called after her. "If you keep throwing up everything you eat you'll get weak." *You'll fade away*, I thought, and I remembered Buddy Holly singing Love is love, "Not Fade Away." I believed that love caused Dee's problems, that her illness resulted from love and sex, not germs.

"North," Dee shouted as a clap of thunder rocked the sky. "You tell anybody I'm sick and I'm telling everyone you stayed out all night with Bill." She used the same threat Uncle Judd had used on me. But I didn't hate her the way I loathed him, her voice a desperate thread.

I wanted to say, *Dee, please, I've seen you do wild things, too, this summer*. I watched her crawl into bed and lie down in the midst of her tangled sheets. Like Jesus's shroud. She stiffened miserably, laying her hand on her forehead. The memory of how differently she lay in Shrimp's arms inside the gazebo resurrected. I saw him thrusting inside her. Dee curled into a fetal position and covered herself with her bedspread and I knew she had become pregnant; Shrimp's baby lay planted deep within Dee. *And he had cried out as he came: Oh, I love you, Deedee.*

On *Friday, a* week after Uncle Judd left for Grosse Pointe, I tried to work on the gum chain while I listened to the radio. The newsman discussed the Communist threat in Southeast Asia. He said America was sending the non-Communist rulers $1,000 per day in aid, and that United States military advisors would continue living in Viet Nam, working with the government soldiers to sharpen their skills against the Communist guerrillas fighting there. I stretched the gum chain across my bed and wondered if one world of peaceful peoples was ever going to be a real possibility.

I rose and walked to my bureau. Someone knocked on my door. I jerked my spine straight. My heart flapped in my throat. My picture of Jackie Kennedy had once been tucked behind the mirror I looked in now. *You look like Jackie Kennedy,* Shrimp had said. I told myself, *Let it be God's truth* and my heartbeat slowed.

"North," Mrs. Graybill called to me. I opened the door and she handed me a letter from my parents; they said they would be coming for me a week from Sunday. On Saturday, a week before that day, my body ached like a giant bruise. When my breasts brushed the bed sheets I felt I would cry from the slightest pressure. My mind filled with morose thoughts of my life echoing Linda Turner's life, of growing up to take a servile job in a place where Uncle Judd would visit at his leisure and order me around.

I barely slept that night. I lay in sheets drenched with sweat wondering when he would return. Sunday morning I listened to an evangelist healing people on a radio station that was broadcast from somewhere in Tennessee. The preacher described a woman limping to the stage on a gangrenous foot. He said the woman had diabetes and her doctors had told her if her foot didn't improve they would have to amputate. When she reached the stage he laid his hands on her, praying loudly in a shaking voice to God and Jesus to heal the woman, but the way he said *heal* it sounded like a dog trainer's command.

Moments later the woman bolted from the stage flanked by her tearfully grateful daughter and husband. That is what the evangelist described in his ecstatic, palsied voice that minutes later asked for contributions to be sent to his Oklahoma mailing address. I wondered if the evangelist could heal invisible problems, if he could lay his hands on my shoulders, pressing the sickness out of my body. I jotted down his address in case my sickness worsened. "Heal, heal," the evangelist commanded over some jackknifed half-dead body. Another supplicant.

A tittering of voices erupted from the front lawn. "Where's Judson?" A woman's voice, loud and honeyed, made me think he could be there in the house now.

I dressed quickly in my U of M T-shirt and my blue madras shorts. I brisked into Dee's room and asked if she wanted to go downstairs with me, but she glared at me from bed. "No, way," she said. I should have known her answer. Mrs. Graybill asked her down for lunch every day but she wouldn't leave her bedroom, where a fetid sickroom smell had set in. Dee told Aunt Joan she didn't want to be bothered because she wanted to read books and get a head start on school next year. "Smart girl," Aunt Joan said, and drifted out of Dee's room like a wraith. She walked sideways down the hall, lilting like smoke. "I always loved reading, too." Her wispy voice lingered behind her.

I tripped on King's rubber hamburger toy in the living room and straight-kicked it under the couch. I peeked out the picture window at the two women who talked to Aunt Joan, pressing my palm against the glass to brace myself. I once had a chameleon in an aquarium who hung by its toes from the side of his cage. I felt unsteady, as if I might fall through glass.

Both women had dressed elegantly, one in a white double-breasted linen suit with a matching pillbox hat and white heels, her

black hair styled in a Jackie Kennedy hairdo. The other woman resembled Marilyn Monroe with her blond hair, huge breasts, and tiny
waist. A black and white knit dress hugged her body. A brown beauty
mark dotted her cheek. Together the women laughed and gestured,
waving their hands. I snuck outside and crouched behind the box-
wood bushes. Shards of broken glass shone in the sunlight like frozen,
shattered sleet.

"Cecile, it's a shame Judson isn't here," the blond woman said.
I breathed a deep relief sigh. "He made such a point of telling us to
stop by."

"I'm sorry, Judson left unexpectedly. But you'd like to stay for
some tea, wouldn't you? And a blueberry muffin." Aunt Joan's eyes
signaled Mrs. Graybill to the kitchen.

"We don't want to trouble you." The dark-haired woman adjusted her white-framed sunglasses. She unbuttoned her jacket and
took it off, revealing her slip of a shirt, her breasts perfect domes
beneath.

"It's no trouble," Mrs. Graybill replied, walking toward the
house.

"Please. Sit down." Aunt Joan extended her arms toward the
wrought iron lawn chairs like a somnambulist.

"The reason we came is we both admire Judson." The woman
who resembled Marilyn Monroe dropped like a handkerchief into a
chair. "You don't mind my calling him Judson, do you, Mrs. Diehl?"

Aunt Joan pulled her fist from her pocket. I'd seen her take pills
from her pocket before. Covering her mouth, palm flat as in an Indian
whoop, she faked a cough, then swallowed.

"Janice, didn't he tell you to call him Judson?" the dark-haired
woman asked.

"Yes. It's a funny story. You know how painful a rhinoplasty can
be. Judson warned me. He said that when he came on rounds the
first day after the operation I'd want to call him something obscene."

"Oh, that's just what he said to me," the dark-haired woman
said. "When he came to see me after my breast implants I wanted to
hug him, except I couldn't hug in my condition. Mrs. Diehl, the operation was my husband's idea. I did it for him, but it made me so

happy. I had no idea how depressing being flat-chested was until I had the implants. I spent the month after the operation buying new clothes."

The blond woman laughed, snorting like a pony.

"It must be wonderful being married to such a talented man." The dark-haired woman accepted a cup of tea and a muffin from Mrs. Graybill.

"Yes," Aunt Joan said, her voice drifty.

"My new nose is a miracle," the blond woman said.

"So are my breasts," the dark-haired woman flattered, sipping her tea.

Uncle Judd had wielded the scalpel while he perfected their bodies. They called him *a performer of miracles. Like God.* I crept over to the side of the house, my hands trembling. *Like God*, I repeated. *God.*

Once inside on the screen porch, I scooped up two *Newsweeks* from the wicker stand, carrying them upstairs to my bedroom. The chattering still filtered in from outside. *Judson this. Judson that.*

The *Newsweek* from July featured an article on a British sex scandal involving high class prostitutes whose clients were famous men. I studied the pictures of the beautiful call girls, one named Christine Keeler. I'd never realized before that prostitutes could be so lovely and innocent looking. I felt instantly sorry for them. *North*, I told myself, *don't let your life end up like this.* My breasts felt full like water balloons. I grew thirsty and fixed myself three lime fizzles in the bathroom, the green trails spiraling up from the discs like colored firework ash.

In the *Newsweek* from August 11th an article described the birth of Jackie Kennedy's baby who had arrived dangerously early for both her and him. The article discussed a miscarriage and also a stillborn baby Jackie Kennedy had had before Caroline was born. Why hadn't I heard about this? Now, Baby Patrick had been born on August 7th in a difficult birth that Jackie Kennedy had survived. Within two days baby Patrick died. I couldn't believe the terrible news, that something so sad had happened to someone so wonderful. She'd been sad for days while I had no knowledge of her tragedy. I wanted to help her.

I saw her eyes, fawn sensitive but farther from me now, as if seen through a layer of the lake. I said to myself, *North, she must have prayed for help but God didn't answer.*

I read on. Before Jackie Kennedy left the hospital at Otis Air Force Base, she gave all the nurses pictures of the White House which she signed, *With deep appreciation, Jacqueline Kennedy.* It was just like her to give someone else a present when she herself felt sad. In the photograph of her and the President leaving the hospital, he grasped her entire hand inside his hand. He'd dressed in a black suit and she wore a light pink shift. The wind swept her hair up on top, and someone in the crowd had said, "They look like a couple of kids." But Jackie Kennedy's face seemed somehow longer and drawn along the bones of her cheeks. I saw a far-off look in her eyes. I didn't think her face would ever look the way she had looked in my picture again after what had happened to her. And I asked myself, *North, how could you ever send her the letter you wrote now?*

That night I awoke around two in the morning with a warm wetness between my legs. Sitting up slowly, I reached over to switch my bedside lamp on. I touched myself there and saw on my fingers what I'd once wanted so badly: my own blood. Pushing my nightgown between my legs, I walked to the bureau where my Kotex was stored.

I ripped open the Kotex box and rummaged the sanitary belt from inside a pair of underpants. I hooked an oblong pad to the belt inside my stained underpants. My image in the mirror surprised me. My breasts rose under my nightgown, two domes of equal size almost as big now as the dark-haired woman's breasts. For a moment I felt I resembled her. As I pulled the pad between my legs, I believed I had become a woman because Uncle Judd had made me one. I thought he had made me a woman when I fell through that ring of fire.

Lost Babies

Baby Patrick Kennedy was buried in Boston, Massachusetts, in a small private ceremony only the closest family members attended. Everyone in our country felt sad. And there was so little you could do about it. I imagined that the strong religious faith of the President and Jackie Kennedy would help sustain them. Although I didn't understand the mysteries of Catholicism, I envisioned the ritual of the funeral passing as they laid their newborn baby to rest. It made my heart ache to think the sun might have been shining.

I decided to write Jackie Kennedy another letter. I tore the first letter into pieces and then began.

Dear Mrs. Kennedy,

I've never heard sadder news than the news of the death of your baby Patrick. I'd thought about you and your baby all summer. I wondered if one day there would be three ponies eating grass on the White House lawn.

Because I'm fifteen years old, I don't know what it feels like to have a baby, or to lose a baby you loved. I guess it would be like having the oxygen sucked out of the air around you, like being inside an airplane that loses its seal up too high in the atmosphere and dives into a tailspin you can't stop for awhile. I want you to know how sorry I am. I think everyone in America sends his and her love to you and the

*President. Words surely are inadequate, but there seems no
other comfort an ordinary person can offer.*
    Sincerely
    North Wagoner
    205 Spring Street
    Ypsilanti, Michigan

Sealing the letter in a white envelope, I addressed it and stamped it
with a stamp that pictured an astronaut in a big white space suit. The
moon shone behind his head, echoing his luminous helmet.

Saturday morning we drove to the Yacht Club in the G-3. The day
was overcast and cool so Dee and I both wore sweaters; hers was an
oversized beige mohair cardigan and mine, a loose navy pullover I
hadn't worn all summer. Today I wanted to be hidden inside loose
dark cloth. Dee came out of seclusion as a result of my storytelling.
I convinced her to believe in my story of Linda Turner's emaciated
baby, about to die a crib death in the upstairs of the Yacht Club. I
said I'd heard from Frank Boyd that she'd maybe had twins, a lie I
didn't mind spinning because I believed it at least partly true.

My parents were supposed to come the next day to pick me up;
they had said so in letters, but somehow I didn't really trust they'd
arrive. Like the clouds overhead and the gray muted day, time blurred
unreliably.

When we passed by Shrimp's cottage Dee refused to look for him.
I tried to follow her example, but when we passed Bill's cottage I
searched the grounds. The empty boat house, with a gray light shawl-
ing it, glowed as silver as an Airstream trailer. I couldn't believe I'd
slept in Bill's speedboat there. Bill had called me a few times, but I
told Mrs. Graybill I didn't want to talk to him.

At the Club we sat at our favorite table, on the glassed-in front
porch. Our waitress, Nancy, wore too much eyeliner. I ordered deep-
fried chicken with French fries but the chicken arrived raw. Dee sent
it back to the kitchen. By the time Nancy brought it out again I didn't
feel hungry as I watched Bill walk into the Club.

"Hi, North, Dee." Bill stopped at our table and pushed his glasses onto the bridge of his nose. I could see his whorl of chest hair through his white T-shirt, like black wool under gauze. I wanted to touch him, then I wanted to run away, seeing him first as friend, then enemy.

"Hello," Dee said, sipping her lemonade.

"North, I called you," Bill said.

"Really?" I picked up the raw chicken leg, hanging it in air, like a Neanderthal woman.

"You didn't know?"

I shrugged my shoulders. "Nah."

"Sorry 'bout that. We're taking our speedboat out of the water today." Bill grinned. "My dad's fanatic about getting the cottage organized for winter before Labor Day." Bill smiled. "You want to go for one last ride in the BelAir?"

"I don't know," I said, fantasizing my finger tracing his chin line.

"North's leaving tomorrow," Dee said and Bill's jaw fell.

"You're going home?" he asked. I almost said, *No, Bill, I'm going to the moon.* "You're going back to Ypsi?"

"Yes," I said, seeking his eyes.

"Maybe I can write to you." Bill sat down in the chair between me and Dee.

"Maybe," I said. *I won't hold my breath until you do. I want you to and I don't.*

Shrimp walked up the front stairs to the Club, his platinum hair bobbing up first announcing his arrival. He came inside and sat down at our table. Dee would not speak to him. Shrimp leaned close to her, almost touching his forearm to her arm until she slapped her hand on the table and gave him the finger. He leaned back in his chair and looked out at the lake, pretending not to notice. Bill stared at Dee, his eyes bulging. He stood up and said softly to me, "Want to take one last ride in the Chevy?"

"Can I drive?"

Bill nodded yes. He led me out to the BelAir and handed me his keys with the black plastic miniature record disc dangling.

"Stay on the straightaway since you don't have a license," Bill said. I started the engine and revved it while Bill turned the radio to WDT where Stevie Wonder's "Fingertips (Part II)" played.

The music escalated. I put the Chevy into gear. Back and forth in the dim gray light of near autumn I drove the BelAir down the straightaway, the big whitewall tires spinning over and over the same ground. I thought I could push everything that had happened during the summer down into the dirt under us. If I drove back and forth I'd bury everything and be O.K. But Bill laid his hand on my thigh. I felt warm. The air in the car thickened, hot like soup. I jerked my leg, throwing Bill's hand off, releasing my foot from the accelerator.

"You're going back to Ypsi just like that?" he said. My hometown's name sounded like a hiccough. "Pull her over here." Bill pointed to a parking spot on the asphalt by the gazebo. I wondered why boys always referred to boats and cars as females. I should have asked Bill then. "Don't run off," he said.

"Dee's not feeling good today," I said. "And I'm not taking off just like that. Summer's just over. You know. Period." I scratched the car seat with my fingernail. "You have any idea where Linda Turner lives? I need to return something I borrowed from her." I asked this with no prior thought.

"She lives in Room Ten upstairs. What do you care? North, Dr. Diehl is a boozer. I know that much. What's the story? You know I didn't want to let you ride with him." Bill's face flushed all up to his temples. *You didn't come through, Bill. And that baby's upstairs wailing. I've got to go to him.* Bill's glasses caught the sun and I couldn't see through to his eyes. The rectangles of light reflected like the lighted spaces on a screen when a projector runs without slides.

"Good-bye, Bill," I said, my voice high-pitched as I jumped out of the Chevy. Turning once to look back at him, I saw him knit his eyebrows down below the rims of his glasses. On the way up the walk of the Club I stopped at the mailbox where I mailed my letter to Jackie Kennedy, suspending it above the dark slit before I let go.

Inside the Club I crouched on the stairs and commandoed my way up to Room Ten. I listened at the door and heard a television tuned into *The Guiding Light*. Hushed voices talked about emergency operations and affairs people were having between surgeries. I heard someone crying, then the honking of a nose. *What about the baby?* I didn't hear him. Not yet. It was Linda inside though, crying. *Linda,*

you've got my permission to kill him before I do it for the two of us.
I knocked on the door then.

"Who is it?" Linda screamed.

"Grocery delivery. Baby food," I said in a man's voice I faked.

"Wrong room. There's no baby here. Go away." Linda turned
up the T.V. which saved me the embarrassment of facing her in a lie.
*The baby was the baby at the car race. If he wasn't here he was
somewhere out in the noisy world of racing cars in the arms of a
redneck mother who screamed at him.*

At the table again I told Dee that Linda Turner lived in Room
Ten and listened to soap operas and cried. I said I hadn't found the
baby, but believed in his existence. I'd seen a premonition of him at
the Speedway in another woman's arms.

"North, you've got water on the brain," Dee said. "Look down
there at those dopes, will you?" She pointed to the shore where Bill
and Shrimp guided Bill's speedboat out of the water using the Club
lift. The boat, cradled in a nest of straps, swung through the air toward the boat trailer parked on shore beside a huge willow. Shrimp
and Don Richardson and Frank Boyd flocked around the boat, extending their arms like religious fanatics, stopping the boat from hitting the tree trunk.

Bill and Shrimp towed the boat away behind Bill's BelAir. Dee
waved Nancy over to our table, asking her to charge our lunch to
Diehl. But Nancy said she wasn't familiar with the Diehl charge ac-
count; she said she'd have to check with the manager.

Linda Turner came to our table. Although I never wanted to see
her again, there she stood dressed in her purple big-sleeved blouse
and black pants and white wool socks, with her hair the color of
September wheat and her look of lost aristocracy.

"Sorry. Nancy's new here," Linda said, sounding secretly glad to
find someone irritated. She looked me up and down. I didn't talk so
she wouldn't connect my voice to the voice outside her door upstairs.
Lolita, she'd called me. Queen Mom had that book and I tried reading
it to find the dirty, arousing parts, passages that could excite me. But
Humbert, who was perverted and liked talking in rhymes, became
obsessed with everything Lolita touched, even her dirty gym socks.

"No problem," Dee said.

Linda lifted our check and turned to carry it to the cash register. A gold bracelet spun down her wrist, like a wheel, a bracelet like the one Uncle Judd had given me. Linda walked away, her false foot hitting the floor, thumping alternately with the *tap tap* of her real foot in an uneven rhythm. Frank Boyd opened the front door of the Yacht Club. Air rushed in rattling the crystal chandelier in the ballroom.

"North," he said, and I thought he spoke to the north wind.

The G-3 skimmed the lake, cool beads of water splashing my face. I'd figured it out in a simple deduction. No puzzlement. Uncle Judd was the cause of Linda Turner's misery. Linda was his slave, the gold bracelet her manacle, her servile job a yoke she wore. Her baby was the baby at the car races. Or he had died. I didn't know which fate loomed worse for the child. Linda had obviously given him up for adoption. I fought the forces that would make my life like Linda's life. The G-3 plowed a seam through the lake, moving us closer to home. The east shore flashed by like a landscape in a speeded-up movie. Pieces of white dock, red speedboat, brown cottage and draping green willow branches flew wildly by.

My *parents came* for me on Sunday at five. The doorbell sounded tinny, far off. Mrs. Graybill answered the door. When I heard my mother greet her, I wanted to run to her the way I did when I skinned my knee as a child. I wanted to tell her I felt sick.

"Where's North?" she said, the sharp edge in her voice blocking my approach. She entered the living room, her head uplifted. My dad followed, his hands slightly raised as if he carried a cathedral train of a wedding gown.

I stood in the middle of the living room, staring down at my tennis shoes, dressed in my navy blue corduroys and my U of M T-shirt. My packed American Tourister stood beside me, the broken clasp spilling a pair of my underpants, wrinkled like skin.

"North, come here," my mother's voice engulfed me as she opened her arms. I was supposed to move inside those arms, but I stood worshipping her throat—not her face, but her throat where she created that voice delivering high expectations. "What kind of hello is this?" She placed a hand on her hip, then approached me and smoothed my shoulder; the smell of Chanel No. 5 and Final Net hair spray rose all around.

"Hello." I raised my shoulders, lifted my head to her face, broad and gleaming, her lips painted bright red. She flashed a smile that demanded a proper response. I forced a grin.

"My God, you've grown," she exclaimed. "Chuck, look at your daughter." She pointed at me with her professional finger, the one that in my dreams metamorphosed into a witch's finger. Then a stick. My dad glanced at me. "You've outgrown your clothes," my mother said. "We'll go shopping." I hoped my new clothes would be dark and loose shapeless shifts.

"Where's Joan?" my mother asked Mrs. Graybill, patting my shoulder as she walked away, the way a coach pats a second-string player. "Don't Joan and Judd have the perfect life?" she said to my father. "Summering in a place where they can rest. And read. That's what we need after all our running around. North, what a treat you've had all summer. I don't know how I'll face school." She sighed, looking at me as if I'd ring the school bell in September.

"Mrs. Diehl's out front." Mrs. Graybill walked out the front door to find Aunt Joan.

"Had a good summer?" My dad looked at me, then turned back to the window, as if the changes in my body startled him.

"Sort of," I said, tapping the toe of my shoe on the floor.

Aunt Joan stumbled into the house, her lipstick smeared and her hair piled high like Marie Antoinette's hair. She twisted her shift with her hands at the waist.

"Mary, Chuck," she said, embracing Queen Mom in a listless hug. "North was such a pleasure." The pleasure of the yellow pills ran palpable in her floating voice.

"Her pleasure, too. Right, North?" My mother looked to me. I cleared my throat reflexively. "Where's Dee?"

"She's upstairs resting." Aunt Joan smoothed the top of her hair. "She hasn't been well. Judd says it's probably a virus."

"Well, everyone says that cancer is the big killer today, but I think viruses are the plague of the twentieth century." My mother spoke with authority while my father and Aunt Joan laughed.

"And Judd?" Her voice swelled with his name.

"In Grosse Pointe," Aunt Joan answered.

"We missed him when we dropped North off, too." My mother pulled the cuff of her ivory lace blouse over her wrist like a schoolgirl fussing before a date. "We have so much to thank him for. To thank all of you for, really. His savvy made our trip possible. Then, you provided for North all summer. She had such a good time she didn't write." My mother poked me in the shoulder blade. "It's always a sign of having a good time when you don't write." She spoke in a sing-song teasing.

Memories of the summer flew through my mind. A flash of sun hit the empty space on the wall where the picture of Jess and me had hung.

"I'm sure he'll be by Ypsi soon enough to advise me on investments. We'll all have a dinner together soon. At our house." My mother smiled.

"A real turn of events—Mary cooking," Dad joked.

But I envisioned Uncle Judd sitting across from me at our dining room table, raising his hands to gesture, his arms lifting. Vulture wings. Dinner turned to carrion. All of us gathered together, him laughing while everyone listened. Only he could fly away. I'd want to run.

I lunged forward, grabbing my suitcase and heading toward the back door, smashing into Mrs. Graybill in the kitchen. She stopped me, her hand gentle on my arm, tan as oak. "You forget something." Mrs. Graybill held up the gold bracelet Uncle Judd had given me. It looked like a bull's nose-ring.

"That must be Dee's. I think she had one just like mine," I lied, my voice like spittle. I coughed and walked out the back door.

I ran to the Mercury, stopped running there, breathing fast, hot, rage breaths and shallowly. My lungs burned. I wanted the car keys so I could drive. *Drive anywhere. Drive over the speed limit.* I didn't care if the police apprehended me. Maybe the cop would pull me over and I'd say, *It's me, Lolita. Humbert's back at the ranch. You know me, Linda Turner's twin sister.*

"I'm ashamed of you. Running out like that." Queen Mom stood over me like a dark Eiffel tower, admonishing. "You didn't even say good-bye. Did you forget your manners?" She drew the heel of her ivory pump through gravel.

"No," I whispered.

"You're out of breath?"

"Just tired," I said, my head down like a work horse on plow.

"Your underwear's showing outside your suitcase. Underwear's private. Especially now. You've developed so." She said the word *developed* like a secret, stained word. She stared at my body and I rounded my shoulders to hide my breasts. "Stand up straight and go back inside. Say good-bye like a lady."

I pulled my spine taut and marched back toward the house. I didn't feel like a lady, though. I felt like a communist Chinese in a Mao camp. I imagined the family dinner my mother had spoken of and my knees shimmied, as if Jell-O. I walked down the field stone path, my quivering legs sinking, deeper and deeper, into a future like quicksand.

Oh Say Can You See Dee

Deedee. I love you Deedee. Don't ever forget Shrimp said that, Dee. I heard a baby crying and it was a howling that scratched my backbone like sharp fingernails. Dee, did you get up in the night? Because he stopped crying and my room flooded with the moon's pure light just like milk fallen from the sky through an unopened window. What are you going to do with the baby, Dee? You can't kill him. They'll try to get you to give him up like Linda Turner did.

Tell Linda Turner I know her baby's lost. But I can find him when I come back to Glass Lake and the state trooper brings his posse to help me track that baby down. We can follow his cries like a trail of crumbs into the woods where it's so dark, Dee. I get lost in the woods looking for the lost babies. You were like my sister but look what happened. You're knocked up and pissed off about it. I don't blame you. I've got my picture hung all over the goddamn world by a flaming asshole. Who happens to be your father. Did he do what he did to me to you, too, Dee? Oh, tell me.

Dee, tell me when the baby first kicks inside you. The Bible called that quickening. God will judge the quick and the dead. No one escapes God. God wants to touch all of us.

"God Save the Queen" is Britain's national anthem, and we used it for "My Country 'Tis of Thee." I need to drive a car. Real fast. Remember how much I loved the Speedway? I'm going to drive fast like Ray Meirs. Maybe get in a car crash. Glass exploding all around me. My face splintered. Then it won't get me the wrong kind of looks anymore, Dee. I'll be maimed but no longer ashamed. Lolita's mother *died in an accident, but Humbert didn't tell her because he wanted to keep her on his string. If you have to do in the baby I want to know about it. Dee. At least tell Shrimp what happened. It's his baby, too. We're all babies when the knife's at our throats. I heard a new song today called "Be My Baby" by the Ronettes.*

Drivers' Training

In our tenth-grade honors government class we scheduled a mock primary campaign and primary elections that would end with a presidential election in the spring. Our teacher, Mr. Ferris, said the project would illustrate how the democratic process worked in America. Everyone had to first choose which candidate he or she would campaign for, which meant deciding whether you would be Democratic or Republican. I chose the Democratic Party, and President Kennedy who was running for re-election in November 1964. Madeline Spears chose the Republican Party and her candidate in the primary was Governor Romney, Michigan's governor. She said she liked him best because she knew about him.

Sally Teague passed the first weeks of September undecided about candidates or parties. She told Mr. Ferris that all the candidates were men the same age who wore clothes that looked indistinguishable and the only one who stood out in her mind was Richard Nixon because of the speech he had made once about Checkers, his dog. Sally said anybody who could talk to the country about his dog was either very empathic or utterly crazy and she would have to take the next two weeks in September to decide which one he was.

I liked President Kennedy best because of all he had done for space travel. I wanted to present a report on his support of the space race; I'd talk about the astronauts who orbited earth. I would describe our preparations to venture to the moon, saying President Kennedy planned for us to beat the Russians there. I decided to write to NASA to see if they could send me a sample space suit that I could model in class while I gave the talk. But when I wrote to NASA asking them to donate a space suit, they wrote me a nice letter back saying space suits were too expensive to send. They enclosed a huge color photograph of an astronaut dressed in a white space suit for me to show the class instead.

The day of my presentation I wore a loose green shift to honor President Kennedy's Irish heritage. After I finished speaking, Mr. Ferris complemented me on the thoroughness of my information. But when a quick vote was taken before the end of class not a single undecided voter had switched to President Kennedy. I felt I had failed him completely.

"North." Sally Teague touched my arm on the way out of class. "I'm going to go for Nixon. Madeline says I can bring her cocker spaniel Ruffles to school to sit beside me when I give my talk." Sally giggled. "Don't you think that would be funny?"

I didn't answer her but I wanted to say, *Sally, you missed the whole point; these elections are important.* I hurried off into the bustling hall with Sally staring after me.

At home my mother complained about cleaning house, so I approached her one evening saying I would clean the house every Saturday if she would give me permission to take drivers' training early.

"You'll still have to keep doing the dishes after dinner," she reminded me and I nodded my head, indicating I would.

"If I take drivers' training now, I'll have more time to drive with you before I turn sixteen." My mother's eyes took on a professorial gleam.

I *needed* to take drivers' training because I was developing a fear of riding in cars. I would sit in the middle of the front seat of Madeline Spears' dad's Pontiac with Madeline sitting beside me and her dad in the driver's seat, when all at once I would start to cough. The coughing made me feel like I had to go to the bathroom so I had to excuse myself and run inside the house to pee.

The first few times this happened Madeline and her father ignored me, but recently Madeline had crossed her eyes at me when I coughed. "What's the matter? You allergic to Pontiacs?" she asked.

"Real funny," I said sharply. But my stomach whirled. Just seeing

Mr. Spears' big flat hands poised confidently on the steering wheel had once triggered my cough. Another time it was hearing "Ring of Fire" playing on the radio. I felt as if layers of cloth were falling over my face, and I wasn't entirely sure if Mr. Spears was Mr. Spears anymore; the black steering wheel seemed to be a dark hole spinning through the air, circling.

The first class of drivers' training was scheduled for Friday, October 4th after school. That afternoon I walked up Spring Street, imagining what it would feel like to drive again. I picked up my pace so that I nearly ran up our driveway until I noticed the extra car parked there. *Oh, God, North*, I said to myself, *that's Uncle Judd's Stingray.* My heart beat in my throat as I looked inside.

Uncle Judd's black sunglasses lay on the dashboard. A pair of beige leather driving gloves lay on the rider's side bucket seat. I looked at the dials and controls on the dashboard, at the clock with its second hand jerking, and all our secret rides from the summer flashed through my mind. I stood in the driveway until my mother opened the front door of the house.

"North, come in, it's cold out there," she called. A gust of wind blew brown oak leaves into geysers around my feet; I walked up the sidewalk.

"Honey, Uncle Judd's here." Her voice sounded unctuous. "He stopped by to work on our investments." She and I stood together in the living room. "We'll be in the study. I left you a snack in the kitchen. Your favorite, chocolate pudding." My stomach turned when I thought about eating.

"North, hello," Uncle Judd said, moving through the arched doorway between the study and the living room. I lifted my head until I saw his smooth white glowing skin, his arctic eyes focusing. "I see you've kept some of your tan from the summer." His eyes seemed to survey every inch of my body. I couldn't speak so I nodded my head, then turned away from him. I bolted up the stairs.

In my bedroom I wrestled on my black turtleneck and black corduroys, all the while hearing their voices filter up the stairs, Uncle Judd's booming laughter, my mother's tittering response. *Oh, Judson.* Then her tinkling laugh.

North, I told myself when my hands began shaking, *North, in a few minutes you'll be driving.* It was almost three o'clock and the class began at three-thirty, so I forced myself downstairs. Uncle Judd's voice grew louder. For a minute I considered stealing the Stingray and driving myself to class. But then I held my breath, forcing myself to walk through the archway to the study. I cleared my throat and Uncle Judd and my mother, who huddled side by side, looked up from the stacks of papers covering her desk.

"What is it?" my mother asked. She wore a green velvet jumper that seemed too formal for a school day. Two half-full wine glasses stood like a married couple together on the desk. A tall bottle of German Riesling towered next to them.

Uncle Judd filled his glass. He lifted it in the air. "To you, Mary. To our endeavors." My mother lifted her glass to touch his, her expression melting rapture. Chink.

"It's time to go to class," I said, my voice a string.

"North, can't you see we're busy?" My mother put her glass down on the desk and smoothed her jumper over her thighs so her muscles showed through.

"You promised."

"So I did. I promised. Judd, I'll have to take her." You could have pulled her voice then, like taffy.

"I could drive her over," Uncle Judd said, standing up, towering like the wine bottle and smelling of Riesling. *Grape face. Booze head.* She smiled into his face, moonlike to the sun. He jingled his car keys in his pocket. He wore a white oxford cloth shirt with a beige cashmere cardigan and a tie with white dots that fell through the blue silk road of the tie like snow.

"North would probably enjoy arriving in a sports car." My mother smiled and laid her hand on Uncle Judd's forearm. Her eyes surveyed my body as if I were a window on *The Price is Right* and she the contestant judging my value. I cleared my throat, drawing my foot in an arc across the carpeting like a ballet dancer.

"My permission slip has to be signed by one of my parents." My words sounded like BBs. Scattering.

"Why don't you come along? We can talk while we drive back together." My mother held Uncle Judd's forearm inside her hand.

"That sounds good to me," Uncle Judd agreed. She let go of him and he walked through the doorway, brushing his thigh against my hip when he passed by; his English Leather left a trail. I pressed myself into the archway and then, when he finished putting his coat on in the living room, I grabbed my navy blue pea coat from the closet, following them to the Mercury.

My mother drove, lacing her hands on the steering wheel. She'd taken off her rings, the diamond and the gold band. White, untanned skin circled her ring finger where they should have been. Uncle Judd sat in the back seat, a shadow behind me. The Mercury stalled at a red light and Queen Mom hit the dashboard.

"Damn it. This car's a wreck." She turned the key, pumping the gas pedal.

"It's prehistoric," Uncle Judd said. "Chuck really should replace it."

"He will. When hell ices over," Queen Mom said.

"When the Pope's a Presbyterian," Uncle Judd said, laughing.

The Mercury engaged and Queen Mom sighed. Wind blew drifts of leaves above the fields and roads. Crimson star-shaped sugar maple leaves whirled and yellow poplar leaves floated like gold feathers over Washtenaw Avenue. Along the horizon the white trunks of the sycamore trees erupted, their brittle branches fingering the sky.

"North's taking drivers' training early so she'll have more time to practice driving before she gets her license." My mother turned down the road that led to the Washtenaw Fairgrounds where our class was scheduled to meet. Her red lipstick glistened in the sunlight, the color of hummingbird syrup.

"I'm sure she'll learn quickly," Uncle Judd said in the doctor's voice that had commanded me all summer. "Won't you?" He tapped me on the shoulder.

"I hope so," I stammered. "There's the 4-H building. That's where class meets," I said. When Queen Mom idled the car looking for a parking place, I jumped from my door and ran inside. Queen Mom signed my permission slip while fast talking with our teacher.

She gestured like an Italian and I buried my face in my textbook. She said she needed to run as she had parked in a tow-zone and asked my uncle to stay with the car. "North. Five-thirty." She gave me the O.K. sign and walked out the big double doors; they reminded me of the swing doors to the hospital emergency room in Alston.

I *sat down* in the very back of class in a desk chair carved with initials of lovers inside hearts surrounded by swear words, as if the two were related. Love made you swear. Or it could have been the opposite. I didn't know. My row of seats was empty. The closest person to me was a girl who wore thick glasses two rows ahead of me. We read the first chapter of our manuals entitled "Becoming Familiar With Cars;" it described aspects of the car interior from rear view mirrors to hood releases to the oil pressure gauge. After the academic part of the class we broke up into five drivers' groups. My group's teacher was Mr. Marshall, who was also my advanced algebra teacher. Our car was a fat green Oldsmobile.

"Debbie, Mark, North and Jean," Mr. Marshall called the names of the students in my driving group. "North Wagoner," he said. "You're up first." I wondered if I had come to his attention because I was nearly failing algebra.

"You ready?" Mr. Marshall's voice sounded like he held a wet washcloth inside his mouth, but actually he chewed tobacco. He had once said in math class it was a habit he picked up when he'd played in the outfield for the Michigan State baseball team. He was tall and when he slid inside the car his head touched the top of the roof inside; his knees buckled against the dashboard.

I sat in the driver's seat, feeling disappointed when I realized the car was an automatic. Mr. Marshall handed me the key. I touched the jagged edge first, coughed once or twice, then slid the key into the ignition and started the car.

Mr. Marshall said that the first month of our driving class would be contained to the fairgrounds where we could avoid *two-car accidents*. He grinned at his own joke then. Debbie, who had breasts like cantaloupes, giggled. Mark smiled at her. I could see them making eyes in the rear view mirror. Mark touched Debbie's thigh, lightly, the way Bill had touched me.

Jean, who sat on the other side of Mark, glared at Debbie. Edging closer to Mark, she raised her skirt slightly above her knees. I pressed the accelerator down and the engine roared.

"Miss Wagoner. Let's not hotrod. I don't think your parents would like you to race their car engine," Mr. Marshall said.

"I didn't mean to do that," I said quietly.

Mr. Marshall reached beneath his car seat and pulled out a glass Coke bottle, placing it upright on the floor mat between his feet.

"Try to keep the bottle standing as you drive, Miss Wagoner," Mr. Marshall said. "By the end of our classes everyone should be able to." His words sounded slurred because of the tobacco. Pulling away from the 4-H building I drove carefully, and the Coke bottle remained upright.

"You drive like you've had practice." Mr. Marshall chewed his tobacco and when he spoke again his breath smelled sweet. "Have you had practice, Miss Wagoner?"

"Just a little bit," I whispered. I thought Mr. Marshall knew what had happened to me. I thought he possessed X-ray vision and could see my breasts through the dark clothes I wore. I thought vignettes of Uncle Judd's hands touching my breasts played in Mr. Marshall's mind and he blamed me for attracting Uncle Judd. He thought my body drew Uncle Judd like an opposite charge. Then I could see the little movies, I could see Uncle Judd's flat pink palm floating toward my breasts as I drove the Oldsmobile to the grandstand where a dirt track circled around.

I turned down the road that ran parallel with the raceway. Glancing over at the dirt track, I saw a vision that seemed real then. I saw Uncle Judd driving the Stingray up the track toward us. I sensed the ring of fire burning. Tongues of fire chased the Oldsmobile, fire that could swallow me. I said to myself, *North, step on it.*

I started driving like Richard Petty racing Ray Meirs after the final turn at the Speedway. The Oldsmobile shivered and jetted forward. The Coke bottle rolled under Mr. Marshall's seat. I pushed the accelerator to the floor and the white fence that ran along the raceway reared up in front of us. I arched my foot to brake, but Mr. Marshall slammed his brake on, stopping us. The white fence caved into a collapsed V. Mark yelled and Debbie screamed.

"You could have killed somebody," Mr. Marshall leaned toward me across the front seat of the car, speaking sternly.

"I'm sorry," I whispered. My legs shimmied under the steering wheel. He said he had no choice but to expel me from the class. Immediately. Then, looking at me more carefully, he must have seen my body shaking, must have noticed the way I quivered like the dead leaves blowing through the sky. Because he stopped reprimanding me. He changed seats with me and backed us up, the fence splintering against the car. Mr. Marshall didn't mention the broken headlight. He drove us to the 4-H building where he dismissed the class early, everyone except me.

"You're crazy," Debbie hissed at me, pulling her sweater down tightly over her breasts.

"Miss Wagoner, what happened to you? You were doing fine. Did you push on the gas by mistake?" he asked.

"I don't know," I answered. How could I tell him of my vision of Uncle Judd's car on the track? How could I say that feeling so sexual during the summer seemed wrong now? How could I say that lusting to drive made me do things I shouldn't have done? I considered asking Mr. Marshall if my thoughts were logical. But then I thought of Uncle Judd back at my house and my mind filled with scattering, leaf-blown thoughts. Mr. Marshall looked at me, his brown eyes glistening.

"Go home and take care of yourself. I'll see you in algebra class," he said.

"O.K.," I whispered. I couldn't look anymore into his eyes. Instead, I stared down at the ridges in my corduroys, the topography of a map to some alien world.

My mother picked me up at five-thirty. I said nothing about what had happened. I looked out the window of the Mercury and saw the sky, blue as robins' eggs, with the autumn leaves falling there like hurled splashes of orange, red, and yellow paint.

"Honey," my mother said as she turned up Spring Street. "Uncle

Judd said to tell you good-bye. He had to leave unexpectedly. One of his patients began to bleed. We'd finished most of our work, luckily. So, we'll have dinner with Dad." My mother pulled into our driveway.

Upstairs in my room after a dinner I couldn't eat because every time the phone rang I thought it was Mr. Marshall calling to say *Your daughter's lost control of herself. She destroyed property. She nearly killed herself and all of us.* I lay down on my bed and turned over on my pillow, hearing a rustling under it. I slid my hand underneath and pulled out a wrinkled piece of paper. A note from Hades read:

I'm sorry we didn't have a chance to take a ride. Until the next time. Love. . . .

He signed his name in a doctor's scribble. *So that it couldn't be recognized,* I thought. The next time I'd demand ransom money from Uncle Judd, the way Linda Turner did. "I need two grand by this afternoon," I'd growl like a gangster on T.V. With two grand I would buy a car and drive away from him. I could drive away from *everything,* from Madeline's shadowing and Sally's irritating desire for boys she couldn't get, football stars and nerds and boys who wore too little deodorant to noon dances. I could drive away, but when I saw myself in flight, the Stingray gained the road behind me, swallowing the space I put between myself and Uncle Judd. My hands shook as I tore the note into tiny pieces and threw it into the wastebasket. *North,* I told myself, *North, today you almost killed yourself along with four innocent people. North, you've got to get a hold of yourself. North.*

Saturday morning I woke early and ate graham crackers for breakfast, then assembled all the equipment I needed to clean the house. I decided to go ahead and clean because I didn't want to tell my mother what had happened at drivers' training. I began in the kitchen, with the dirty pots and pans, scrubbing with an SOS pad on the spaghetti cauldron. My dad came in the kitchen, carrying his camera equipment.

"I'm going to shoot some photos on campus. Want to come along?" he asked. "Take some pictures of you under the big elm trees?"

"Lots of those trees are infected with Dutch elm disease," I said. "They have big yellow Xs painted on them. Any day now they'll be cut down." I scrubbed the spaghetti cauldron harder.

"All the more reason to take a picture," he said. Although I had once found my dad's artistic banter interesting, I didn't want to listen to him now; I didn't want to be in any more photographs.

"I'm supposed to clean house," I said, seeing how he'd lost weight while in Europe; his dark winter coat swallowed him.

"You're like Cinderella," he joked.

"Funny. Ha!" I flicked dishwater off my fingers at him.

"Who's the prince?" he laughed, shaking a hand.

"The princes all turned into frogs."

"Ribbet, ribbet," he said. "See you in the bog, frog."

"There's no prince," I shouted, as he crossed the white linoleum toward the back door.

"Oh, North," he sighed over his shoulder.

I almost ran after him to say, *Wait, there's one prince left. President Kennedy. And his queen Jacqueline. Together they will slay the dragons of the world.*

At the back door my dad fumbled with his equipment, his hands looking too large. I watched out the front window as he drove off in the Mercury. Then I ran into his darkroom, pulling open his filing drawers and rummaging through the pictures of me. Each curve of my flesh, even the crook of my elbows, looked seductive. Even when I was very young my private parts—a bun turned sideways, my breasts two welts risen on my chest.

I hurled the pictures into a pile and then sliced them into narrow pieces with my dad's paper cutter. Then I threw them away with the other trash I had accumulated in the kitchen in a trash bag.

Feeling more calm I cleaned the study, wiping off the chair Uncle Judd sat in. Light brown hairs, the color of his hair, curled and twisted over the furniture everywhere. I wiped them away and they flew through the air, falling to the carpeting. I brought out the vacuum and swept them up, remembering the big wads of fur that fell off King when he scratched his flanks with his back feet during the summer.

I turned on the radio in the study, with the volume loud. WDT played the Beach Boys. I used Spic-n-Span on the damp mop in the bathroom, keeping time with the music. "Go Away Little Girl," Del Shannon's song played. It was a song about an older man who finds a young girl attractive; he says he says he wants to be with the little girl all the time. He talked about the girl being too hard to resist. The mop clattered to the shiny tile floor. The song played until I ran to the radio and switched the station to WBJ where Rosemary Clooney sang of unrequited love. I knelt on the bathroom floor and with Comet and an old fashioned scrub brush in hand began washing the floor a second time.

Homecoming

I stood at the drinking fountain between government and algebra class, a drop of water sliding down my chin. Leaning over, I worried that my slip might show and I wished that the school's dress code had allowed girls to wear pants to school. Many times I thought about writing Jackie Kennedy to ask her to plead the case for pants in our school with Mr. Knight, our principal. She wore elegant slacks in Palm Beach, Florida, even when she attended church. Some newspaper columnists were very critical of her casualness. But I didn't think God would have minded in the least bit. She could have told Mr. Knight that allowing women to wear pants in public proved a society progressive. But each time I considered writing her I thought of how sad she must feel about losing her baby and decided against it.

"I know about your secret, North," Madeline said brightly. She stood so close beside me at the drinking fountain I inhaled her Emerade perfume.

"O." My mouth formed the shape of the letter. My secret? In my mind I saw Uncle Judd's hands moving over my breasts. I pulled the hem of my shift down my legs as far as it would go.

"I know why you're acting weird." Madeline's dark hair streamed down her back as straight as the hair on a paintbrush falling over the mauve-colored Villager sweater she wore.

"I don't know what you're talking about." I walked away toward algebra class with Madeline shadowing.

"My friend Shelly lives in Grosse Pointe." Madeline's breath hit my shoulder. "She's the one whose cottage is next to ours in Traverse City. She called and told me about this rich girl who dropped out of school this fall. All of a sudden. She flew to some foreign country or New York City to have an operation."

My shoes pounded the shiny linoleum of the hall like the boots of a marching Nazi. Images of Dee, in her many metamorphic stages throughout the summer, ran through my mind. Sexy, pretty, athletic Dee. Then Dee sick in the bathroom, the fluorescent light casting a green sheen on her face.

"So what are you trying to tell me?" I snapped from the doorway to algebra class. Mr. Marshall stared at me.

"Dee's P.G. Everyone at Grosse Pointe High's talking about it. They think she had an affair with an older man, a sailor or something." Madeline leaned toward me, looking like a witch at Halloween.

"That's a lie, Madeline. Stop lying to me." I wanted to say it was Shrimp who created a baby with Dee. It was Shrimp, and when he held her after they made love he had shouted, *I love you Deedee.* I wanted to say, *Dee's baby is not the baby of an older man!*

"No, it's true," Madeline whispered. I felt everyone in the class was staring at me. Any minute the bell would ring. "She's having an abortion. You must know all about it."

"I don't know anything," I said as the bell rang. I wandered toward my desk in the last row where kids with names at the end of the alphabet sat.

All through algebra class I thought about Dee and her baby and the things Madeline had said. When Mr. Marshall asked me to tell the class what absolute zero was, I couldn't speak. My lips froze shut and my mind soared to another plane where absolute zero became the temperature of my body, even during the summertime. Where absolute zero became the temperature of my skin all the times Uncle Judd had touched me.

On *Thursday before* government class both Madeline and Sally Teague approached me. Looking down at their feet, I saw the pennies inside Sally's loafers shining.

"Who are you going to vote for Homecoming Queen?" Madeline asked. "I can't decide between Mindy Leighton and Chris Norman." The Homecoming Queen would be crowned during half-time at the football game. Madeline reminded us that tomorrow she would be selected from a group of senior girls by an all-school ballot. I didn't know any of the candidates except Mindy Leighton who was the head cheerleader. I swayed back and forth, my legs feeling like brittle sticks inside my oxford shoes.

"I think Mindy will win," Sally said, "but I won't be at the dance to watch her on her throne."

"You mean no boy has asked you?" Madeline's eyes opened wide.

"Not one." Sally spun a blond curl from the side of her head on her finger and looked down at the floor.

"You're crazy to care," I blurted out. "It's just a dance after a game where boys run around like Roman gladiators ruining their knees. No boy has asked me to homecoming and I'm glad because I don't want to go." I nearly stomped my foot as I spoke. But then I wished I hadn't spoken so freely with Sally and Madeline because they squawked at me like mad chickens.

"North, you're the crazy one. You're lying. You'd go if some boy asked you," Madeline said.

"That's right, you're just pretending you don't care." Sally pinched her mouth up as she spoke. Then she and Madeline huddled along the green plaster wall of the hall beside me waiting for my response. I lifted my notebook from government class closer to my chest. I thought about President Kennedy sending a rocket to the moon. I didn't notice at first when Peter Vanderhaven strutted over toward me.

"Just who I wanted to run into," he said.

I saw his Nordic face, so white, and his wavy blond hair clipped clean all around, his eyes blue as sky. I looked at him but I didn't say anything. I didn't want to talk to a football star who wanted to talk to me.

"Say *hi*," Madeline whispered, elbowing me.

"North, would you like to go to homecoming?" Peter asked in a loud voice. Madeline and Sally bent over toward the wall like poppies in the wind.

"I, I don't know," I stammered. "I think I might have something to do that night with church fellowship." I looked down the hall, away from Peter, knowing I lied.

"She means yes. She can make up church fellowship," Madeline said quickly. "North always means *yes* when she says *I don't know.*" Sally nearly stared through me as I stood there mute. *You can have Peter, I thought. You can have him with his shoulder pads on and everything*. I saw Mr. Ferris glaring from inside government class and I froze in place, letting my head nod as if I agreed with Madeline.

"I'll pick you up after I shower after the game. I'll call you to-morrow to get directions to your house." Peter smiled at me as if I were not entirely human. As if I were some place he wanted to get to, like a goal post or the ten-yard line. Then slowly, with his thighs brushing together, he walked away.

"God, I can't believe this. Vanderheaven asked you," Madeline gasped. And I thought, *Vanderheaven, Vanderhell*. I walked through the doorway to government class, trying not to make eye contact with Mr. Ferris.

During the homecoming game I sat alone in my black corduroy pants and my winter jacket that looked like a Victorian rug. I watched from a spot halfway up The Hill which was a hillside beside the stands in the stadium. I sat on The Hill because I had suddenly felt claustro-phobic while sitting in the stands. So I told Madeline and Ted that I would go buy myself pop and a hot dog. That I would return later, that for some reason I felt terribly hungry.

As I watched the game, Peter's hands, huge as baseball gloves, swatted down the ball all over the field as he made dramatic runs and lunges. I tried not to think of going out with him. A boy beside me shouted about the field goal Chuck Teague, Sally's brother, kicked and a boy in chinos pulled his girlfriend down The Hill in front of me, rolling her over ground that was wet from rain earlier in the week.

After Peter scored his third touchdown an oafish boy who had been sitting behind me rolled against my back, pushing me down onto a muddy place on The Hill where two lovers had tangled moments before. I slid down, mud splattering my body. Stopping myself with my hands I lay there for a moment, then pulled myself to my feet. I walked back up to a drier spot on The Hill where I sat down. I began remembering Bill Hamilton's letter. He had said he missed me. *When I ride in the BelAir now and listen to the Beach Boys singing "Surfer Girl," I can't help but think about you.* I sensed the floating feeling I'd felt when I first met him, but the din of the football crowd cheering absorbed the feeling and the memory.

On the sidelines at half-time Mindy Leighton hung from Greg Bowman's arm; he was the captain of the football team so he wore his yellow Ypsi High uniform even as her escort. Mindy wore an emerald satin prom dress with spaghetti straps and emerald satin shoes. She looked like Alice in Wonderland. I thought she might grow bigger or smaller right in front of our eyes.

The announcer said the queen from last year, Sharon Richards, would crown this year's queen. Sharon had been slim in high school but now her body bulged from inside her turquoise wool suit.

The girls and all their escorts were introduced over the loud-speaker, and groups of fans cheered for the different girls as their names were said. Each pair walked to the middle of the field, forming an upside down letter V, centered on the fifty-yard line. "Now the moment has come to crown Ypsilanti High's 1963 Homecoming Queen," the announcer said. Sharon Richards walked onto the field, circling behind different girls and stopping to almost crown them. She held the crown over Renee Gordon's head and Renee wiped tears from her eyes.

The crowd oohed and ahhed as they watched Sharon, the sound of their sighs seeming muffled like a man's voice making an obscene phone call. Kids rolled all around me down The Hill, every one of them covered in mud and severed blades of grass. Finally, Sharon stopped in back of Mindy Leighton and in slow motion she let the rhinestone crown float through the cool darkness, hooking it into Mindy's hair, where the rhinestones glittered like pieces of glass sprinkled through black wool.

Mindy began to cry and Greg Bowman kissed her for a long time. Hot flashes sparked down my legs. He pulled his face away and Mindy sobbed. Greg had to hold her around the waist like an effigy when they walked off the field.

Mindy moved over the grass in Greg's arms and her body seemed to change into another body. One minute she was Mindy Leighton, Homecoming Queen, with the rhinestone crown slipping down over her milky white forehead. Then the crown dug into her skin. She changed into another body like a reflector scene inside a Cheerios box that when you turned it one way showed Donald Duck jumping and when you turned it the other way showed Porky Pig eating chocolate cake.

Mindy changed forms like that in front of me while Greg turned her in his arms. And her rhinestone crown looked like a crown of sticks sprayed silver by the flood lights blazing high above the field. Her emerald dress paled to a white sheen and grew longer, fluttering over her flexed knees.

Madeline and Ted dropped me off at home between the game and the dance. I found my mother in her study, correcting papers. Quietly I entered and stood waiting for her to notice me. She looked up slowly over her silver reading glasses.

"North, you're covered with mud." She let the glasses fall and hang around her neck by the glasses chain.

"Someone pushed me down The Hill," I whispered. "I feel sick. I don't think I should go to the dance. I think if I call now I can catch Peter at home."

"What's wrong with you?" Queen Mom's face tightened.

Mindy Leighton turned into a wraith after Greg Bowman kissed her like Rudolph Valentino. Lover boy. Face man. Lover boy.

"My stomach aches," I said.

"It's probably something you ate at the game. And the excitement. I had butterflies before every big dance." My mother smiled broadly.

"I didn't eat at the game," I said. "Last summer you said not to get distracted by boys." I coughed and a patch of dried mud fell from my coat to the carpeting, breaking to dust there.

"Last summer you grew up. Look in the mirror. Dating's inevitable. Most girls would be happy to be so attractive." There was a knife in her voice when she said *Look*. Setting her reading glasses back on her nose, she gazed down at the papers.

"Really I feel sick," I said quietly.

"That will pass as soon as you get to the dance, I'm sure." My mother glanced up at me. "Get ready."

I took a long shower in water as hot as I could stand it, so hot it turned my legs red. I scrubbed myself with a bar of Fels Naphtha soap. The water pelting the white porcelain tub sounded like sleet when it first starts falling. I remembered Uncle Judd's note: *until the next time,* he'd said.

I felt cold, despite the steamy heat in the shower, the misty clouds surrounding my head. I stayed cold until I jumped out of the shower and threw my white terry cloth bathrobe on.

As I dressed for the dance my heart thrummed like a bird's heart under its feathers. My feathers were turquoise brocade, a floral sheath with a wide belt studded with rhinestones—a dress my mother had chosen for me. She had the shoes dyed turquoise, two sleek slippers the color of robins' eggs. I thought they might break over my feet.

I stood in front of the full-length mirror inside the door of my closet. My shoulders sloped gently down, the muscle in my legs and my wrists with their delicate bones curved like relics.

I heard my dad arrive downstairs with his friend Evan, who was also a photographer. Evan's high-pitched laugh carried up the stairs. My mother laughed too. I wished they would be quiet, so I could think about something far off. Something distant, like the constellations, so I could imagine the stars of Orion shining from inside the rhinestones on my belt.

I dabbed a dot of Shalimar perfume on each wrist and heard the doorbell ring. My mother answered with a flittering voice I'd heard her use with Uncle Judd.

"Please come in. You must be Peter," she said. Then she called me downstairs. I stepped carefully with my hand on the railing.

"Hi, North. You look fantastic," Peter spoke in a gravelly voice. I nodded slightly, thinking how a nod of my head got me into this date in the first place. "You ready?" he asked, tapping his foot.

"Yes," I answered, speaking in monosyllables. I wanted to say to him, *Duh, duh, coach*. In the kitchen Evan and my dad talked intensely. I heard ice hit inside their glasses. Rising laughter.

"This is a fine house. Real fine." Peter looked at the walls of the vestibule as if our house were Monticello.

"Thank you," my mother said when I didn't respond. She dropped my white rabbit's fur stole over my shoulders. I fastened the hook and eye in front. Peter opened the door for me and we walked out to his dad's gray Lincoln Continental.

On the way to the dance he turned the radio on. Haley Mills sang "Let's Get Together." We sped down Washtenaw Avenue.

I hadn't driven since drivers' training. I needed to hold the cool circle of the steering wheel inside my fingers, to sense the forward movement of the car. Very few people knew about my reckless driving at drivers' training class. I'd told my mother I couldn't remain in the class because there were too many students enrolled and our teacher decided to remove the younger students. Mr. Marshall never mentioned my near accident to my parents. Maybe he'd pitied me as he gazed out into the algebra class, full of moony adolescent faces, and saw my face, drawn and thin.

Peter carried my stole to the cloak room which was in the converted girl's locker room beside the gym. He returned, wrapping my hand and forearm around his and escorting me into the gym, the same way that Greg Bowman led Mindy Leighton onto the football field.

Up on the stage at the end of the gym Mindy Leighton and the homecoming court, along with their escorts, sat in wooden fold-down chairs borrowed from the funeral parlor. Madeline Spears ran up to me and grabbed my free arm, her rhinestone earrings glittering like Mindy's crown.

"Isn't Mindy gorgeous? Could you believe how she sobbed on the field?" Madeline's eyes shimmered like Jell-O. Ted joined us then.

"Mindy's queen for a year," I said in a soft voice as if I spoke in church. Ted smiled at me and took Madeline's hand inside his. I gazed up at Mindy who appeared so calm now. In the blue floodlights that shone from the foot of the stage she glowed, her skin blue with reflected light, her emerald green dress iridescent.

"Great game, Peter." Ted let go of Madeline's hand, and punched Peter in the arm muscle.

"No big deal," Peter said, lightly shoving Ted backwards, kicking the floor with his wing tip shoe.

Ray Denney, Ypsilanti High's aspiring disc jockey, announced Mindy as our 1963 Homecoming Queen; she and Greg floated onto the gym floor. In the changing colors of the overhead spotlights we watched Mindy and Greg dance the first dance alone to "Stranger on the Shore," a slow clarinet piece.

When Ray Denney said everyone should join Greg and Mindy, Peter pulled me onto the gym floor, which glistened from shellac the way Shrimp's Chris Craft had glistened in the sunlight all summer. Beneath the festooned false ceiling of yellow and black crepe paper, Peter and I turned with the music. Madeline and Ted whirled off into the center of the dance floor.

Peter and I turned like two dancers inside the plastic bubble of a musical toy. I held myself at a distance the way the girl dancer in the toy's bubble would stand, stiffening my arms like a mannequin. I resisted the pressure of Peter's flesh, the tickle from the hairs of his hands as they brushed my hands. Now and then Peter's skin felt too warm and I pulled away to sway separately on the dance floor.

When Ray played "Blue Velvet" with the volume loud over the speaker system, Peter drew me out on the floor inside the wide loop of his arms. He pulled me in and pressed me close to his chest. I felt the wool of his sport jacket scratch my neck like a beard; I smelled his Old Spice cologne filling the air around me. Feeling dizzy, I untangled my body from his. I put my hand to my forehead and excused myself to the bathroom.

• • •

At ten-thirty we left the dance for Renee Gordon's house. As we entered the living room I heard a girl whisper: "Vanderheaven, he's a dream." But my legs and arms ached from staving off Peter's looming body during the dance. The air in Renee's living room hung heavy with heat and pressing bodies and the smell of perfume mixed with perspiration. I could barely see because only one tiny lamp glowed and a girl's red chiffon scarf had been draped over it.

Peter pulled me in through the living room toward an oversized couch. As my eyes adjusted to the darkness I saw Renee Gordon lying on the wall-to-wall carpeting near the picture window, her body caught up in Greg Bowman's arms. *Where was Mindy?* I watched Greg kiss her harder and harder. I wanted to run, but Peter pulled me down on the couch, his hands pressing my ribs. I felt like part of a renaissance sculpture of ensnared, rapacious bodies. Then his lips, tasting of stale beer, touched mine.

"Take me home," I said, pulling away. But it was like talking to the night. Boys groped under the dresses of girls who sat on the couches and the floor and the chairs all around me. They were all juniors and seniors. Everyone's hair looked tangled and wild as if they had driven to Renee's house from Chicago in convertibles.

"Oh, honey," Peter said, his breath covering my face. Shoving his hand down the top of my sheath, he grabbed my breast as if it were a tiny football. I heard Renee Gordon giggle when Greg pressed her against the picture window. But her laugh, signaling my ears from across the room, sounded like a whimper.

Peter's tongue whipped like a snake's tongue whipping reflexively. All of a sudden I felt a rise of energy, a propulsion like that of a jet airplane lifting. I jabbed my right arm through Peter's elbow and caught him off guard. He recoiled like an astonished lineman, his mouth dropping open. Running through the living room toward the front door, I fled. The kissing bodies I passed stiffened into postures of permanent arousal like the lovers found covered by lava in the volcanic eruption at Pompeii.

I outran Peter all the way to his father's car as he shouted, "Stop, North." Each *stop* he screamed propelled me. Throwing myself into the front seat behind the steering wheel, I power locked the doors. Peter knocked on the window, screaming, "North, North, open up." I felt my strapless bra scratching my ribs and holding my breasts up like puddings. *I'm Peter's piece, I'm Peter's piece.* I considered driving, imagining myself behind the steering wheel of the Continental, the car lunging forward.

"Give me the keys," I spoke in that assured voice I'd found during the summer with Uncle Judd. I spoke through the driver's side window that Peter had left cracked open.

"Open up," Peter shouted, pounding the door.

"After you give me the keys."

"The door first." Peter dangled the keys against the window.

"You give me the keys," I insisted. Peter frowned, slowly dropping the keys through the window; I started the engine.

"Hey, what are you doing?" he asked excitedly.

"I'm going to drive home. I could leave without you. But if you'll let me drive I'll open the door." I smiled slightly and saw Peter's face, as white as ice, the floodlights from Renee's house beaming over him, the wind tossing his hair high in circles.

"Please," his voice staccatoed.

"Don't try to stop me." I pressed on the accelerator.

"Oh, damn it, all right," he agreed. I opened the door and he slid inside. "But don't ever tell anyone I let you. My dad would kill me."

"I won't say a thing," I said, backing out the driveway. Turning the radio on, I drove away from Renee's house and up the streets and avenues, turning the wheel in perfect half circles, pressing the accelerator and the brake to the floor, rhythmically. "Come Go With Me," a song by Dion, played and I became another North, the North who could see her past as a road far away in the distance.

"Do you know what you're doing?" Peter asked, as I revved the engine at the stoplight on Washtenaw Avenue, a cloud of exhaust billowing up behind the Continental. "Are you all right?" his voice trembled.

"I'm fine now," I said. "I was a little too excited at Renee's house. My mother says girls get excited when they go to dances." I accelerated, skidding around the corner to Spring Street, nearly hitting a parked V.W.

"Jesus, watch it," Peter shouted. Within minutes we sat parked in my driveway.

"Thanks for letting me drive." I handed Peter the keys.

"I didn't have much choice," he said, walking me to the doorstep where he leaned over me. I thought about all the things that happen to people, things they don't choose.

Peter's hair looked white beneath the porch light, his head brightly outlined. He leaned closer, darkness engulfing his face. I pivoted away from him and opened the front door, lurching inside, then turned to face him.

"My parents don't allow boys inside this late at night," I said, my knees weakening. He stared at me as I lifted my hand to wave. Glancing down at my shoes, I noticed my legs were splashed with mud from running across Renee's lawn. "Oh, God, I'm all dirty," I said, closing the door on Peter and locking it.

The North Wind

The next morning I told my mother my date with Peter had gone well, that because the football team won the game by such a wide margin the dance had become a victory celebration. I said nothing about driving, nothing at all. But if I closed my eyes I could still feel the circle of the steering wheel pressed inside my fingers, and when I walked by the Mercury in the driveway on the way to the station wagon, I felt an urge to slip inside and drive away on my own.

On Monday at school Peter walked toward me in the hall like John Wayne walking to his horse, the gigantic yellow Y on his varsity jacket luminous. He veered in my direction, lifting his hand to wave. I ran into the bathroom, squeezing behind the two girls who walked beside me.

Standing in front of the mirror, I washed my hands twice with pink soap pumped from the wall dispenser. My fingers looked long, thin and white.

"I saw Vanderheaven out in the hall waving to you," Madeline said, appearing out of a stall. "You didn't wave back. How was your date? I heard about a makeout party at Renee Gordon's house." Madeline smiled, knowingly.

"I didn't see Peter." I dried my hands and felt my fingers tremble slightly. I dotted my face with tan Cover Girl make-up and rubbed it in. I dusted on top with soft beige powder. My lipstick, Crystal Violet, was a light lavender color that made me look as if I'd been visited by Count Dracula. "I have to get my hair fixed straight like yours," I whispered to Madeline. I thought my hair, so curly and dark, drew too much attention. I wanted to look like the other girls in school, girls who had smooth, straight hair with the crown expertly teased.

"See what I mean," I said, pulling my fingers through my dark curls, my hand caught in the snarls. "I can't even get my hand through my hair."

"Try big rollers or ironing it. That's what girls in California who want to look like surfer girls do." Madeline smiled as she stood beside me, brushing and teasing the crown of her naturally straight hair with ease. "If you want me to, I'll help you do it on Saturday."

"Thanks for the idea," I said, snapping my purse shut. *I'd do it tonight. The sooner the better.* I hurried out of the bathroom with Madeline in my wake.

In government class a debate between the supporters of the various Republican candidates in the mock primary elections broke out. The argument centered on who could best defeat President Kennedy in the 1964 election. Near the end of the discussion the Republican kids who were arguing finally agreed that President Kennedy was handling the civil rights movement poorly. Madeline Spears said he did too much for Negroes, and Larry Denty said he didn't do enough. Other kids joined in, back and forth, some shouting. Someone said the Negroes wanted too much freedom too quickly; someone else said they deserved it. Sally Teague said they already possessed the right to vote, and wasn't that something?

Nobody else but me supported President Kennedy. I wanted to enter the discussion to defend him but no one left a space for another opinion. I daydreamed of Jackie. I'd read an article in *Newsweek* about her traveling with her sister Lee Radziwill, who was a princess, to Greece. There she'd cruised the Mediterranean Sea in a gigantic yacht owned by a Greek shipping magnate. In honor of her he had the boat decorated from bow to stern with red roses and gladiolas.

I thought Jackie Kennedy had traveled to that far-off place I'd seen in her eyes in the picture when she left the hospital. I hoped that being in a foreign country allowed her to feel that she was another person besides the person who had experienced so much loss. But then I noticed that she wore sunglasses in all the photographs, and although the sun was surely bright in Greece, I wondered if she wept behind the shield of the dark lenses.

The debate grew louder around me. Larry Denty hit his fist against his desk top; he criticized President Kennedy for not sending federal troops to the southern states quickly enough to protect the Negroes demonstrating there. I wanted so much to defend President Kennedy for all his attempts to make the world more fair. But the conversation grew so wild I couldn't get anyone's attention, so I sat quietly at my desk until class ended.

In algebra class Mr. Marshall wrote equations on the overhead projector for us to solve. I tried to follow along but I couldn't factor equations. I couldn't expand. I couldn't solve for X and Y and I couldn't apply equations to story problems. Instead of focusing on the question the math problem asked I became absorbed in the story.

One story problem asked: *If it takes a farmer using four baling machines thirty hours to bale eight hundred bales of hay, how many bales of hay would the farmer produce using six baling machines for twenty hours?* Instead of concentrating on bales of hay I imagined the farmer's family. The farmer had a beautiful daughter, who boys called on the telephone asking her to meet them in the hay loft of the family barn on Friday nights. I pictured her there, her hair teased and glinting, the color of straw. When Mr. Marshall called on me for the answer to the problem I told him I hadn't arrived at the answer. He instructed me to try again. I did, but still couldn't solve the problem. He asked me to speak with him after class.

"Miss Wagoner," he said. I stood beside his desk staring at the equations scrawled across the transparency on his overhead projector screen. "You aren't concentrating. Do you have any idea why?"

"My mind just wanders off," I said. I wanted to say that if I could drive again, if I could get my license early, then I might be able to make sense of math and the world again. I wanted to ask him to let me back into drivers' training.

"You need to concentrate if you're going to keep up in here." He wiped a rag over the transparency, blurring the last equation to a black cloud.

"I'll work on it," I said. Madeline stared at me from the doorway where she waited. Ever since my date with Peter, Madeline seemed to be wherever I was in the school, my double, my twin, shadowing me. Smoothing my hand over the wrinkles in my skirt, I walked toward her, attempting to smile.

That evening I went to the basement and set up the ironing board; the white cover, clean and stiff, smelled of first starch because my mother so rarely used it. I set the iron on steam, then knelt on the seat of a card table chair I set in front of the ironing board. Spreading my hair over the flat surface, I straightened the curls with my hairbrush and began ironing, starting near my scalp. Pushing the tip of the iron too close to my skin, I burned my forehead at the hairline. I smelled hot singed hair, and sat up to look at myself in the make-up mirror I'd brought down to the basement. A little triangular welt rose up like pink dough on my forehead. I watched it turn red, then knelt back down and ironed my whole head of hair.

Once finished, my look pleased me. My curls flattened to dark waves that lay close to my head. I looked like someone other than myself, like a movie star extra from the 1940s. Or a singer with a big band. But even as I looked in the mirror the curls rebounded, bursting up around my head. I shouldn't have used steam, my hair turned into a hedge when it rained. I changed the setting to dry heat.

"What are you doing?" my mother called to me from the kitchen.

"Ironing my hair."

"What?"

"Ironing my hair."

"What ever for?"

"Straight hair's in style. I'm ironing it straight," I shouted solidly.

"Be stylish, then," she shouted back to me. "But don't burn yourself."

I have already, and it's a little triangle shaped like the tip of the iron. The Bermuda Triangle of my forehead covering all the whirling thoughts. I let the welt hide under my hair like a secret. I continued ironing, without steam. And if I held the iron down too long the burning smell filled the air again, and I remembered when Shrimp singed the tips of the new boat ropes in the summer to keep them from unraveling.

Afterwards my hair looked dull and dry but straighter than ever. I teased it high at the crown. The next day at school I felt anonymous. Incognito. But on Wednesday after study hall as I walked out of school to the bus through a snow that changed to rain, my hair curled into wild snarls. I sat on the army green seat in the bus, rubbing my hair between my fingers, moist dark curls that if cut and pressed between two sheets of wax paper would form the shapes of Os and Cs.

For the next five nights I slept on huge pink plastic rollers secured by bobby pins that stuck into my scalp when I rolled in bed. Every night I awoke from discomfort and my heart began to pound. *Until the next time*, Uncle Judd's note had said.

The fifth night when I awoke I sat up in bed and turned my bedside lamp on. I dove my hands through my hair, stripping out the pink rollers that fell to the floor, scattering like miniature pink tunnel toys.

The second week in November I received a letter from the White House. I couldn't believe such a wonderful thing could still happen to me. My mother handed it to me when I arrived home from school.

"You're communicating with people in high places." She gave me a rare smile.

"Research for government class," I said, shooting up the stairs. In my bedroom I opened the letter, addressed to me with my name and address and the date spelled perfectly in deep black type.

Dear North Wagoner,

President Kennedy and I wish to thank you for the letter of sympathy you sent concerning the death of our son Patrick. Your expression of sorrow strengthens us and reveals a maturity of character at your age, to have thought so deeply about the lives of people other than yourself. President Kennedy has often asked the young people in this country to think about the things they can do for this nation and for the world. He believes the decisions and actions of our youth will shape the world to come. I feel certain that you will grow up to accomplish some remarkable things for which you, your family, and others in our country will be proud.

> *Sincerely,*
> *Jacqueline B. Kennedy.*

Oh, baby Patrick, I thought, *baby Patrick, in heaven where you must be, you had a wonderful mother you hardly knew.*

On Thursday night, the twenty-first of November, I sat in my bedroom at my desk, studying for an algebra quiz with the radio on low volume. The newsman talked about President Kennedy's trip to Dallas. Jackie Kennedy would accompany him, now that she'd returned from Greece. This was to be their first big trip together since they lost baby Patrick. She could wear her sunglasses in Texas if she needed to because the sun could be brilliant there. Cowboys wore big hats to shield their faces.

I remembered all the jokes President Kennedy had told, saying that he suspected audiences came more to see Jackie than to listen to him speak. She'd handle all the eyes with a shy smile.

But Texas seemed like such a huge place, a state that stretched out flat and indivisible as far as the eyes could see. A state of cowboys with six guns slung on their hips and *yippy kay yay little doggy* songs on their lips. A state that had always seemed like another country, where men like Jim Bowie and Davie Crockett fought at the Alamo, dying for the independence of Texans.

I opened my drawer and fingered the letter from Jackie Kennedy, tracing the American eagle embossed on the letterhead. The paper rustled between my fingers; her words of encouragement repeated in my mind.

She'd said I would contribute to the world, but I felt certain my contribution wouldn't be in mathematics. I struggled to factor equations. I decided to make a list of my strengths and weaknesses so I could best decide what contribution to concentrate on. I tore a sheet of paper from my scratch pad and began listing, my weaknesses first.

Distractibility, I wrote, then *poor nutrition. Attractive.* My writing changed, the letters slanting. I wondered what Jackie Kennedy would think about being attractive, whether she would see this as a weakness or a strength in me. Maybe *attractive* did not belong in the weakness category, because Jackie Kennedy herself was beautiful; I found her face so calming and satisfying to see. Maybe one person's strength *was* another person's weakness, as Queen Mom so often said.

I heard voices downstairs where my father was developing photographs and my mother grading papers. But another voice sounded, a loud, booming voice punctuating their voices like a drum. I looked out my window at the driveway where snow dusted the asphalt. The floodlights from our house beamed like three tiny moons. The Stingray stood parked and shining red behind the Mercury, steam rising from its still hot engine, mist like breath against the falling snow.

I held Jackie Kennedy's letter, bending the edges without wanting to. Equations blurred in the opened text on my desk. The voices downstairs grew louder.

"North," my mother called. "Come here."

I couldn't move.

"North, honey." The walls of my room pressed in on me. "We're going out." I walked to the top of the stairs and saw my mother at the bottom, diminished, like an image viewed through a camera lens.

"Uncle Judd stopped by and we're all going to see Dad's show at the Gallery." Pictures of me? I'd destroyed some prints, but my dad had not mentioned finding them gone. Maybe he had copies. I hadn't destroyed the negatives. Did he make new prints? Or would he show the pictures Uncle Judd had taken?

I ran to the bathroom where my head whirled; all the swear words I could hurl spun through my mind in long phrases, colored streaks.

"North. Are you all right alone?" my mother called from the front vestibule.

"Yes," I shouted, gripping the rim of the sink. Then I heard the rumblings of car engines starting outside.

· · ·

A light snow swirled in spirals, lifting, then falling through the sky outside my window, illuminated by slants of flooding light. I gave up on my algebra homework and lay listening to the radio playing songs from last summer. When I heard "One Fine Day" I closed my eyes to picture Bill's face. But I remembered Uncle Judd's laugh tonight from downstairs. I pressed the curve of my calves against the bed sheets. I wanted to drive. I bolted up, went to the window. The drive-way was empty, the tire tracks from the Stingray already heaped with newly fallen snow.

Lying down on my bed again I reassured myself I was alone. I closed my eyes and slept. I dreamed that a Martian had pushed me down on a tarmac. He was taking me to Mars to be his wife. He'd been drinking. He said having one wife wasn't enough and I screamed *No!* My hair turned electric green and stood on end. Then a weight pressed me further. A faint smell of liquor wreathed the air. My eyes fluttered open. I saw the light green walls of my bedroom, no longer a dream.

"Just want to say goodnight." Uncle Judd began to kiss me, his lips nibbling my cheek. Then his lips pressed my lips, his tongue dart-ing in. I rolled away from him to the far side of the bed and knotted myself up there. He knelt on the floor, his hands lying in the impres-sion my body had left in the sheets. *Alone. Alone. Dee had said it all summer. Leave me alone. Now she didn't answer my letters written in code. Pig Latin. Ou-yay regnant-pay? s-Iay t-iay rue-tay?*

"The show was beautiful. You should see it. You're beautiful. I haven't seen you in so long." His voice trembled. "I just want to kiss you goodnight the way I did last summer. Maybe take a few pic-tures." He raised his camera bag by the strap, his arm like a crane. *Those were French kisses. Humbert kisses. Not the kind you get from an uncle. Son of a bitch. Where's Linda's baby? Did you get Dee pregnant or was it really Shrimp?* My voice didn't come. He leaned toward me, unsnapping the camera bag.

I sat up, leaned back against the wall. One small lamp burned in my room and the moonlight fell in from outside. Light fell in silver coronas around my head. *Martyrs had haloes around their heads and so did all those who had died in grace.*

Through the window, the sifting snow.

I felt as if I lived inside a little scene encased in a glass bubble that you shake to make the snow fall. The snow falls over the little house and the fir trees inside the glass bubble. The snow covers the house so no one can see what's happening inside.

"No more pictures." That sure part of me rose up from somewhere outside the glass. I crawled to the end of the bed, my nightgown catching on my toes. Uncle Judd leaned and caught my foot in his hand, pulling me to him like a piece of driftwood. The cotton of my nightgown climbed my thighs. His fingers slipped over my underpants and rubbed.

"Just one kiss." Uncle Judd's head moved down over me in one long, purposeful arc like an X-ray machine. His lips pressed mine. Taste of bourbon. He moved his hands everywhere. The top half of me flashed warm, but the bottom half sunk down cold, deep into the bed sheets, ice sheets. I shivered with cold. His tongue lashed. My arms rose and fell across the bed, as if I were making a snow angel. His fingers read my breasts like Braille.

I imagined a star shining somewhere far off. At Orion's feet. In my mind I flew toward the star until I hung in the sky too, looking down at another North, lying in the scattered bed sheets, kicking her foot. The scar on her heel glinting in the darkness. Like another star. A tiny star.

I fell back down to merge with the North there. Uncle Judd pressed his face against mine. The camera lay on the bed. *North, do something*. My legs fluttered, at first gently and then with great snapping motions at the knees.

"Stop that," Uncle Judd said, his face inches from my face. I kicked harder. "No one's home," he said. My arms flailed in arcs like two helicopter blades, aimed at Uncle Judd's arms. I hit his wrist on top of the Swiss watch wishing I could shatter it, and all the times it glittered in the light hypnotizing me. I kicked the camera to the floor with one knee snap. It skittered over the wood, hit against the far wall.

"Damn you," I shouted, lunging from the bed. I ran out of my bedroom, my nightgown falling down around my shoulders. Leaping down steps by twos, I heard footsteps, keys jingling. Thrusting my arms back into the sleeves of my nightgown, I grabbed my father's army coat from the front closet and jammed my feet into his snow boots. I ran outside the back door to hide behind the shed in the back yard. A gust of wind blew drifting snow over my footprints.

"You're going to freeze. North, I need to talk to you," Uncle Judd called from the driveway. I saw snow whirl over his head in circles, his camel hair coat bleached to an ivory color by the flood-lights. "North, you can't hide from me." He began walking into the backyard, toward the shed. I pulled my coat up over my mouth so my breath would not rise in plumes. A blast of cold wind ripped past the shed. Uncle Judd shivered.

"North, where are you?" Hugging his arms close around his chest, he turned and walked to the Stingray. He shivered again. Then he slid inside the Stingray and drove away, leaving me his voice: "You can't hide from me."

Yes, I can hide. I did hide and I'm hiding right now like the wind. I'm hiding around the corner of this shed where you can't find me. You can't touch me. I'm the cold, cold North wind.

The sounds of tires slushing through the snow on the street woke me to the night and my legs red with the cold, to the clinging wet hem of my nightgown. Wrapping my own arms around myself, I stumbled toward the house, misty ghosts of my breath rising into the night air.

The Yellow Rose of Texas

Dee, you didn't *write me. I know the baby's dead. Wrapped in a hospital blanket thrown in the ground. Or in a trash bin. Dead. I don't know why he followed me into the woods. In my bedroom the moon fell in the window and broke into shards. Like glass. Splintered all around. The car wrecked, Dee, and I was driving.*

I can't call you on the phone because he might answer. The father of all the babies. But Dee, you've got to know this: Lolita didn't die. She went into hiding. Like one of those Nazi war criminals who had to have his face operated on so he could hide from his crimes. Except, what had her crime been? She went into hiding like a war criminal. That's what she did, Dee. Humbert doesn't know any of this. Please don't tell anyone. Not even God. Lolita's mother was in love with Humbert. But Humbert loved Lolita instead. He loved Lolita enough to kill her mother so he could have her. One time he made her have sex with him when she had the flu. Dee, I can't stand it.

The only person in the world who can help us is Jackie Kennedy. She lost babies. And Dee, she wrote to me. I think I can stand anything when I touch her letter. I read about an opera singer who had cancer and he sang arias while they radiated him. Jackie Kennedy is going to Texas. A boy at school told me The Yellow Rose of Texas was a whore. But she saved the Alamo.

Going through the windshield was like falling into the Devil's Hole. You and Shrimp and Bill weren't there, but the devil was.

Chambered Clouds

In the morning my mother called me to breakfast, but her voice seemed to sound from somewhere far off. The white winter light filled my bedroom with strands like floating gauze.

"North, hurry up," my mother shouted. I felt a sharp pain deep inside me. Did Uncle Judd's hands move over me still? Or perhaps move me like a puppet? I didn't know anymore who decided what would happen next. If he could be in my own bedroom in Ypsi he could be anywhere. He might even call me out of class at school.

"North." My name, my mother's voice, echoed against the walls around me. Dressing in my dark navy jumper and a black turtleneck, I breathed the cold air of the room. My hair flew in wild angles around my face but I did not brush it. I gathered my notebooks, forcing myself down the stairs.

The bowl of corn flakes my mother set on our white enamel table seemed to float on a surface of snow. When I touched the spoon, it clattered. Everything felt cold, ice cold, as my mother bustled around me in the kitchen.

"The show looked fabulous, and then Dad and I stopped at Gino's for chili. Judd had to leave from the Gallery because of the roads. What a snowstorm!" She sipped hot coffee and I envisioned Uncle Judd on the freeway, the Stingray spinning out of control, a truck speeding toward him in the outside lane. I fantasized the phone ringing any minute, a cool voice saying he was dead. I could see my mother sobbing then.

"You're not eating." My mother stared at me. "Oh, look at the time." She grabbed her purse. I sat at the table thinking, *move your feet, North*. Stiffly, I rose and found my coat, gathered my books and papers with my name scrawled on them as if in another person's handwriting.

From inside the Mercury I watched the snow fall in spirals. My mother scraped the ice from the windshield, moving inside a whirl of white, pushing, forcing the blade against glass.

The hallway I passed through at school on my way to science class tunneled around me. I stopped to admire the photograph of Ron Williams in the Hall of Fame; he had graduated the year before, winning in math. Sally Teague's brother said Ron counted the pencils on his desk and lined them up in a row before class. I wished I could learn to do such orderly things. A flood of cold light poured in through the clerestory windows behind me, blotting out Ron Williams' face and replacing it with a reflection of my own face swimming inside the pooled light. My lips, slightly parted, looked violet-pink. And I didn't know who I was anymore. I was North, but I wasn't North.

My hands shook as if on some other girl's body. I turned to hurry toward science class when a boy approached me. "Can I walk you to science?" he asked, holding his books against his chest like a girl.

"I don't think I've met you," I said, my eyes averted.

"Oh, yeah, you have, North. C'mon," he said loudly. "I'm Richard Sellers." I heard him say, "C'mon. You have to know who I am" as I scurried down the hall.

In science class Mrs. Gilker called on Terry Brennan to give a demonstration of his science project, a cloud chamber he had made from a big glass jug with a cork in the top. Two tubes entered the bottle through the cork, and when Terry Brennan shot water through one of the tubes, then closed it off, a tiny white cloud formed inside the bottle like an act of God.

Everybody oohed and aahed, and Mrs. Gilker smiled broadly. She said she thought Terry might be asked to take the cloud chamber to the state science fair in Lansing, his project was so good. Terry shrugged his shoulders. He wore a black and white wool shirt. I stared at the checked pattern as Mr. Knight's quivering voice came over the loudspeaker. At first, I couldn't understand Mr. Knight. I only knew that there was a huge emergency. I thought maybe there had been an air raid; the Russians were bombing Detroit, trying to demolish all the car companies. A recording of "The Star Spangled Banner" played, and Mr. Knight spoke through the music, his words broken as if by otherworldly static.

"At 12:30 Central Standard Time, President Kennedy was shot while riding through Dallas, Texas, in a motorcade."

North, this can't really be happening. No, Mr. Knight, you're lying. "He was taken to Parkland Hospital where doctors attempted to save his life, but due to the President's extensive head wounds their efforts were in vain. At 1 P.M. the President was pronounced dead. Ypsilanti High will close now in honor of John Fitzgerald Kennedy."

Don't tell us, Mr. Knight, Jackie Kennedy is dead, too. Both of them killed by some crazy person. Tears formed in my eyes and the checked pattern in Terry Brennan's shirt blurred. I looked at Terry's cloud chamber. The cloud inside Terry's cloud chamber started to rain little oval drops, as smooth as tears. The faces of the kids all around me glistened. Nobody had any Kleenex so a wild flurry of sniffling filled the room. Mrs. Gilker started crying when she said, "Class dismissed."

Terry Brennan left his cloud chamber on the front desk where he had placed it for the demonstration. Nobody wanted to touch anything; nobody wanted to move the objects in the room because changing something might have been a sign of irreverence. Maybe if the cloud formed again, if the cloud chamber could look like it did before Mr. Knight's announcement, we could have President Kennedy back for a minute or two. I closed my eyes wishfully and heard a girl sob from the back of the room. When I opened my eyes the cloud still rained, though lightly now.

We filed out of class quietly, but once we gathered in the halls girls huddled together along lockers, the most distraught among them holding each other. Handkerchiefs and Kleenexes materialized from nowhere. I thought maybe the school nurse had brought them up from the sick room.

Beside my locker Madeline Spears fell into my arms, her green mohair sweater like moss touching my shoulders. "Oh, North, this is horrible," she whimpered. I couldn't say anything. I dragged Madeline down the hall in my arms the way Greg Bowman had dragged Mindy Leighton off the football field. When we reached a group of girls I deposited Madeline in their outstretched arms.

"Where are you going?" Sally Teague shouted to me.

"I don't know," I shouted, as I reached the outside door. I stumbled a bit as I loped down the concrete steps. I didn't walk to the bus. How could I ride inside that warm quiet? *God, how did you let this happen?* Clothed in my rug coat and my black knee-high boots with the fake fur I pulled my black knit gloves on. I should have been warm, but a chill spread up from deep inside me.

Walking toward campus town, the dead leaves rustled around my boots, sound of falling sleet. My breath rose in white plumes. A cold wind ripped through the streets, twisting my hair around my face. The branches of all the bare trees along the avenue scraped the sky like skeletons of arms. The darkness of winter fell over me.

At home I walked into the living room where my mother sat in her Bentwood rocker, watching T.V. Wads of used green Kleenex lay mounded in her lap.

"A madman shot President Kennedy," she whimpered, bolting up. She walked to me and drew me into her arms, then let go quickly, her arms falling limp at her sides. The skin on her face looked shiny.

Behind her the T.V. news showed a scene in Dallas, picturing President Kennedy giving a speech early in the morning. As he waited for Jackie Kennedy to join him, he joked, "Mrs. Kennedy is organizing herself." Everyone burst out laughing. Perhaps they remembered that, when in Paris, he had described himself as *the man who accompanied Jackie Kennedy to Europe*. "It takes her longer," he continued, "but of course she looks better than I do after she does it." Laughter sounded again all around. Then Jackie Kennedy appeared, looking radiant and standing bathed in sunlight. She flashed her quick smile for all the photographers. This was no longer Greece, and she didn't wear her sunglasses to shield herself from the cameras. She smiled at them for him. Although I did not see the grief for her baby in her face then, I believed it lay just under the surface, that it rose and fell of its own life like breath. It rose and fell and grew the way he had once grown inside her.

I glanced into the study and back to the T.V. where a film of the motorcade in Dallas played. President Kennedy and Jackie smiled broadly, waving their hands like big Xs in the sky. President Kennedy's hair flew in the breeze, and Jackie Kennedy wore a tailored suit with a nappy weave and a matching pillbox hat.

Then the gunshots were fired. I couldn't hear them, but I saw the President crumple into Jackie Kennedy's lap. She held him and cradled his head. Then, turning her head, looking confused, she laid him down on the seat. She crawled desperately across the back of the limousine, extending her arm to a Secret Service man who ran toward her. When they locked grips she pulled him into the car. Then everything quickened like a movie shown on rapid speed. I couldn't see Jackie Kennedy in focus. She blurred on the screen as the limousine sped off, spilling yellow roses.

The room darkened around my mother and me. I glanced over to the study. I remembered Uncle Judd standing there with my mother. I backed away from my mother's arms. *Uncle Judd could arrive here any moment. You didn't know what would happen next anymore.* I remembered last night. Because he hated Democrats and President Kennedy, he probably felt no pain from his murder. Maybe he was secretly glad. *Last night. Any night. Until the next time. You can't hide from me.* My head spun with his words.

I ran upstairs. I lay on my bed, trying to remember the picture of Jackie Kennedy I had lost last summer. How would it feel to hold her image against my chest again? Would my heart slow down? Was her dress green or blue, satin or velvet? Did she wear a tiara that sparked with light, or did my memory place it there?

During the evening, the T.V. churned out news of the President's death and the world's reactions, minute by minute. Jackie Kennedy was pictured emerging from the rear exit of Air Force One, walking beside the President's coffin with Bobby Kennedy, her suit still splattered with the President's blood. I saw shock on her face, and even if our T.V. had been color her skin would have looked ghostly white.

Jackie Kennedy's face, frozen and wide-eyed, filled with dignified sadness. In her letter to me her words had sounded so strong, but I didn't see how she could hold up under this much grief. His bullet-torn head in her lap, and no way to mend him.

I leaned forward as more pictures of Jackie Kennedy came on. I longed to be close to her; I wanted to touch her. *Anything could happen. Anything.* I saw the film of her standing beside the President at the Dallas airport before the assassination; she looked so beautiful, with *welcome* signs all around her saying: *JFK* and *LBJ* and *Dallas Loves You, Jackie.* I stood and walked to the television set. Now she was standing beside Lyndon Johnson as he took the presidential oath, his palm raised high. I touched her image on the screen, warm, with light that glowed between my fingers.

The phone rang in the study and my mother rose to answer it. She said hello. "Oh, Judd," she said, her voice lifting excitedly. Then there was silence for some time. "I'm so sick about Kennedy." She ran a hand back through her hair at the temple. Her fingers got lost there. Her fingernails peeked out from her dark nest of hair, red as clotted blood.

"Thanksgiving dinner? I forgot all about it." Her voice expanded. "You're coming here." She nodded. "Yes, that's what we decided. Yes, I'm looking forward to seeing you, too."

I looked into the study where he would stand again. There where my mother stood. Where he had stood beside her so often. As he always stood with my mother.

Jackie Kennedy's image flashed across the screen again. She still wore the pink suit. I lay my hand across the warm surface that divided us. Tomorrow, as I watched her, the sunlight would fall in through the windows behind me, warm on my legs. *Like the sun from another country.*

The world would watch Jackie Kennedy, and she would carry the world's burden. She would walk out in front of the funeral procession by herself, raising her head and taking long, athletic strides. She would never yield to her full grief in public.

I looked at her face on the television screen. I touched her image and raised my chin. My mother hung up the phone and walked back toward the living room.

I told my mother on Thanksgiving, before Dee and all her family arrived, that he'd come to me in the snowstorm after the gallery preview. As the sky filled with white frozen tears he touched me in the places you saved for the right boy. It was like Humbert touching Lolita, I said, even when she was sick. He fondled her gym socks. I told her about the bathing suit Uncle Judd gave me.

"North, you've got a big imagination," she said, her lipstick smudging her teeth in front as she smiled, her lips curling snakishly back. "He wouldn't. I know him better than you think." Love for him glowed in her eyes. "Your summer reading list was too long. Your fantasy's running away with you." She turned to walk away toward the kitchen. Dad hadn't come downstairs yet. He was probably hungover. If I'd been married to her, I'd have wanted to throw the bottle at her and bolt. But he stayed.

"Listen to me." That sure voice rose up from inside me, the voice I thought I had lost to the cold of winter and his hands.

"I listened. And now you hear me. Judd's attractive. You've twisted things. It's a crush. You've got a crush on him. North, you're upset. Stop watching the assassination on T.V." *My crush on him? Crush. Crush him. Yes.* Violent words twisted, wild vines in my mind.

"It's true," I said, fisting my hands at my sides. "Someday you'll know it like . . . like . . . Hamlet's mother. Too late."

"You're getting very literary, North. How *recherché*." She laughed a hyena laugh.

"You don't believe me," I shouted into the space of the house that felt like the space of outerspace, where stars exploded and fell to pieces in the slated darkness.

"Oh, North, please stop this." She stomped her foot on the carpet. "I believe *you* believe it. That's what I believe."

"Jackie Kennedy's right," I said in a near whisper, a voice as soft as Jackie's voice. Oh, and when Jackie Kennedy talked in her soft voice everyone listened.

"Jackie Kennedy?" My mother dropped her jaw, rolled her eyes like a comedian.

"In a dream. She told me."

Jackie Kennedy wore her black mourning suit and veil. We walked into the White House together and sat on a burgundy, velvet-covered love seat. She dropped her veil to her shoulders. A tear trailed through the black netting like a falling drop of rain. But the sun was shining. Oh, God, the sun was shining so brightly outside. A scream of yellow light.

I told her what Uncle Judd did and she pulled me into her arms. I said I was so very sorry the President died. It wasn't fair the way she had to be in front of a television camera while it all happened. Oh, I was so sorry for that, but I had watched because I needed to see her there before me. Living.

We wept. She said she would never forget the President or her babies who had died. I said I thought Dee's baby had died not long after her Patrick, and that she had had an abortion and probably didn't tell Shrimp. I said Linda Turner's baby might still be alive, but I didn't know where to find him. Or her. It could have been a her. I said I felt like a baby now.

You're alive, she said. Her eyes were swollen nearly shut from crying by then. I said I wanted a mother. I wanted my mother to help me. She told me I could tell my mother what Uncle Judd did, but she might not help me. Some mothers never did. But God would comfort me in ways I could not understand. She said, when your mother didn't help you you found another mother.

Next time somebody tried to take a picture I didn't like I could break the camera. She had broken a few cameras. She said I should travel around the world and see how other people lived. The people in India died in the streets and were sent down the Ganges River on barges. Flowers domed their bodies. They burned on funeral pyres. God was not ever visible. But the United States of America was still one, indivisible country under God. Although God couldn't step in. That's why President Kennedy died in Dallas, Texas.

"You dream of Jackie?" My mother slapped her palm to her forehead. Her wedding ring glistened as if wet.

"You wouldn't understand," I said. I felt my eyes flame.

"Dream what you like. But stop the other stuff. About Judson. Turn off the T.V. and come to the kitchen. We'll stuff the turkey." She walked into the kitchen where yellow light pooled on the linoleum floor. Like a mirage.

The television showed Jackie Kennedy in her pink suit, after the assassination. She moved across the tarmacs at the airfields in Dallas and in Washington, moving through her fear like a gazelle. Eyes wide. Heart in her face.

Oh, Jackie. You held the world together. Oh, Jackie. You held me. If I looked at your face, I believed in goodness. And beauty. And maybe even truth.

I knew one thing. In truth I knew of another candidate for stuffing. His name rhymed with stud. He was the father of some of the dead babies, and maybe one baby lost out in the world who might still be alive. He was the devil in the Devil's Hole. The devil who would win the girl with the blue dress on every time because she wanted to drive. But I wasn't wearing a blue dress. No. I was wearing black. And I could hide. I was the wind now. The cold North wind. And I would whirl away when he arrived. You can be somewhere in your body and not be there inside. I'd be like that if I had to see him. I'd be half there like a Buddhist monk who could walk on hot coals without feeling pain. I'd transcend like a monk. And I wouldn't feel his hand when he touched my breast. Just the way I saw his hand detach from his body, I'd break away from mine. Like Humpty Dumpty.

Until so many years later, when I left home and could tell my story and take my pink suit off. Jackie Kennedy lived in New York City the year I married. I had my babies. I'd never forget the dead. Never forget I loved Dee. Like a sister. Oh, and Shrimp loved you, Deedee.

The devil lives in the darkness of Hell.

Oh, Jackie. If I hadn't had you I wouldn't have survived.